A SHOOT ON
MARTHA'S VINEYARD

Also by Philip R. Craig
in Large Print:

A Deadly Vineyard Holiday

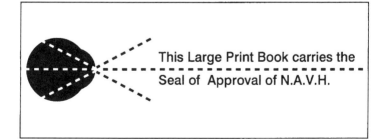

This Large Print Book carries the
Seal of Approval of N.A.V.H.

A SHOOT ON MARTHA'S VINEYARD

Philip R. Craig

Thorndike Press • Thorndike, Maine

Published in 1999 by arrangement with Scribner, an imprint of Simon & Schuster, Inc.

Thorndike Large Print ® Mystery Series.

The tree indicium is a trademark of Thorndike Press.

The text of this Large Print edition is unabridged. Other aspects of the book may vary from the original edition.

Set in 16 pt. Plantin by Rick Gundberg.

Printed in the United States on permanent paper.

Library of Congress Cataloging in Publication Data

Craig, Philip R., 1933–
  A shoot on Martha's Vineyard : a Martha's Vineyard mystery / Philip R. Craig.
    p.   cm.
  ISBN 0-7862-1614-X (lg. print : hc : alk. paper)
  1. Jackson, Jeff (Fictitious character) — Fiction. 2. Private investigators — Massachusetts — Martha's Vineyard — Fiction. 3. Martha's Vineyard (Mass.) — Fiction. 4. Large type books. I. Title.
  [PS3553.R23S56   1999]
  813′.54—dc21   98-34902

*For the Nereid
who lives with me on her island:
my wife, Shirley*

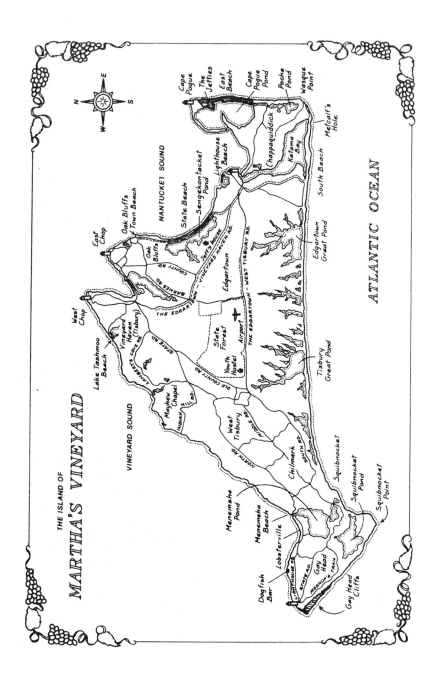

THE ISLAND OF

MARTHA'S VINEYARD

"Twain are the gates of shadowy dreams,
The one is made of horn, the other of
   ivory;
Such dreams as pass the portals of ivory
Are deceitful, and bear tidings that are
   unfulfilled.
But the dreams that pass through the gate
   of horn
Bring true issue to whoever of mortals
   beholds them."
— PENELOPE to ODYSSEUS
The Odyssey

$$— 1 —$$

There have always been pirates on Martha's Vineyard. Some came ashore in the seventeenth and eighteenth centuries with cutlasses and pistols; others are arriving right now with briefcases and California smiles. There's not a whisker of moral difference between them.

Zee and I first heard about Hollywood's latest plans for the Vineyard in early June. According to rumor, first noted in the *Martha's Vineyard Times* and later rather breathlessly reported in the *Gazette*, it was to be a film about a modern treasure hunt for ancient pirate gold buried on the island.

The movie makers were to do the filming in September, which Zee and I agreed was probably a good idea since, aside from the occasional hurricane that finds its way to New England in September, fall is often the loveliest time of the island year. Not only have most summer people returned home so their children can go back to school, but the weather is good, the water is still warm, and the bluefish are coming back.

From the wide-eyed tones of local reporters, we gathered that the producers, directors, and stars of the film were famous folk, but since Zee and I rarely went to the movies, they were unknown to us.

We actually liked movies, but it took really good ones to get us to go to island theaters, where every showing was an adventure due to ancient projection equipment and cost cutting by the theater owners.

If the managers remembered to turn the houselights on before the showing of the film, they often forgot to turn them off after the movie started. Screens routinely went black at key moments and stayed black while audiences hooted and stamped and, to their credit, laughed. Sound and image would fail to correspond. Whole reels were out of focus or occasionally omitted entirely. Sometimes there was only one projectionist for the two theaters in Oak Bluffs, and he left one audience waiting while he got things going across the street, then rushed back to start the other movie, and continued to run back and forth all evening, changing reels or doing whatever it is those guys are supposed to do up there in the projection booth.

Island residents who are seriously interested in movies sometimes go over to America so they can see them in real theaters. But other people love the island theaters precisely because they are what they are. For them, the shabbiness, the broken seats, soggy popcorn, and the projection mishaps are part of the entertainment, the theater being a sort of stage on which they themselves are players, and as much a part of the island's summer ambiance as are the golden beaches, the sun, the trees and gardens, and the harbors full of sailboats.

It was only when we felt slightly wacky that Zee and I were willing to shell out the required dollars to sit in sticky seats and participate in the living theater of Vineyard cinema. If we really wanted to see a movie, we rented one, usually an elderly one, and watched it on the television that had come to the house when Zee moved in.

"Part of my dowry," she had explained. "Like the cellular phone."

The cellular phone had been kept in her little Jeep when she'd been single, but was now in my Land Cruiser, since that was the vehicle we usually drove on the beach. I had never used it, and didn't plan to, but it was there "just in case."

I'd never had a television in the house before we got married, but was glad to have this one since we could now watch an occasional Red Sox game without driving all the way to Boston. I built a shelf on the wall for the television set and its accompanying VCR, and that became our movie theater if we really wanted one.

So it was that we were both notably ignorant of the famous names that were mentioned in the press, and it was August before we met any of them.

"They're going to hire local people for bit parts and extras," said Zee, her nose in the *Times*. "That should be fun. If we see the movie, we can look for the people we know."

It would not be the first movie to be made on Martha's Vineyard. The most notable earlier one was a famous fishy thriller that, decades before, had kept a lot of shark-fearing people out of the water for at least one summer, and had entertained hundreds of islanders, who were less interested in the great white villain of the film than in spotting Uncle George as part of the background crowd, or little Petie and Sally on the beach with the other extras. *So cute! And now they're all grown up! Time flies!*

"They'll definitely want to hire you," I said. Zee was the most beautiful woman I had ever seen.

"And you, too," said Zee. "And Joshua, for sure."

We looked at Joshua, who looked back with his big eyes. He and Zee were star material without a doubt.

"Immortal fame and wealth beyond our wildest dreams will be ours at last," I said.

Zee nodded. "And about time, too."

Joshua agreed, and no doubt Oliver Underfoot and Velcro, the two cats, would have too, had they been asked.

Joshua, having arrived on the Vineyard in May, was an alimentary canal with lungs. His face reminded me of a cross between Edward G. Robinson's and Winston Churchill's, but he was a generally cheerful fellow with a winning smile, and we were delighted to have him in our house. An award winner, for sure.

And Zee, who had toted him around single-handed all winter before delivering him into the outer world, was lovelier than ever, as many women are after they produce their offspring. With her deep, dark eyes and her long blue-black hair, she was Gaea, earth goddess, mother of at least one potential Titan, sleek as an otter, graceful as a panther.

"Setting fame and fortune aside for the moment," she now said, "and paying attention to more important things, such as the new tide tables, I note that if we leave right now, we can fetch Wasque Point just in time to fish the last two hours of the west tide.

"What do you say?"

"Done."

For reasons known only to Neptune, the bluefish, which normally would be visiting Nova Scotia in late August, were, instead, still here in Vineyard waters, delighting the island fisherpeople, of whom we were two.

I put down my living room book and went out to load fishing gear into my faithful, rusty, old Land Cruiser. Rods on the roof rack, tackle boxes and fish box in the back, drinks in a cooler, and a quick check to see if our car books were there just in case the bluefish didn't show up. I also put in Joshua's stuff: a car seat, his homemade beach chair so he could watch his parents fish and learn a few tricks of the trade (you can't start too young), an umbrella so he wouldn't burn his delicate skin, and my personally designed baby pack, good for carrying him on my back or my chest, depending on how I rigged it up, in case I decided to tote him down the beach while I fished.

By the time this was done, Zee had the diapers, lotions, bottles, and other Joshua gear together, and had slipped into her shorts and a shirt she knotted over her once-again-flat belly, and had her hair done up in the blue bandanna she liked to wear when she was fishing.

I ogled her. "Maybe we should send Josh on ahead and the two of us can sort of linger here for a while. We can catch up with him later."

"He's too young to drive alone," said Zee, lifting him off her hip and buckling him into the car seat. "Besides, you know how it is when you give your kid the keys. He goes to some girl's house and shows off, and the first thing you know, the cops are calling your house telling you to come down and pick him up at the jail because he tried to use a fake ID to buy beer."

We drove out our sandy driveway to the highway, took a left, and went into Edgartown. The A & P–Al's Package Store traffic jam, perhaps the island's worst, thanks entirely to people making left-hand turns off and onto the main road, was only half bad since it was still fairly early in the morning, and we were soon past and headed out of town toward Katama. There, at the end of the pavement, we turned east and drove over the sands toward Chappy.

The Norton's Point barrier beach hooking Chappaquiddick to the rest of the island was once again open to off road vehicle traffic, after having been closed since Memorial Day on the orders of Lawrence Ingalls, a state biologist for the state's Department of Environmental Protection. Ingalls was the object of both loathing and adoration by many islanders for closing the beach during plover nesting and fledging season.

Now that the chicks had finally flown, ORVs could once again ply the sands as in the good old pre-Ingalls days, so trucks filled with fisherpeople, picnickers, bathers, and shellfishers were ranging to the far corners of the beach, where their drivers and passengers could, in late August, pursue their traditional pleasures.

As we drove along the beach, we could see Edgartown far away through the narrows of Katama Pond to our north. To our south, the waves of the Atlantic rolled in from countless uninterrupted miles and crashed on the yellow-white sands. We saw oystercatchers, terns, gulls, ospreys and snowy egrets, and pointed them out to Joshua, whose Vineyard bird lore was scant since he hadn't been on the island for long.

The closing of the beach was a hot and heavy issue on the Vineyard, with ardent moralists on both sides of the argument, as might be expected. I should know, for I was one of them, myself.

On one side, my side, were the drivers of

off-road vehicles, who, like their parents and grandparents, had always driven over the sands to the Vineyard's fabled but faraway fishing, shellfishing, and picnicking spots, and who saw no reason why they shouldn't keep on doing it. On the other side were people who saw themselves as environmentalists, as protectors of a fragile ecology, and as defenders of threatened species such as the innocent piping plover, the Vineyard's equivalent of the snail darter.

Never the twain did meet, and for the many summers of what some still thought of as the Plover Wars, the environmentalists carried the day, led by Lawrence Ingalls, who, as far as the many members of the losing side were concerned, was, as was each of his supporters, an irrational bleep.

The environmentalists' principal reason for closing the beach was their belief that ORVs were destroying the habitat of the plovers and thus needed to be banned during the birds' nesting and fledgling seasons. The state biologist accordingly interpreted DEP regulations to mean that no vehicle could drive within a hundred yards of any plover nest during these crucial weeks. And since the Norton's Point barrier beach was only a couple of hundred yards wide at the point where one plover pair happened to have established a nest, the whole beach was closed to traffic for June, July, and most of August, the very months when most over-sand drivers used it.

The drivers saw themselves as lovers of birds and the beach, and resented being considered the enemies of plovers. They reminded anyone who would listen that only one plover had been killed by an ORV in the year before the beach was closed, and that one had also been killed the year after it was closed, by a truck driven by one of the beach's hired plover protectors; they argued that the plover eggs and fledglings that had been destroyed during the years when the beach had been open to traffic had been done in not by trucks but by skunks, gulls, and other natural plover predators; they considered Lawrence Ingalls to be a fool and a totalitarian bureaucrat, and spoke his name with loathing for having deprived them of their traditional joys for no reason other than ideological whim.

For years, members of both the environmentalist and ORV groups thought wild thoughts and made wild statements, and for years violence was feared or threatened by members of both factions. Some plover lovers believed that the plover nests would be systematically destroyed by ardent ORV drivers, and pointed to anti-plover T-shirts that had emerged on the Vineyard's summer scene, and to the popularity of the lyric, "I'm running over a piping plover"; some drivers spoke of getting all of the ORVs on the island together at Katama and then driving, en masse, from one end of Norton's Beach to the other, ridding the beach of every last plover nest, and arguing that if there were no more plovers, there would be no plover problem. Zack Delwood, who was a fine fisherman but also a bully and a hater who shared no more love for me than I for him, was even more specific. His favorite proclamation was "No goddamned plover lovers, no more plover problem!"

But none of the wild threats or imaginings actually took place. The drivers had fumed and the environmentalists had ignored them and their arguments.

"Don't frown," said Zee, reading my mind as she often does. "Forget Ingalls. The beach is finally open. Enjoy the day."

Good advice, and I took it.

It was only later that murder was done.

— 2 —

We passed about a dozen parked ORVs on our way to Wasque. Most were owned by morning sunbathers, but a couple of picnics had already gotten started on the Katama Pond side, and I could see some clammers and quahoggers at work in the shallows of the pond.

But we were not shellfishing today, we were after the wily August bluefish, who had decided to summer on the Vineyard, and there was no better place to hunt them than at Wasque Point during the last two hours of the falling tide.

There was a line of Jeeps at the point when we got there, and there were bluefish under every one of them. Rods were bent and everyone was happy, even though the fishermen were shoulder to shoulder. The fish were in, and clearly had been for some time.

"Wow!" cried Zee. "Look at that!"

I found a parking spot farther to the left than I usually like to be and pulled in beside the almost new truck that belonged to Moonbeam Berube. Moonbeam and his ethereally beautiful son, Jason junior, were hauling in the fish, just like everyone else, which was a good thing because it meant that there'd be food on the Berube table that night, which was not always the situation.

Moonbeam was reputed to be the product of a long line of incestuous ancestors, and was, at any rate, one of the Vineyard's sad cases. He and his wife and many children lived in a hovel up in Chilmark. All of his children were nearly beautiful, with fine bones and delicate skin. But their eyes were dim and their prospects dimmer. Moonbeam was sly, but was bad at everything but fishing, and his family was a constant concern to social workers, teachers, cops, and other toilers in the public realm. Where he'd gotten the money for his truck was a mystery to many, but no one cared enough to ask him to solve it.

There was nothing I could do for Moonbeam except be friendly, so I waved at him and turned to Zee. "Grab your rod and get down there," I said. "You can't catch 'em from up here!"

But she hesitated. "You go. I'll take care of Joshua first."

"No. I was nailing them here the morning

21

after Joshua showed up and the two of you were still in the hospital. I'll take care of him now. Get going!"

Still she hesitated.

"They won't wait," I said. "Jeez, look at that one. Must be twelve pounds!"

Zee looked at the fish flopping on the sand, then at me, then at Joshua, then back at me.

"Go!" I said.

"Okay!"

She got out, snagged her rod off the roof rack, and trotted down to the surf, looking like a dark Venus. She made her cast and the lure arched far out over the surf. As the lure hit the water, there was an immediate explosion of white as a fish hit the lure, and her rod bent as she set the hook.

"Now, pay attention," I said to Joshua, as Zee began the fight to bring the fish in. "You want to know how to fish, you watch your mom."

We watched as she hauled back, reeled down, and hauled back again, leaning against the strength of the fish, controlling it, never giving it that instant when it could snap the line or throw the hook.

There is a beauty in anything being done well, be it a good carpenter swinging a hammer, a good musician at work, or a good short-order cook producing food for a diner full of customers. You see it when an athlete is running well, when a dancer is one with the dance, or when someone makes a good hunting shot or handles a boat well. And it's not only in humans that you see this, but in animals and birds as well. In the deer bounding into the forest, an osprey soaring above the beach, or in the stalking cat intent upon its prey. It has to do with economy of motion and the perfect coordination between action and intent. And when a beautiful creature like Zee is performing beautifully, the experience can be extraordinary.

So it was that dull Moonbeam and duller Jason, and the other fishermen nearest to Zee, held their casts and watched her bring in her bluefish. Gradually, more fishermen on either side of her stopped and watched as she worked the big fish in, as if they'd never seen a fish landed before, as if they were seeing a sea nymph, a Nereid, perhaps Amphitrite, herself.

She was unaware of her audience, concentrating totally on the fish, and when she brought it, thrashing and heaving, up through the last surge of water onto the sand, a sort of sigh of wonder seemed to pass among her observers.

Then she grinned at them and punched a

fist of triumph through the air and the moment of magic was gone. She was no longer a goddess but just another one of them, one of the fisherpeople who had landed a big one during a blitz, so one by one they took their eyes away and went back to their own happy work.

"Now, that," I said to Joshua, "is the right way to bring one in."

Joshua said he'd remember.

I was out of the Land Cruiser when Zee brought the fish up. She was happy and breathless.

"This guy gave me a real tussle!"

She got the hook out of the fish's mouth and smiled at Joshua. He stared back with his big eyes.

"Get another one," I said to Zee, as I set up Joshua's custom-made beach and lounge chair, which I'd made by adding legs, a table space, and an attached umbrella to a plastic car seat. When Joshua was in it, he was about high-chair height above the ground and could play with a couple of toys too big to get into his mouth, watch what was going on, or take a nap. The sun couldn't get to him, but Zee and I could keep an eye on him at the same time that we were fishing. It was one of my better furniture designs. My only one, in fact.

I put Joshua into his chair.

"Well, what do you think? Can you see everything?"

Joshua said he was fine, so I got my rod off the roof rack and went down to the surf, where Zee was already on again.

"Cast!" she said, flashing her white grin. "They're queued up out there, waiting to get on your line!"

I made my cast and had taken only a half-dozen turns on the reel when I saw the swirl and felt the fish hit my redheaded Roberts. I set the hook and joined the line of people with bent rods. Dynamite!

It was a genuine blitz, with fish thicker than a state biologist's head. And they were hitting anything you threw, so after a couple of casts, both Zee and I exchanged our good Roberts for junk lures we wouldn't mind losing so much if we got cut off. For people were losing lures, as is often the case when the razor-toothed blues are in a feeding frenzy. The ocean bottom at Wasque Point must be covered with lures cut off over the years, and no small number of them are mine and Zee's, so we played it safe today and caught fish anyway.

Joshua approved of our decision, and took a real interest in the fish we brought in, but between my sixth and seventh blue he suddenly smelled of serious low tide, so I parked my rod and changed his diaper in the back of the Land Cruiser. Zee came up before I was through and bent over him and smiled. He gurgled and pissed straight up into her face.

"Wretched child!" She wiped her face and laughed.

"It's penis envy," I explained to him. "Girls can't do that. It's a manly talent." I pinned his diaper.

"I'm getting outnumbered by you guys," said Zee. "I need another girl in the family to even things out." She ran a hand down across my chest; I felt that thrill that was always there when she touched me, and was surer than ever that motherhood had made her not only more beautiful than before, but more sensual.

She raised her dark eyes to mine, and I saw something smoldering deep down inside them. She let her hand fall farther.

"I do believe you've got something alive in your pants," she said.

Behind me George Martin's voice said, "Hey, is that the latest Jackson? Let's have a look."

Zee removed her hand and smiled up at me. I picked Joshua up and we turned to greet George as he came to us, rod in hand, followed by a sun-bronzed man I'd never seen before. He looked like some kind of Greek god.

George was in his sixties and spent as much time as he could manage on the beach. He had retired rich, but on the democratic surf-casting sands of Martha's Vineyard, no one cared how much money he or anyone else had or didn't have. George and Moonbeam were judged by the same standards. All the regulars cared about was how you handled yourself: whether you could cast without crossing everybody else's lines. It was even better if you were kidding when you bragged, instead of one of those jerks who really meant it; whether you liked a joke, even if it was on you; and whether you took your losses without self-pity. George passed the tests. He was a good guy, and we had known him for years.

He took a long look at Joshua, who stared back, as he tended to do when people stared at him.

"Boy doesn't look a bit like you, J.W., which is a good thing, all in all."

"You got that right." I gave him my Robinson-Churchill interpretation of the lad's face.

"He does not look like Edward G. Robinson or Winston Churchill, either," said Zee, only half-feigning maternal annoyance. "I think he looks like a little angel. You do, don't you, Joshua?"

27

Zee dropped her eyes to look at her son as I raised mine to find George's companion's eyes wide and staring as he looked at Zee. I'd observed the expression before in the faces of other men who saw her. I'd no doubt had it on my own face, and probably still did from time to time. It was a look of astonishment and wonder, mixed with wild imaginings.

He stared, then became aware of my eyes on his face, and, with effort, looked at me instead of her. His tan may or may not have reddened. He put a grin on his face and held out his hand. There was a golden watch on his wrist and a golden chain around his neck. His perfect teeth flashed in the sun. I knew, suddenly, that he was from California.

"Drew Mondry," he said in a rich baritone voice. "Great-looking boy. They're never too young to start learning to fish."

His grip was firm and so was mine. "J. W. Jackson," I said.

"I'm forgetting my manners," said George. "Zee, this is Drew Mondry. Drew, this is Zee Jackson."

Zee looked at Drew and Drew looked at Zee. They shook hands.

"How do you do?" he said, his hand holding hers a heartbeat longer than need be.

She didn't seem to notice the heartbeat. "How do you do?" She smiled.

His hand released hers. "Your son is a beauty," he said, flicking his bright blue eyes down to Joshua and then back up.

She smiled some more. "Yes. We got it right the first time."

"You have no other children?"

"Not yet."

Love me, love my child, I thought sourly.

"Drew's here looking over locations," said George. "I thought he should see what the island's really like, so I brought him out here."

"It's terrific." Mondry grinned. "I never saw anything like it. All these people catching fish like this. It's amazing!"

"He even got himself one," said George. "Not bad, for his first time surf casting."

"Fish about wore me out," said Mondry, who didn't look at all worn out. "I've trolled out of San Diego, but I never tried this kind of fishing before. I can see how it could become addictive."

"Locations," said Zee. "You must be tied in with that movie business we've been reading about."

He grinned a grin as white as her own. "That's right. I'm one of the guys who scouts areas for the other people who actually make the movie. The more they know about possible shooting areas, the more time and

29

money they save. And with the cost of films these days, they want to save all they can. There are going to be a lot of outdoor shots for this movie, so I'll be here for quite a while, taking a look at things."

"I'd keep the cameras away from Wasque in September," I said, putting in an unrequested two cents.

He kept the grin on his face and looked at me. "Why's that?"

"Derby time. There'll be this many guys and more down here fishing. They wouldn't want anything interrupting them."

"Well," he said, "we wouldn't want that."

"No," I said. "You wouldn't."

Lawrence Ingalls, state biologist, appeared in my mind. Loathsome Lawrence, who had interrupted more Vineyard fishing than anyone in history.

But Drew Mondry already had a new thought. "On the other hand, you've given me an idea. This is just the sort of shot we need to establish island ambiance." He put his hands on his hips and swept the fisherman-filled beach with his eyes. "Yeah! Great idea! They'll love this scene."

Terrific.

"I think it'd be wonderful," said Zee. "You could hire some of the regulars as extras and pay them to fish, which was what they'll be doing anyway. You can start with George. Now, he's what I'd call local color."

George pretended dismay. "You mean I don't get the lead?"

Drew Mondry's bright eyes swept back to Zee as though drawn by a magnet. "We will be hiring local people. How about you, Mrs. Jackson? Are you interested?"

Zee knows that people find her attractive, but has no idea why they do. She hesitated. "Well . . ."

I sniffed Joshua's behind, found the fragrance satisfactory, and returned him to his lounge chair. Then I took my rod off the rack and nodded to Mondry. "Nice meeting you. Good luck with your project."

I went down to the surf. As I went, I heard him say, "May I call you Zee? Thanks. Are you in the book? I think you'd have a lot of fun being an extra, and that you'd photograph very well. Think it over. I'll phone you later."

I made my cast. The lure arched far out into the water. No swirl surrounded it. No fish took it as I reeled in. I thought that Drew Mondry might be having better luck.

"Well, what do you think? Do I have a future on the silver screen?"

Zee sipped her Luksusowa martini, and looked out over the garden and the pond to the far barrier beach, where the very last of the day's swimmers and tanners were packing up and heading home.

I took more than a sip of my own drink (perfectly prepared, as usual: vodka and chilled glasses from the freezer, a splash of vermouth spilled into each glass, swirled, then tossed out; two green olives into my glass, two black ones into Zee's, and Luksusowa to the brim).

"You can probably have a lot of fun finding out," I said. "And when Joshua is a little older, he can watch your reruns on the VCR."

"I can see the headlines now," said Zee, waving a languid arm. "Humble island housewife transformed into glamorous cinema queen, but Academy Award winner never forgets her simple island roots." She sipped some more, then gave me her dazzling smile. "Really, what do you think?"

"As one who's ogled women since puberty, I bow to none as an expert on good-looking women, so you can take it from me that you're at least a ten in any man's book. And I've never known a woman who wasn't an actress part of the time. If that's what it takes to make a star, you've got it made."

She reached out her strong brown arm and took my hand in hers. "I've got it made right here."

We were on our balcony, and Joshua, after his long day on the beach, was snoozing down below in our bedroom. The window was open, and we took turns running downstairs to make sure that he was okay. We were still in the stage where we worried that he was dying when he cried or that he was dead when he was quiet. Like all beginning parents, we were amateurs at the job, and like all amateurs, we used up a lot of worry-energy to no useful end.

I liked having Zee's hand in mine. I liked being married to her, and having Joshua making us three. I didn't want to do anything to unbalance us.

One of the things I liked about our marriage was that it was stuck together without any coercion of any kind. There was no "We have

33

to stay together because we said we would" or "You owe me" or "You promised me you'd love me" stuff or, now, any "Think of the children" stuff, either, even though we had said we'd stick together, and we did owe each other more than we could say, and we did love each other and, now, we did have Joshua to think about.

Basically Zee and I were married because we wanted to be married, and for no other reason.

I wondered why I was thinking such thoughts, and suspected that it was because of two things: the first was a sort of restlessness that had come over Zee since Joshua had made his appearance. Her usual confidence and independence were occasionally less pronounced, occasionally more; her normal fearlessness was sometimes replaced by an uneasiness that I'd not seen in her before, and at other times she became almost fierce.

A postpartum transformation of some kind? I didn't know. Maybe she saw the same things in me, and all that either of us was seeing was the fretting of new parents who didn't really know how to do their job and were worried that they were doing it wrong.

The second thing bothering me was more easily identified. It was Drew Mondry.

Him, Tarzan; Zee, Jane.

34

They even looked like Tarzan and Jane. Both were suntanned and spectacularly made, with his blond hair and brilliant blue eyes contrasting well indeed with her dark eyes and long, blue-black hair. Golden Tarz; bronze Jane.

And there was that little charged current that had run between them this morning.

May I call you Zee? I'll phone you later.

But why shouldn't there be electricity between them? She was a great beauty who left only blind men unscathed, and he was a handsome man with two bright eyes. And didn't I still eyeball female beauties while married to Zee? What was so different about Drew Mondry being fascinated by Zee and her being interested in him?

Or was I only imagining things? Was I just being jealous?

"Come to think of it," Zee now said, looking at me with a parody of a frown, "what do you mean when you say all women are actresses? What sort of a sexist thing is that for a nineties kind of guy to say?"

"I'm a *late* nineties kind of guy. I'm in my post-sensitive period."

"I see. And when were you in your sensitive period?"

"It happened fast. You had to be watching for it."

Her hand squeezed mine. "I don't think you've quite left it yet. But what's this actress notion you have?"

"How about women faking orgasms because guys fake foreplay?"

She sniffed. "Oh, that . . ."

I became conscious of silence in Joshua's room. "I'll be right back," I said, and trotted downstairs.

Joshua was snoozing, not dead. He looked soft and sweet. I gave him a kiss on the forehead and went back upstairs.

I decided to change the subject while I had a chance. "I saw Manny Fonseca downtown when I was selling the fish, and we talked about this and that. He sends his regards and wonders if you might want to do some more practice tomorrow."

To everyone's surprise, especially her own, Zee had fairly recently discovered that she had an amazing knack for shooting the very pistols she had always viewed with distrust and alarm. With Manny, the local gun fanatic, as her mentor, she had quickly become a far better shot than I had ever learned to be, in spite of my training in the military and the Boston PD, and had, in fact, started attracting attention at contests Manny had persuaded her to enter. As she continued to practice and compete, her enthusiasm had mounted. She was, as Manny often said, a natural, and after Joshua had been born, he'd not waited long before luring her to the pistol range once more.

Now she looked at me. "Tomorrow will be fine. I have to get ready for that October competition."

"I'll stick cotton in Joshua's ears," I said, "and we'll both watch you pop those targets."

She gave me a smile. "Pistol-packin' momma?"

"When the other kids learn about your gunslinging, nobody at school will try to beat up our boy. I could have used a mom like you when I was a kid."

Her smile got bigger, more genuine. "I'm sure nobody ever beat you up. You probably beat them up, if they tried."

"Like my sister says: There's never a bronc that's never been rode, and never a rider who's never been throwed. I got pounded a few times."

My sister Margarite lives near Santa Fe, and, like many Eastern transplants, prides herself on her knowledge of Western lore.

Neither of us had had a mom for long, ours having died when we were young, and our father, a one-woman man, never having remarried.

"I like shooting that forty-five Manny's got

me using," said Zee. "My only problem is that I feel I should be with Joshua all the time even though I know that I can't be. I keep hoping that if I keep shooting, it'll wean me. I have to be weaned sooner or later."

Zee had taken a two-month maternity leave from the hospital where she worked as a nurse, but now was back at work part-time.

"You don't have to shoot or go back to work if you don't want to," I said. "We've got enough dough stashed away to keep us alive for a year or two, as long as we don't live too high off the hog. Besides, if I absolutely have to, I can get a regular job."

In the years since I'd retired from the Boston PD and moved to the island, I had managed to avoid anything resembling a steady job. Like a lot of people on Martha's Vineyard, I had, instead, brought in money in a variety of ways: looking after other people's boats and houses during the winter, doing commercial fishing and shellfishing, and taking the occasional odd job. These incomes, combined with small disability pensions from the Feds and Boston (the first for shrapnel wounds contributed by a Vietnamese mortar, the second for a bullet, still nestled near my spine, the gift of a frightened thief trying to escape the scene of the crime), had allowed me to live as well as any bachelor needs to live. I ate a lot of fish and shellfish, grew a garden, which gave me fresh veggies all summer and canned and frozen ones all winter, got fed a lot of meals by women who thought it their duty to feed such as me, and thrived.

But now I was a married man and a father to boot, and maybe it was time for me to change my ways.

On the other hand, maybe not, because Zee now said, "But I want to shoot and I want to go back to work. I love my work. I'm not going to spend Joshua's college fund just so I can stay home and cuddle him."

Joshua's college fund?

"How about staying home and cuddling me, then?" I asked.

"If you go out and get a steady job, you won't be home to cuddle either one of us," said Zee. "It's better the way you do things now. You can take Joshua with you whenever I'm not here, and vice versa."

That was true. For centuries women have known how to handle work and babies at the same time, and I didn't see any reason why I couldn't do it too, so I had made some preparations to help myself out.

The baby pack I'd made, along with a knapsack full of baby stuff, allowed me to go anywhere I normally went on land and do all

the things I normally do. If I had to tempo-
rarily put Joshua aside for any reason, I could
put him in his snappy beach lounge chair. If I
went shellfishing, I could put him in the
mini-raft I'd rigged from inner tubes, and he
could float beside me as I worked.

"No problem," I said, meaning it. Unless
Joshua cried for no reason, in which case I
was in trouble.

I knew most of the cries: the hungry cry, the
load-in-the-diaper cry, the need-to-burp cry,
the mad cry, the I-need-to-be-cuddled cry,
and the I'm-frustrated-about-something-but-
I-can't-figure-out-what-it-is cry; but the cry-
for-no-reason was always a bummer and
always scared me.

Fortunately, Joshua rarely resorted to his
no-reason howl, and usually quieted down
anyway, after some snuggling, so I hadn't yet
been obliged to tear my hair out.

"I'm glad you like being a dad," Zee now
said.

"It's not bad," I said. "How's mom-
ming?"

"If you were named Molly, I'd burst out in
a chorus of 'My Blue Heaven.' "

We listened to the sounds of the evening as
darkness came at us from the east. There were
birds in the air, and the wind hushed through
the woods on three sides of us. On the far side

of Nantucket Sound the lights of Cape Cod began to flicker.

We went down to eat. Grilled bluefish, fresh-made bread, a rice and bean salad, and the house sauvignon blanc. Delish. Such stuff does not go to waste in our house. We wolfed it down.

Zee patted her lips with her napkin. "And what else did Manny have to say to you this afternoon, other than wanting me to pick up my trusty shooting iron and head for the target range? What's new in Edgartown?"

Manny's woodworking shop was on Fuller Street, and customers and friends were wandering in and out all day, so he was always more up on current downtown happenings than were we, who lived up in the woods and only went into the village when we had to.

"Well, it seems Edgartown is going to have a visitor from America," I said, forcing myself to speak in an even tone and avoid expletives. "Maybe you'll want to go down and shake his hand."

"Who might it be? Anyone I know? I understand the president is vacationing out west this year, so it's probably not him." She narrowed her eyes and looked at me. "Do you plan to shake hands with this person, Jefferson?"

"I think not. I don't even want to get into

41

spitting distance of him."

She thought, then arched a brow, then frowned. "I can only think of one person who'd put that look on your face. You don't mean . . . you know who?"

"Yes. Him."

"Not Lawrence Ingalls, state biologist!"

"Shocking, but true. What gall. After keeping the beach closed for three summers, he has the nerve to show up in Edgartown!"

, "What ever for? Doesn't he know that there are dartboards in this town with his face on them?"

"I think he'd be glad if he knew. He'd take it as more evidence that people who disagree with him are crackpots like that wacko Zack Delwood. He's down here to talk to the No Foundation."

Zee found a toothpick and stuck it in her mouth. "The No Foundation, eh? He'll have a friendly crowd, anyway."

The No Foundation was really the Marshall Lea Foundation, and was composed of a private group of citizens who raised money and purchased pieces of Vineyard property for the announced purpose of preserving the land for future generations to enjoy.

Cynics had given them their No name because of the signs the foundation erected on all of their territories, informing readers that there was to be no hunting, no fishing, no trapping, no picnicking, no use of bicycles, etc., and sometimes no trespassing at all.

It was, thus, no surprise to me that Loathsome Lawrence was to speak to the No's. They were his kind of people. The kind known to their critics as No People People, who didn't want any human beings walking around except where and when the No People People wanted them to walk. Naturally, the No People People also didn't want ORVs on the beach.

The critics of the No People People wanted to walk and drive where and when they themselves wanted to walk and drive, and viewed Loathsome Lawrence and his ilk with — what else? — loathing.

I was one of them. I sometimes thought that Zack Delwood was right: that Lawrence Ingalls should probably be shot. It was about the only thing Zack and I agreed about. We not only rubbed each other wrong, but rumor had it that in his cups he had confided a desire to flatten my face just as he had flattened others in several barroom brawls. I made it a point to stay clear of him, because I had problems enough without having a flat face, to boot.

The most irksome of these problems was, of course, Lawrence Ingalls. Maybe he shouldn't be shot, but just be fired or given some job where he could never again have any affect on the lives of other human beings.

Yeah, that was probably better. There was too much shooting in the world already.

This was not a universally held view, as was soon apparent.

— 4 —

If you have to go into downtown Edgartown in the summer, the best time to do it is about seven in the morning. The streets are empty of pedestrians, you can always find a parking place, the dreaded meter maids are not yet at work, and the lovely houses and gardens are bright with morning light and there just for you. You can walk everywhere and see things at your own pace without having to share space with cars, bikes, mopeds, or other sightseers.

And you can get breakfast at the Dock Street Coffee Shop, where the cook has magic hands that can keep a steady stream of satisfied customers from waiting long for their food. His hands and arms move like those of an Oriental dancer as he plies his art. I sometimes take guests down there not only for the good breakfasts, but so they can watch the perfect grace and economy of his motions. He is like a conductor directing a symphony of food.

Zee and I had found three stools together, and had put Joshua in his lounge on the one between us. The waitress looked at him.

"I know your folks want juice and coffee to start with," she said. "How about you?"

Joshua said he'd already eaten.

"You don't look a thing like J.W.," said the waitress. "I'll give you credit for that."

Joshua said he'd heard that before and blew her a bubble.

The waitress brought juice and coffee for two and took Zee's order for a bagel and mine for the full-bloat breakfast — eggs over light, sausages, rye toast, and hash browns.

You'll find a lot of local people and a few touristas at the coffee shop in the early morning, and there are always copies of the *Globe* and *Herald* scattered along the counter, so if you want to know what's going on, you can usually catch up with the latest news and gossip.

Today the principal subject of conversation was the Red Sox, who had so far suffered no real major-league slump and thus still had aficionados and lesser fans enthusiastic about their prospects; the other subjects were the movie people on the island and Lawrence Ingalls's appearance in town.

Zee, who had strong skeptical opinions about this year's edition of the Sox, was quickly engaged in conversation with the guy next to her, who was looking at the *Globe* sports page.

"No D," she was saying. "They can hit, but they can't stop a ground ball. It's always been a problem with them. Like a genetic deficiency passed down through a family."

The guy thought that the problem was with the bull pen. No middle relievers. But their D was no worse than a lot of other teams' he could name, so they had as good a shot as anybody.

Zee was not convinced. "They've never ever been great fielders. Remember Dick Stuart at first? Dr. Strangeglove? He could hit a ton but couldn't catch a cold. The Sox always have at least one guy like that playing the infield, and they've got two this year."

"The real problem is they ain't got no fourth starter," said a guy two stools over. "They got Clemens, who's past his prime, and Wakefield and that other guy, but who they got after that? Nobody. They ought to trade Clemens for a couple of young arms while they can still get something for him."

Zee looked at him across the belly of the guy with the sports page. "Get rid of Roger? That's nuts. The guy they should get rid of is that second baseman who thinks he's playing soccer instead of baseball. He kicks the ball so well he should be playing for Liverpool."

I ate my high-cholesterol meal. I was happy. What could be more pleasantly American than high-fat food and baseball? Joshua couldn't have agreed more. I touched his nose with my forefinger and he smiled. I let my ears roam along the counter.

"They say this movie's about hunting buried treasure. I heard about a real buried treasure that was supposed to be up there by the drawbridge in Vineyard Haven. A couple of sea captains buried it there, then dug up half of it and left the rest. My dad used to talk about it. I think maybe some ancestor of his was part of the crew or something. Name of the boat was the *Splendid*, or some such thing. All happened back in 1850 or so . . ."

"You don't have to go all the way up to Vineyard Haven," replied another voice. "You just have to go over to Chappy and find the Blue Rock. There's a treasure right there. All you have to do is dig it up."

I recognized the voice. It belonged to Moonbeam Berube. What was he doing downtown at breakfast-time? Had Connie thrown him out of the house again? She was a tiger when it came to protecting her children, and didn't tolerate Moonbeam's sometimes heavy-handed notions of parenthood, although so far she'd always taken him back after first kicking him out of the house for a few days.

"The Blue Rock," said another voice. "I never heard of that one. How come you haven't dug it up yourself?"

Laughter from listeners. "You got to know the story," said Moonbeam. "This farmer was chasing a cow when he sees these here pirates burying a big chest in a hole near the beach. He hides behind the Blue Rock and watches. When the chest is in the hole, the chief pirate shoots the two guys helping him and dumps them in the hole. Then he pulls out some sort of package and calls on the devil to help him out and tosses the package into the hole. There's flame and smoke and the farmer faints.

"When he wakes up, the hole's been filled in and there's no pirates in sight. Since then, a lot of people have tried to dig up the chest, but every time they do, demons or some such keep them from finding it."

More laughter. "That's a good one, Moonbeam. Now, where'd you say this Blue Rock is?"

"If I knew, I sure wouldn't be sitting here telling you thieves this story. I'd have dug up that box long ago and be living on Water Street instead of eating here with you guys."

"Not afraid of the devil himself, eh, Moonbeam?"

"Depends on how much money's involved."

Moonbeam would do about anything for money. Even work, if he had no other choice.

"I'll drink to that," said someone.

"Speaking of the devil himself," said a third man, "you read that that bleeping Lawrence Ingalls is in town?"

A number of unflattering remarks filled the air, attracting the attention of tourists, for whom Ingalls's name meant nothing.

"Somebody's going to shoot that son of a bitch," said a voice I recognized as Zack Delwood's. "Goddamned fool. Who does he think he is?"

"Closes the beach every damned summer!" said another voice. "No more morning fishing, no more Sunday picnics, no more shellfishing! Guy should be in jail, but no! He's actually come here, to this very town! My God!"

It was a familiar litany.

The man beside me leaned toward me. "What's all that about? I'd hate to be this Ingalls fellow, whoever he is."

Clearly a tourist.

I sipped my coffee. My own hackles had risen at the very mention of Ingalls's name, and I wanted time to lower them before answering. In my calmest voice, I reviewed the issue of beach closure, and the arguments on both sides.

"Sounds to me like Ingalls may have a point," said the tourist tentatively.

"The only point Ingalls has is the one on his head," growled the man on the other side of him, going on to describe Ingalls in a number of colorful ways.

The tourist wisely said no more.

I waved a fatherly finger at Joshua, who had been listening to everything. "Now, no matter what these guys say, Joshua, I want you to leave Ingalls alone while he's down here. I know he deserves to be run over by a truck, but you're too young to drive, so just stay out of it. Remember that God is just and will take care of him and his kind in due time. In their next lives they're all going to be plover fledglings on Norton's Point, surrounded by skunks and gulls and other creatures who love to eat plover eggs and little plovers. And they won't have any predator fences to protect them."

"I'm glad you've decided to let God take care of him instead of shooting him yourself," said Zee approvingly. She exchanged big smiles with Joshua. "Your dad apparently has a religious side that no one has known about up till now. Isn't that nice? Maybe he'll join the church and become a deacon or an elder or something. You and I could go and watch him every Sunday morning, wearing his robes and passing around the collection plate. Would you like that, Joshua?"

Joshua said he'd think about it.

"You're so cute," said his totally unprejudiced mom, letting him hold on to her finger. "Oh, what a grip you have!"

"Like father, like son," I said modestly.

The guy with the sports page folded it, pushed back his empty plate, looked at Zee, and said, "Have faith. They're only three games out," and left.

"Talk to me in October," Zee called after him.

"I thought you told me you thought they had a real chance this year," I said.

"Yeah, but I couldn't tell him that. Besides, they do have a leaky infield and you know it."

A man came past us and sat down in the seat the Sox fan had just left. The waitress cleared away the fan's plate and cup, gave the counter a fast wipe, smiled at him, and asked him what he'd have.

He'd have tea, juice, and a bagel. Healthy food, of course. His voice was deep and manly. I'd heard it before. Tarzan had seated himself beside us. The waitress smiled some more and headed for the juice dispenser. Tarz had whatever it took to make women like him on sight. Zee and I both looked at him. Zee smiled.

"Well, hello," she said.

"Hi," said Drew Mondry. Then he leaned toward Joshua. "And how are you, partner? Anybody ever tell you you're the best-looking kid on the block?"

Joshua smiled his wide smile and gurgled.

What better way for Tarz to win Jane's maternal heart? Better even than roses and champagne, probably. Zee's smile grew wider.

"He is a cutie," she agreed, beaming at her son. "Aren't you, sweetie?"

Sweetie could not deny it.

"Beautiful day," said Mondry. "I took an early run up to Oak Bluffs and back, and the ocean was shot with fire when the sun came up. I can see why people love it here." He looked at me. "George Martin tells me you really know your way around the island. Any chance you might find time to do some work with me?"

I had been thinking sourly about people who ran up to Oak Bluffs and back before breakfast, and was caught quite off guard by the question. I chewed a sausage and swallowed before answering in the most casual voice I could manage.

"What kind of work?"

"I'm still checking possible locations and I need a guide to show me around. George has to go off island for a few days to tend to some business, so he won't be available. He suggested you. I'll make it worth your while." Then he laughed. "That is to say the company will make it worth your while. I get to spend it, but it's their money. George told me to get you if I could. He gave you quite a recommendation."

There are people who are naturally charismatic and have no need to practice or polish their charm. Drew Mondry was one such. I felt his power now, and was annoyed to discover that I was responding to it. My impulse to resist, however, was countered by my interest in making some money.

I looked at Joshua. "What do you think, Josh? You want to do some sight-seeing?"

Sure, said Joshua.

"Any objection to me coming along too?" asked Zee.

"Love to have you," said Drew Mondry. "It'll give me a chance to talk you into being an extra."

Terrific. But I forced that reaction away. Why shouldn't Zee be an extra if she wanted to? It would probably be a lot of fun for her.

"And I'll tell you what else," said Mondry, giving Joshua a grin. "You might be an extra too, little guy." He glanced at Zee. "How old is he?"

"He arrived in May," said Zee, flashing her great smile.

Mondry turned back to Joshua and gave him a California grin. "You'll be a star before you're six months old! How does that sound?"

Joshua didn't ask me my opinion of this offer. He thought being a star sounded just fine, as long as he didn't have to leave his mom to do it.

"When do you want to start?" I asked Mondry.

"You'll do it? Great!" He leaned back and behind Zee's back stuck out a hand that I couldn't not shake. "I really appreciate this, J.W.!"

For a moment I actually felt like I was doing some sort of great service for mankind. Charm can do that to you.

"Just tell me when you're ready to go," I said.

"How about today?"

How about that?

"Why not?" I said, then wondered if a time would come when I might be sorry to learn the answer to that question.

— 5 —

"I like this," said Mondry, stepping out of the Range Rover in front of our house. He looked around, his brilliant eyes taking in the flowers along the fence and in the hanging baskets, the garden with its late-summer veggies, the bird feeders, and the house itself, with its screened porch and its balcony. "Yeah, this is really nice."

A lot of people say that when they first see the place, but I often wonder how many would actually enjoy living in an old hunting camp that had only recently been spruced up enough to count as a house. For most of its career, it had been more of a wooden tent.

My tent. Now our house.

Still, like much that Mondry had a knack for doing, he had said the right thing. How can you be mad at somebody who really seems to like a house that you like yourself?

"Hi," said Zee, coming out of the house with Joshua on her hip. "Are you ready for your exploration?"

"Raring to go," he answered, flashing his white grin. "I thought we could take my Rover, here, if that's okay. It's got beach stickers if we need them."

I had been looking at the windows of the Range Rover. Whoever owned it had stickers for about every beach or parking area on the island. The stickers on my old Toyota Land Cruiser and Zee's little Jeep were limited to Edgartown's beach offerings.

The Range Rover was also new and shiny, unlike our cars.

"The Rover will be fine," I said.

"Why don't you drive," he said. "That way you won't have to be telling me where to turn all the time, and I can eyeball the scenery instead of just the road."

He could also chat with Zee while I was busy at the wheel.

"Fair enough," I said.

I got Joshua's car seat and strapped it into the backseat of the Range Rover while Zee fetched the baby bag from the house.

Drew Mondry took the bag from her and carried it to the car as I wondered if my skin was literally turning green.

"What do you want to see?" I asked. "Anything in particular?"

"Everything but Chappy, I guess. George took me out to the very end of the Cape

Pogue Reservation, all the way to the gut. So I've seen that area. Then he showed me the Japanese garden there by the Dyke Bridge, and took me around to some other places on Chappaquiddick. But I haven't seen much else."

"The two-wheel-drive tour seems to be in order," said Zee, strapping Joshua into his seat and climbing in beside him.

"We can start with that, at least," I said.

I got behind the wheel and Mondry climbed in beside me. He had a clipboard and camera close at hand as we headed up our driveway toward the paved road.

I give two Vineyard tours to visitors: the four-wheel-drive tour out around the far beaches of Chappy, and the two-wheel-drive tour around the rest of the island. Each takes about two hours at least, but can last a lot longer, depending on how often my guests want to stop to eat or pee or sight-see in more detail. Real restaurant/restroom tours can take half a day.

I explained this to Mondry as we headed for Edgartown and he laughed. "My belly and bladder are in pretty good shape," he said, "but I may want some photo ops or I might even want to get out and look around a bit. If we don't get everything done today, we'll go out again later, if that's all right with you."

58

"If you've got the money, honey, I've got the time."

He grinned. "I've got the money, and we're already in my Cadillac."

Son of a gun. Another C and W fan. Didn't he have any flaws at all?

"I know you're looking for possible sites for shooting this movie," said Zee. "But how do you know when you've found one?"

He turned and put an arm on the back of his seat. "I have a copy of the screenplay and I've got notes with me here on this clipboard. I want to do two things right now: spot scenes that we might use for atmosphere and background stuff — the ferry coming in, the beaches full of people, Wasque and the fishermen, the village streets, and like that; and I also want to find places like a beach where they can dig for the buried treasure, and a good road for the car chase scene. That sort of stuff."

"I hear that it costs a lot of money to make a movie these days," said Zee.

He nodded. "Especially if they're made on location. It would be a lot cheaper if we could shoot this in a studio, but then it wouldn't be the real Vineyard, would it?"

"No, I don't think you can fit the Vineyard into a studio." She laughed.

I have a pretty standard spiel that I give on

my island tours: odd and not-so-odd observations about what we're looking at, so newcomers will know something about what they're seeing. I gave it now as I drove down through Edgartown, showing Mondry the yacht club, the On Time ferry, which was always on time because it had no schedule, and the town wharf, with its walkway topsides where you could get a good look at the harbor, which was full of yachts.

I took him up North Water Street, past the library — a favorite hangout — and the huge captains' houses, which were each set slightly cockeyed to the street for reasons I have never had explained to me. We hooked away from the lighthouse, rounded out of Starbuck's Neck onto Fuller Street, and passed Emily Post's house and lovely flower garden. I took Main down to the four corners again, then went right on South Water, passed under the giant pagoda tree, then took a left down to Reading Room and Collins Beach, where the locals, including Zee and me, keep their dinghies chained to the bulwark to prevent them from being stolen by visiting gentlemen yachtsmen and other thieves.

Then I drove him up Cooke Street and along other narrow, flower-lined streets, past the white and weathered-shingle houses of the village, until we popped out on Peases

Point Way and I headed south toward Katama.

"Beautiful," said Mondry.

Indeed.

I drove to South Beach, where already the Late-August People were parking and putting up their umbrellas and morning kites. I showed him the Great Plains, the herring run and the ruins of the old herring factory. As we passed the little Katama airport, I told him the tale of the wife who, wearing only a bathing suit, had flown in with her husband so she could sunbathe on the beach while he attended to a couple of hours of business in Edgartown, but who had ended up buying a whole wardrobe and spending three days in town because of a sudden thick fog that kept her husband grounded.

Then we drove back through Edgartown, where the traffic jam was already in place between Al's Package Store and the A & P. Creeping free, finally, we went up the beach road to Oak Bluffs, where I pointed out the island's entry in the farthest-north-statue-of-a-Confederate-soldier contest, which was actually a gray-painted statue of a soldier in a Union uniform. Then we crawled up honky-tonk Circuit Avenue and I showed him the tabernacle and the gingerbread houses of the campground. I told him of the old-time camp

61

meetings, of the town's racially integrated citizenry — in stark contrast to that of almost lily-white Edgartown — and of its importance as a summer resort for nonwhite doctors, lawyers, merchants, and other wealthy folk, many of whose families had been coming there for generations.

Mondry asked questions and took notes. I modified my earlier notion that he wanted to ride shotgun only because it would give him the opportunity to dazzle Zee. He seemed to be doing the job he was supposed to be doing.

I drove him around East Chop, over the Oak Bluffs bluffs, and told him of the time when I was a little kid, that the sound had frozen a third of the way out from the island and a third of the way out from the far Cape Cod shore, leaving only a channel down the middle of the sound.

"No kidding," said Mondry, glancing at the blue August waters. "You'd never guess that now."

"If you look at photos taken in the old days," said Zee, "you see pictures of wagons and sledges out on the ice unloading square riggers. It really got cold back then."

We drove past the hospital where Joshua had been born, and went over the drawbridge and past the island's only red light. The *Shenandoah*, which sails out of Vineyard

Haven harbor, had her square foresails up and was heading out before a small following wind. She looked like something from an earlier century.

I drove up Main Street and out onto West Chop. There, at the far end, I told him the tale of the island's most famous murder and showed him the buildings associated with that never-solved crime.

"It captured people's attention because the victim and the suspect were both involved with a theater company," said Zee. "The guy they charged was found not guilty, but even afterward a lot of people were sure he was the one who done it."

"Just like modern times," said Drew Mondry. "People love to know about scandals involving theater people."

I ducked down to the Lake Tashmoo landing, then drove out to the entrance to the pond, where mussels grow on the rock jetties and I've caught more than one bass and bluefish. Across Vineyard Sound, the Elizabeth Islands seemed close enough to hit with a stone from my slingshot.

Then it was up-island, via Lambert's Cove Road, Christiantown, and North Road, to Menemsha, a fishing village that looks like it was built by Walt Disney as a set for a movie about a fishing village. Drew Mondry, seeing

63

the obvious, got out and snapped several pictures and came back full of enthusiasm.

"We'll shoot here, for sure!"

Joshua, less impressed, had taken advantage of the stop to pass that morning's breakfast along to his diaper, requiring a change of clothing by his mother, who didn't mind because she'd seen Menemsha lots of times but still barely knew Joshua and his habits.

"Why do you call it up-island?" Mondry asked.

I told him about the two explanations I'd heard: that it was up-island because the prevailing winds were westerlies and you usually had to sail up-wind to get there from down-island, and vice versa; and that it was a longitude matter, with Gay Head being a higher number than, say, Edgartown.

"I favor explanation number one," I said, "because I've beat my way up the sound more than once, but I've never met anybody who knows the longitude of Edgartown or Gay Head."

"And that's why you go down Maine, I guess."

"I guess that, too. Down Maine and up to Boston. Of course, I've never sailed to Maine and back again, so what do I know?"

"You seem to know quite a bit," said Mondry. "If you ever decide to go into a new line of work, you might consider buying yourself a bus and running your own tour of the island."

Quel horror!

"How you doing?" I asked Joshua, who once again smelled sweet.

He said he was hungry. What a kid. As soon as his belly was empty, he wanted it filled again.

"I'll tend to his lunch," said Zee, and she did that while I drove us past Beetlebung Corner and on toward Gay Head. I paused at the overlook where you can get the great view of Quitsa and Menemsha Pond, with Menemsha Village way over on the far side, then cut through the gateway in the stone wall on the opposite side of the road and parked so we could walk down and see the Quitsa Quoit, one of the island's oddest stone structures.

"What is it?" asked Mondry, as we came into the little clearing and saw the quoit.

"A genuine Vineyard mystery," said Zee, taking him up to the structure while Joshua and I went down to see the little fire pit at the bottom of the grassy area. Mondry was busy with his camera.

The Quitsa Quoit, also known as the Chilmark dolmen, consists of low, vertical supporting stones topped by a slab of rock that pretty apparently didn't get there by chance. I've seen photos and read of quoits in Great Britain, and the resemblance is considerable. But American and British antiquarians, archaeologists, and historians differ greatly about their interpretations of such sites. The British are quick to say that their dolmens are prehistoric structures (the current favorite theory being that they were originally the interiors of burial mounds from which the earth has long since washed away), while the American scholars dismiss such claims about their country's quoits and are inclined to say they are either fakes built by beguilers or are storage chambers built by early settlers who just never got around to mentioning them in their writings.

Zee had apparently brought Mondry up to date on the various theories, for as we walked back to the car together he was saying, "Storage chambers? Burial mounds? That doesn't look like a storage chamber or a burial mound to me."

"John Skye couldn't agree with you more," I said. "He thinks both theories are bunk."

"Who's John Skye?" asked Mondry.

"John Skye is a friend of ours who summers on a farm in Edgartown," said Zee. "In the wintertime he teaches up in Weststock College, up north of Boston. Medieval lit. He goes over to England whenever he can get the college to pay for it, and spends his time in libraries and out in cow pastures looking at standing stones. He says that if the quoits were originally covered with dirt, there should still be a lot of that dirt right there around them. But there isn't."

"For years he's been working on the ultimate translation and interpretation of *Gawain and the Green Knight*," I said.

"So what's he think of this quoit here?" asked Mondry.

"You'll have to ask him."

"Will you introduce me?"

"Sure. If you need to know anything that happened before fifteen hundred, he's your man. He's not so good on things that have happened since."

"I'd like to meet him," said Mondry. "I'm not sure if I can figure a way to get this quoit into the film, but I like it. Do you know who owns this land? I'd like to talk with him."

I'd heard the owner's name, but I didn't know him.

"We can find out," I said.

We got back into the car and headed for Gay Head, where the Wampanoags, after centuries of being hard-pressed by the Anglos, were now hoping to do quite well, thank you, from the profits of their proposed mainland bingo joint. Toni and Joe Begay, she a native of Gay Head and he a long way from the Navajo country of his grandfathers, lived up near the cliffs, and I thought it might be a good thing for Drew Mondry to meet two real live Indians.

— 6 —

Gay Head has some of the finest bass and bluefish grounds on the island. Squibnocket, Lobsterville, Dogfish Bar, and other sites are famous among East Coast surf casters. The town lies on the western tip of the Vineyard, famous for the multicolored cliffs whose bright-hued clays give those cliffs and the town their name. Gay Head is a lovely place of rolling hills, fine beaches, and ancient Wampanoag traditions, but I consider it to be an unfriendly town because of its politics. I mean, you not only can't park beside its roads to go fishing or lie on the beach, there are signs that forbid even pausing to unload passengers. Worse yet, the town parking lot charges two arms and a leg to park there, and the only public toilets are pay toilets. Any place with pay toilets is a place to avoid, such facilities being an affront to God herself.

But Zee and I didn't completely bypass that end of the island. The fishing was too good, and we had friends who lived up there and who let us park in their yards when we wanted to fish under the cliffs, thus allowing us to avoid the clutches of the ever avaricious Gay Head distributors of parking tickets.

Two of these friends were Toni and Joe Begay. Joe, whose folks still lived out in Arizona, near Oraibi, had, long ago, been my sergeant in an Oriental war, but now, after a long and little-discussed career in odd parts of the world, he had settled down with island-born Toni in a house not far from the famous cliffs. They and their new girl-child Hanna lived a quiet life while Joe and Toni, like Zee and I, tried to figure out how to play the parenting game. Toni and Zee had grown close even before both had become pregnant, and now that they were the mothers of actual living and breathing children about whose care they knew not too much, they were even closer, and inclined, as new mothers often are, to participate in long mom talks about their babies and the trials and pleasures of motherhood. The failure of males to be enthralled by such conversations was, as Zee observed with tart sympathy, another liability of the Y chromosome.

I took Drew Mondry first to Squibnocket Beach, where, after the daytime sun seekers have gone home, the bass fishermen love to prowl, then on to Lobsterville Beach, where there's more good fishing (if you can find a parking place), then up to the cliffs themselves. There, after making thrce circles before I could find a free place to park, I led Mondry up between the fast-food joints and the shops selling Taiwan-made Gay Head souvenirs, past Toni Begay's shop, which actually sold American Indian crafts, to the lookout at clifftop. From there, looking to our right, we could see the bright clay precipice, see across the sound to Cuttyhunk and, far away, the edges of America itself.

To the south lay No Mans Land, that curious island which at one time had been a combination of bird sanctuary and navy bombing range. What a mixture of uses. Now the navy had gone away, but even before that the birds had thrived there in spite of the bombs. Recalling this, I immediately thought of wretched Lawrence Ingalls, who had closed Norton's Point because of his misplaced conviction that ORVs were responsible for the dearth of piping plovers on those sands. Loathsome Lawrence.

"You're clouding," said Zee, looking up at me when I stopped talking. "What are you thinking about?"

"Nothing," I said, pushing the cloud off my face and putting on an artificial smile.

She frowned, not fooled. "It's something."

"I'm thinking about Immanuel Kant," I said. Immanuel had once observed that the possession of power inevitably spoils the free use of reason. Maybe that was what had happened to Lawrence Ingalls. Maybe he'd been fine before he'd gotten to be a state biologist. If so, he wasn't the first person whose brain shrank as his power grew. Old Immanuel's generalization was a good one.

Zee decided to let it go. She put a finger under Joshua's chin and smiled down at him. "Immanuel Kant, eh? Well, if Immanuel can't, who can?"

Joshua laughed and drooled. Apparently he'd not heard that old one before.

"We'll go there next," I said to Mondry, pointing down to the narrow beach at the foot of the cliffs. "On the way I'll introduce you to a couple of people who live up this way."

"That might make a good setting," he said. "I would like to get closer to it."

"You can negotiate with the Gay Headers," I said. "I don't know if they want anybody making movies down there."

"I'm just an idea man," he said, with a smile. "Somebody else can do the negotiating if it needs to be done."

As we passed Toni Begay's shop, I put my head inside and saw her little sister Maggie. "Toni at home with the family?"

"Oh, hi," she said. "Yes, everybody's there. Since Hanna showed up, it's hard to get my sister out of the house. I think she's afraid that Hanna will break if she takes her outside."

It was a now familiar fear that I hadn't known existed before Joshua was born. I was working hard to overcome it, but wasn't out of the woods yet. I suspected that I might never be, that as a parent I was doomed to worry about my children forever.

"And speaking of babies," Maggie went on, "how is Wyatt Urp?"

"Wyatt is right outside," I said. "See for yourself."

She did that, and I made introductions.

"Maggie, this is Drew Mondry of the Hollywood Mondrys. Drew, this is Maggie Vanderbeck of the Gay Head Vanderbecks."

Maggie and Mondry exchanged hellos.

"Hollywood," said Maggie. "Are you with that movie outfit I've been reading about?"

"I'm afraid so."

Maggie was cute. "Are you looking for genuine Native American extras to give your film a touch of authenticity? I can use some fame and fortune."

He laughed. "I don't think authenticity has a lot to do with movies these days, but I'll keep you in mind."

Then Maggie and Zee cooed over Joshua

73

until a customer came by and Maggie had to go back to work.

"Maggie and I work together at the hospital," said Zee to Mondry. "She's studying to be a nurse."

"A noble profession," said Drew Mondry.

Zee nodded. "It is. Once I thought I'd go to medical school and become a doctor, but I decided that being a nurse was more important. I think I made the right choice."

"Indeed." He nodded.

It was beginning to take effort to dislike him. After all, his only problems were that he looked like a leading man, acted like a gentleman, and was fascinated by Zee; and who could blame him for any of those things?

We drove toward Lobsterville and turned off into Joe and Toni Begay's yard. Joe's truck and Toni's car were parked there, and there was a pretty new Ford Bronco there, too.

Toni Begay came to the door and, seeing Zee and me, came right out and gave us hugs.

"What a nice surprise!"

I introduced Drew Mondry to Toni and Toni to Drew Mondry. "I'm giving the twenty-five-cent tour of the island," I said, "and I want Drew to see the cliffs from the bottom looking up."

Toni waved toward the path that led to the beach. "You two go look at the cliffs. Zee and

I will stay here and make plans for Joshua and Hanna's wedding."

"But Hanna is an older woman," I said. Hanna had been born ten weeks before Joshua.

"Women should always get their men young and raise 'em the way they want them," said Zee. "Everybody's happier that way."

"You didn't do it that way."

"I made a mistake, myself, but it's not too late to save my son." Zee put her nose against Joshua's. "Is it, you little sweetie?"

"You'll probably meet Joe and his friend Larry and Larry's assistant on your walk," said Toni. "They're out strolling the beach. Come on in, Zee."

Drew Mondry looked appreciatively after them. "Now, there are two women who make you think there's hope for America. You and your friend Joe are two lucky guys."

True.

We walked west along the sandy trail until we came to the beach. To our left the cliffs began to rise. We went that way, with the waves slapping at the sand beside us.

"A lot of bass have been caught under these cliffs," I said. "And a lot of people like to take mud baths in the clay that washes down onto the beach. For years nobody thought much about it, but now it's very politically incorrect, and they've got people with badges patrolling the beach to protect the cliffs."

"You sound like you aren't too sympathetic with the badge wearers."

"I'm getting crotchety in my old age. I don't like people telling other people that they can't do harmless things they've always done."

"Maybe the mud baths aren't harmless. I imagine the police are just trying to protect the cliffs."

Sweet reason.

"It'll take more than a few mud bathers to tear down the Gay Head cliffs," I said. "I'm not a mud bather myself, but I'm on their side."

From the direction of the cliffs, two men and a woman were walking toward us. I recognized the taller one as Joe Begay. His companions were shorter and slighter and were strangers to me. They seemed deep in conversation.

"I think the argument is that there have to be rules that keep people from wrecking the environment," Drew Mondry was saying.

I wasn't opposed to that thought, but felt a surge of familiar stubbornness. "Yeah, but who's going to decide what the rules are and who's going to be the enforcer? Those are the questions. Personally, I don't think I need anybody else telling me how to save the planet."

"I think that I'll just ease out of this subject," said Mondry with a grin.

The grin was infectious and I found a smile on my own face. "Both of us will ease out of it."

Ahead of us Joe Begay and his companions seemed to notice us for the first time. Actually, I suspected that Joe had taken note of us before I had seen them. There was little that escaped Joe's eye. Now I saw him raise a hand, and raised my own in reply.

"Joe Begay," I said to Mondry. "We met in Vietnam."

"Quite a while back."

"Yeah. It's in the history books these days, the way World War Two was when I was a kid."

The five of us came together and paused. Begay raised an eyebrow.

"Are you alone, or are our ladies at the house admiring their children?"

"They're there. Joe, this is Drew Mondry. He's scouting locations for that movie outfit that's coming here in the fall. Drew, this is Joe Begay, Toni's husband."

They shook hands. Then Mondry shook hands with one of Begay's companions.

"Call me Drew," he said.

"Larry," said the other man. "This is my assistant, Beth."

He was slim, clean-cut, and wearing pressed jeans and a short-sleeved shirt. He wore wire-rimmed glasses and had thinning brown hair above intelligent blue eyes. Everything about him was clean and neat.

"Hi," said Beth. She was young and outdoorsy looking.

There was a little smile lurking somewhere in Joe Begay's scarred bronze face.

"And this is a friend of mine, J.W.," he said. "I don't think you've met. Larry, this is J. W. Jackson."

Larry put out his hand and I took it. It was sinewy and brown. A working hand.

"And, J.W., this is Larry Ingalls," Begay's amused voice continued. "Larry works for the state. He's down here to give a talk."

Larry Ingalls. Works for the state.

Lawrence Ingalls, state biologist. Plover lover. Eco-terrorist. Beach closer.

"Pleased to meet you," said Loathsome Lawrence.

— 7 —

"Larry's down from Boston," said Begay.

"That makes you a stranger in a strange land," I said, looking at Ingalls.

Ingalls shook his head. "Not really. I'm based in the city, but I have a place here. I get down whenever I can."

"Larry works for the Department of Environmental Protection," Begay said to Mondry, enjoying the situation. He then turned to Ingalls. "J.W. is one of our local surf casters."

"When I can get to the surf to cast," I said.

Ingalls, apparently used to being warmly received by his audiences, gave me a second look.

"Well," he said, "there's certainly plenty of surf on the Vineyard."

"Not as much as there used to be," I said. "Some idiot up in Boston has closed down Norton's Point Beach for the past several summers because of his asinine notion that ORVs were killing off piping plovers. There's a lot of local sentiment to the effect that whoever made that decision should either be shot to put him out of his misery, or institutionalized because he's delusionary."

Beth looked startled, and Ingalls's eyes got hard. "The law is the law. And the plan worked. The plovers are thriving and the beach is open again."

From the corner of my vision I could see the smile on Begay's face, but I kept my own eyes cold.

"Everybody but this seven-letter word from Boston knows the plovers are thriving because the beach patrol built predator fences around the plover nests, not because there weren't any ORVs going down the beach. But this fanatic, whoever he is, is one of those eco-terrorists you read about: he's got himself a list of commandments straight from God, and one of them is that ORVs are plover killers. He reminds me of that bastard Oliver Cromwell."

Was Ingalls running seven-letter words through his mind? I couldn't tell.

"I'm the guy in Boston," he said coldly. "This island is a fragile place, and we protect its ecology, including its wildlife. Irreparable harm can be done! And a lot of studies show that ORVs have been a principal cause of destroying the natural habitat of plovers and other shorebirds!"

I put my face a little closer to his. "There's no evidence at all that the plovers on Norton's Point are any better off because you banned ORVs, you know."

"I do not know!"

"You probably don't know a lot of things," I said. I was on a roll. "Before you closed it, the county cleared about forty thousand dollars a year selling ORV stickers to that beach! Since you closed it down, they've had to spend more than that just to hire people to enforce your worthless regulations! It works out to about two thousand dollars a plover, and by the ounce that's more than the price of gold!"

"We're sensitive to the revenue issues," said Ingalls, putting his nose up toward mine. "But if vehicles aren't managed on that beach, the ecological consequences will be extremely adverse!"

"The ecological consequences will be extremely adverse, eh? The only time I ever heard anybody string together a phrase like that was when he was reading it out of a book. You must have memorized those tablets God showed you when he gave you the job of leading us heathen out of the wilderness!"

"Don't raise your voice to me, Mr. Jackson!" he said, raising his voice. "It costs money to enforce the law, and there are no laws more important than those protecting our environment!"

I was beginning to feel pretty good.

"Nobody needs you or your idiotic notions about what it takes to protect the environment!" I said, raising the voice he'd ordered me not to raise. "The scariest thing about you is that you actually believe what you say!" I turned to Begay and winked and said, "Joe, what are you doing hanging around with an arrogant idiot like this guy?"

I turned back and was surprised to find Lawrence Ingalls swinging a wild right hand at my chin. It was easy to slip it, and I felt sorry for him until he belted my jaw with a hard left and the world turned gray-black. My knees went watery and I realized too late that the right had only been a feint and that Lawrence Ingalls was a boxer. Although only a middleweight, he knew how to put shoulder behind his punches, and that one such punch in the right place has put better men than me down for the count. I got my hands up just in time for him to step in under them and put a hard combination into my gut. Although I was a couple of weight classes heavier than he was, I sagged some more.

If he'd stepped back then and taken his time, he might have put me down, or I might have just kept falling until I hit the ground.

But, instead, his temper kept him close, throwing more punches at my belly, and I was able to lurch forward and get my arms around him. I put my chin on his shoulder and let him hold me up while he banged on my kidneys. Slowly my head began to clear and my knees got some starch back into them.

I tightened my arms around him. The surf was off to my right, and I dragged him down to it while he kept thumping my kidneys. But I was a lot bigger than he was, and in spite of his best efforts to stop me, I walked him out into the water and shoved his head under.

He thrashed like a bluefish, but I held him there.

Somewhere off in the distance I heard Begay saying, "Now, now, J.W., if you're going to drown him, it'd be better if you did it without any witnesses around."

"Let him up," said Beth's voice. "You'll kill him!"

"Somebody probably will," I said. "Why not me?"

Ingalls seemed to be weakening. I pulled his head up and he choked and gasped and grabbed at me.

"You shouldn't pick fights with strangers," I said. "They're not all as nice as I am. The next one may hand you your head on a plate."

I dragged him back to shore and dropped

him on the beach. He didn't look as ironed as he had before.

"I thought he had your number there for a minute," said Begay. "You must have forty pounds on him, but he still almost cleaned your clock. You're getting old."

"He never laid a glove on me," I said, panting.

Beth was kneeling beside Ingalls, who was coughing salt water out of his lungs. She looked up at me with furious eyes.

"I'll have you arrested for assault, you big bully! You almost killed him!"

"He's not even half dead," I said. "Besides, he threw the first punch, so I should be the suer, not the sue-ee. Ask your witnesses." I waved a hand at Mondry and Begay.

Ingalls got to his hands and knees. He was still coughing, but looked like he'd live.

"You'd better take your boyfriend back to Boston," I said to Beth. "This island isn't good for his health."

"You won't get away with this," she said. "I'll make sure you don't!"

Ingalls sat back on his heels. By some miracle, his glasses were still on his face.

"Why don't you two keep going on your walk," said Begay. "Beth and I will get Larry back to the house."

That seemed like a good idea. "Come on,"

I said to Drew Mondry. "We'll check out the cliffs from the beach."

"Stay away about an hour, at least," said Begay, with a reasonably straight face.

"I'll remember you," said Ingalls, coughing. "We'll meet again!"

"You'd better hope not," I said, and walked away up the beach. Snappy dialogue is my forte.

Mondry walked beside me, saying nothing.

After a while, I looked back and saw that Begay, Beth, and Ingalls were gone.

"Well," said Mondry.

"I know, I know," I said. "The whole thing was stupid."

"I wasn't going to say a thing, but now that you mention it . . ."

"If my face isn't red, it should be."

"These things happen," said Mondry.

"I don't like them happening to me," I said.

A couple of times in the past, when I'd been injured or afraid, a crimson curtain had fallen over my eyes and turned the world the color of blood, and I'd come close to really hurting people. I didn't ever want that to happen again, and wondered now how far away that red world had been when Ingalls had hit me.

"Your friend Begay is an interesting guy," said Mondry. "He didn't seem too worried about either of you."

"Joe has seen too much to worry about a spat like this one."

I was soaked, but that didn't mean much since I was decked out in my normal duds: shorts, a T-shirt, and Tevas, the first two being products of the Edgartown thrift shop; if you live on an island, you have to expect to get wet now and then, either on purpose or accidentally. Besides, my clothes were already drying in the summer sun.

"Where did your friend see all that stuff?"

"You can ask him when we get back to the house. He might tell you, but I wouldn't count on it."

We walked along the beach as the cliffs rose higher and higher above us, and passed the place where people like to take mud baths.

I said, "This is the place I was telling you about. When I was a little kid, nobody cared if you wallowed around down here in the wet clay, and we used to climb up and down the cliffs. I think it would take a lot of people a lot of time to wear away these cliffs, but they're Gay Head's cliffs, not mine, and if they want to keep people off them, it's okay with me."

"You're pretty testy today," said Mondry.

He was right. I tried to put my testiness away.

We walked to the far end of the cliffs, then back again, passing the rocks where sometimes there are big bass lying in wait for your lure. The only problem with hooking a really big bass at the foot of the cliffs is that you have to somehow tote it back to your truck, which is a long walk. It is a difficulty gladly accepted by bass fishermen.

"We could bring a boat in close and get shots of this beach," said Mondry, looking first out to sea, then up at the sky. "And I should take a look at the cliffs from a helicopter, too. In fact, I should take a look at the whole island from the air. You know anybody with a helicopter?"

"It costs a lot of money to rent a helicopter."

He smiled his California smile. "Money is no problem."

I thought of Zorba's observation that life is a problem; only death is no problem.

"I can find you a helicopter," I said.

"Good man."

Our hour was up, so we walked back to the Begays' house. Loathsome Lawrence and his helper were gone.

Zee narrowed one eye and looked at me. "What happened out there? All Joe will say is that you and Larry Ingalls had an argument. But Larry was soaked when he got here and I can see that you got pretty wet yourself. What happened?"

She had Joshua on her hip. I was almost dry by then, so I took him and put him on mine. Babies fit on women's hips better than on men's, but Josh did not seem discontent. He grabbed my T-shirt and tried to get it in his mouth.

"Nothing happened," I said. "We both jumped into the water, that's all."

"Jumped into the water, eh? You both jumped into the water?"

"We were having a hot argument, so we jumped into the water to cool off."

"With your clothes on."

"There was a lady present. We had to stay decent."

Zee came up to me and put a finger lightly against the bruise on my jaw. "I can see I'm going to have to take you home alone before I get the truth out of you."

I smiled over her head at Toni Begay. "She never beats me up in public. Only in private."

"I understand," said Toni. "I'm the same way. I'm just waiting for you guys to leave so I can pound the truth out of Joe."

"In fear of my life, I plan to hold tight to Hanna as a human shield," said Begay, bouncing his daughter on his knee.

Mondry, the only man there without a woman, looked from one of us to the other. He had an odd, almost covetous look in his eye.

"Do you have a wife to keep you in line?" I asked him.

Quick as a card sharp, he produced his wallet and a photo of a woman and a girl. "This is my wife, Emily, and our daughter, Carly. They're out in L.A."

"You should always keep your wife close at hand," said Zee.

"I'll be back there before too long," said Mondry. He looked at the photo and then put it away.

"Meanwhile," I said, "Toni can tell you all about Gay Head. She knows more about it than the rest of us do because she's a genuine born-and-bred Vineyard native and we're just off-island ginks — except for Hanna and Joshua, of course; they qualify as genuine islanders, too, but they're not talking much yet."

Joe Begay and I took Joshua and Hanna and a couple of beers outside so the babies could discuss their betrothal with their fathers.

Begay rolled himself a cigarette and lit up. Smoking was a habit he had not yet licked, but he was past buying ready-rolled cigarettes, at least.

"What's with you and Ingalls?" I asked. "I don't think I ever heard you mention him before."

"I was trying to spare your tender sensibilities," said Begay. "I've heard you saying nasty things about him over the last several years, and I didn't want to get you all worked up. Anyway, he's down here to give a talk to the Marshall Lea Foundation tonight. I met him the last time he came down to talk with them."

"And you've been showing him the cliffs."

He tried to blow a smoke ring, but the wind forbade it. "That among other things. We've got the same environmental problems here that the rest of the island has, and no long-range plans to take care of them. Larry has some ideas that might help, so he's been talking and I've been listening. You two didn't seem to hit it off."

"I don't like dictatorial bureaucrats."

He smiled. "Especially when they close you off from your fishing grounds, eh?"

"Especially."

He tried another smoke ring without more success. "I like a man who operates on high moral principles."

His irony was clear, particularly since he knew that I distrust people who see themselves as acting on high moral principles.

People acting on principle have probably done more damage to the earth and its creatures than all of the unprincipled people combined.

"When somebody finally shoots that guy," I said, "there'll be so many suspects that they won't be able to solve the crime."

"You're a hard case," said Begay. He laughed, and after a minute so did I. I wondered if life is absurd all by itself, or if we just make it that way. We meaning me. Begay and I drank our beers and watched Joshua and Hanna paw at each other and eat a little dirt, which they seemed to enjoy.

When the others came out of the house later, Mondry claimed to know more about Gay Head than he had known he could know. He and Zee and Joshua and I then climbed into the Range Rover and drove back down-island.

At our house, the Jacksons got out of the Range Rover and Mondry got into the driver's seat.

"A good time was had by all," said Zee, flashing her dazzling smile. She took Joshua's wrist and waved his hand. "Say good-bye, Joshua."

"Good-bye, Joshua," said Mondry, waving back. "Thanks for coming along."

Joshua and Zee went into the house.

"Thanks a lot for the tour," said Mondry to me.

"There's more you haven't seen. The Vineyard doesn't look very big on maps, but not many people, including me, have seen all of it."

"Will you show more of it to me?"

"Sure."

"And you'll find a helicopter?"

"Sure."

"Great." He hesitated. "And there's one thing more."

"What's that?"

He hesitated again, then said, "I want your permission to take your wife out to lunch. I want to talk to her about —"

He stopped as I held up a hand.

"You don't need my permission to talk to Zee. She's my wife, not my property. If you want to ask her to lunch, ask her, not me."

He opened his mouth, then closed it. Then he opened it again. "I just want to do this right. I don't want to go behind your back."

I wondered what my face was showing him. "I appreciate that," I said, "but Zee is her own boss and decides what she'll do or won't do. I don't own slaves."

"But she's your wife. Don't you care what she does?"

I cared. "I want her to be happy. If having

92

lunch with you makes her happy, I want her to have lunch with you. But she decides, not me."

He stared at me. "Are you sure about this?"

"I'm sure."

"Well, then, I'll give her a call. Is this going to prevent you from showing me the island? I don't want you to feel that —"

"The one thing has nothing to do with the other."

He took a deep breath and nodded. "Tomorrow morning, then?"

"I'll be here."

He drove away, and I went into the house. One of my demons was the desire to keep Zee only to myself. There were other devils in me, but none were stronger than that one. Had I believed in God, I would have prayed daily to keep the imp in check; sometimes I prayed anyway.

— 8 —

Joshua was nodding on my lap and I was sitting on the balcony with Zee. Across Sengekontacket Pond, car lights were moving back and forth along the road on the barrier beach between Edgartown and Oak Bluffs. Beyond them, on the far side of Nantucket Sound, the lights on Cape Cod gleamed at us, and to the southeast we could see Cape Pogue light. Above us, the summer stars glittered and the Milky Way arched from horizon to horizon. There was a soft wind that made the trees sigh and brought us the sounds of night birds and other nocturnal creatures.

Zee's hand found my knee. "How's the heir?"

"The heir is almost asleep. He's a sweetheart, just like his old man. Never gives anybody any trouble."

"That's odd. I thought *you* were his father." Zee's fingers gave me a sharp squeeze. "What happened up there in Gay Head?"

I told her.

She sighed. "Men!"

"Let's have no sexist remarks," I said. "Remember Zenobia and Boadicea and Morgan le Fey and those other killer women. All I did was dunk Loathsome Lawrence in the drink."

"Morgan le Fey was fiction."

"How about Ma Barker, then? Or Belle Starr? Don't give me this 'men are violent, but women are sugar and spice' stuff."

She snuggled nearer. "But I'm a woman and I'm sugar and spice. I know you can't see them, but I'm fluttering my eyelashes even as I speak."

I got one arm loose from now snoozing Joshua and put it around her. "Any woman with fluttering eyelashes can wrap me around her finger."

We looked at the stars for a while, and I felt good, with Joshua in one arm and Zee in the other. After a while, we went downstairs and put the lad in bed.

Zee beamed down at him. "It's hard to believe that he'll ever be a terrible two."

"I was never a terrible two," I whispered. "Maybe he'll be like me: a perfect child all the way."

"Didn't some psychologist theorize that if we don't get our childishness out of our systems while we're little, we'll be stuck with it when we're big?"

"It's a good theory. It's true of everybody I know except me."

We went out into the living room, where I sat down on the couch and Zee lay down and put her head in my lap.

"Drew Mondry's coming by again tomorrow," I said. "I'm going to continue the grand tour. He wants me to find him a helicopter, too, so he can look at things from the air."

"I like him," said Zee. "He seems like a nice guy."

Great.

"Don't you think he is?" she asked.

I couldn't think of anything to make me think he wasn't.

"Sure," I said.

"I have to work tomorrow. Maybe you should get one of the twins to take Joshua for the day."

"No, I'll take him with me."

John and Mattie Skye's twin daughters, Jill and Jen, doted on Joshua, and would care for him at the drop of a hat. But I didn't drop the hat too often, since I figured that I was going to be Joshua's father as long as I lived and I'd better get used to having him around. Besides, I liked being with him even though I knew little about babies in general and not much more about him in particular.

"Drew Mondry said he wanted to talk with you about something," I said.

"Oh? What?"

"I don't know. Maybe this business about getting you into the movies."

She laughed. "Oh, that. I think it would be fun to be an extra, though. Don't you?"

"Maybe I could carry a spear or something."

"I don't think this is a spear-carrying film. A quahog rake, maybe. I know! You and I can be American Gothic, only we'll stand in front of a clam shack and you can wear waders instead of coveralls and hold that quahog rake instead of a pitchfork. It'll be great. We'll be the background for something that happens in the foreground. A steamy sex scene, maybe, with us standing there as contrast. What do you think?"

"Maybe we can do the foreground scene instead."

"Ah," she said. "Maybe we could, at that."

"Of course, we'd need to rehearse."

Later, as she lay beside me in the darkness of our bedroom, her voice was sleepy. "Maybe I *could* learn to do this in front of a camera crew, after all. Maybe there *is* a place for me in Hollywood. I feel like a star right now."

I ran a lazy finger down over her face,

tracing her forehead and nose, getting the finger kissed as it crossed her lips, passing it over her chin and down her throat, down between her breasts, over her flat, sweaty stomach until my hand rested on her lower belly, damp and musky from lovemaking.

She put her hands on top of mine, then shivered and rolled toward me and wrapped me in her arms.

The next morning I made some phone calls and found a helicopter outfit on the mainland that would be glad to ferry Drew Mondry anywhere he wanted to go, as long as Drew didn't mind paying for the pleasure. Since money seemed to be no problem to Drew, I told the guy on the phone that I'd get back to him. I imagine he had his doubts about whether I actually would, since he probably had gotten a lot of calls from people who couldn't afford him but were too shy to admit it.

Drew Mondry showed up on schedule, and was openly disappointed by Zee's absence.

"She's a working girl," I said. "If you want to spend more time with her, get yourself hurt enough to go to the emergency ward at the hospital."

"I'll give it some thought," said Mondry.

"Of course, there are some other nurses up

there, too," I said, loading Joshua and his gear into the Range Rover. "You might get one of them instead."

"Drat," said Mondry. "I guess I'll have to stay well."

We spent the day driving back roads and walking paths through reservation areas.

"I thought you were mad at the environmentalists and the conservationists," said Mondry as we stood on a sandy trail beneath tall trees and admired a brook that tumbled over rocks at our feet, then disappeared beyond a grassy embankment. "I could have sworn that you dunked one of them in the Atlantic Ocean just yesterday."

"If I could afford it," I said, "I'd buy this whole island and keep as much as I could looking just like this. But I wouldn't keep people locked away from it. Every beach would be public, and I wouldn't keep people from hunting and fishing and blueberry picking and doing the things they've always done on the land."

He jabbed the needle. "How about lumberjacking and building gas stations and more houses?"

"They farm trees in a lot of places," I said. "They could probably farm them here, too. You plant them and grow them and cut them down and plant new ones, so you always have the trees you need. The same goes for shellfishing. If I owned the place, I'd have shellfishing farms in some of the ponds. As far as the houses are concerned, everybody wants to be the last person to own here, but actually there's a lot of room on this island for more houses. The problem is that I'm not so sure there's enough water for too many more people. I guess I'd go for individual homes, but not for developments."

"No constraints?"

I don't like constraints. "No more than need be," I said.

"What about those gas stations? What about more people coming every year and more cars coming and all that stuff I keep hearing about?"

"When I own the island, there won't be any more of that stuff."

"How about since you don't own the island?"

One reason I'd given up being a cop and come to the Vineyard to live a quiet life was because I'd grown tired of trying and failing to make the world a better place. I'd decided to get away from society's problems, but like the guy says, there is no "away."

"How should I know?" I now said. "You don't let go, do you?"

"I don't get paid to give up," he said, and I

knew then that he would, indeed, be telephoning Zee to invite her to lunch.

We walked on along the trail with Joshua out of his backpack and in my arms, sucking on a bottle.

"Are there roads into these places where we've been walking? If there aren't, I don't know how we could do location work in them, even though they're beautiful."

"There are old roads all over this island, and the conservation groups that own these places always need money. If you offer them enough and can convince them that you can get your trucks or whatever in and out without damaging things, you might be able to make a deal."

"Can you put me in touch with the people in charge?"

What an irony. Me contacting the very people whose policies I had criticized so often in the past.

"I can do that," I said.

His smile revealed his awareness of the contrast between my feelings and my promise of action. "You don't mind being a go-between for me and your enemies?"

It is a truism that we judge groups we don't belong to by their least desirable characteristics, and hold their most extreme members as being typical of their fellows. I wasn't immune to such stupidity, but I tried to fight it.

"I don't mind," I said. "Besides, they're not my enemies."

"Not even Lawrence Ingalls?"

"Every group has its jerks," I said. "He's theirs. I'll talk to some other people, but if you want to talk to him, you can do it yourself." But even as I spoke, I realized I was no longer angry with Ingalls. As sometimes happens, once blows had been taken and returned, anger had gone away. Loathsome Lawrence was no longer a person I hated, but only a guy who held views I couldn't abide. The difference was a great one. Hatred is an exhausting emotion, and I was glad to find mine gone.

At the end of the day, we drove back to our house. Zee came out and took Joshua, who was glad to see her. Madonna and child.

"Seen enough?" I asked Mondry.

"No," he said, and I saw that he was looking at Zee. Then he realized that I was talking about the island, and forced his eyes away from her. "Enough from the ground. For the moment, at least. Can we fly tomorrow? Maybe after that, I'll want to see some places I don't know about yet."

"I'll call the helicopter outfit," I said.

"Good. Have them meet us at the airport in the morning."

Drew Mondry drove away.

"Well, how did it go?" asked Zee.

"Fine." We went inside and I told her about our travels.

"And tomorrow you're going to fly. I've never been in a helicopter. It must be fun!"

I had been in a few that weren't fun while in Vietnam, but that had been long, long ago.

While Zee and Joshua exchanged gossip and hugs in the living room, I phoned the helicopter outfit and surprised the guy I'd talked to earlier by hiring one of his planes and a pilot. Then I called Drew Mondry and told him when to be at the airport. Then I got to work in the kitchen, finishing making the supper that Zee had already started: stuffed bluefish and fresh garden salad.

It was our last fresh bluefish, which meant that a surf-casting trip was at the top of our list of things to do. Not a bad duty, as I pointed out to Zee, as we polished off our meal.

"Well, blast and damn!" said Zee, looking at the tide tables. "The last two hours of the west tide at Wasque are after I go to work in the morning!"

"I, on the other hand, am free until ten o'clock," I said. "Joshua and I can be down there and back again in time to be at the airport when the helo comes in."

Zee was telling Joshua about the unfairness of life, when the phone rang. She answered it, and I began washing the supper dishes. I was nearly through when she came back into the kitchen, Joshua on her hip.

"That was Drew Mondry," she said, brushing at her son's mostly imaginary hair. "He wants to have lunch with me."

I put a last plate into the drainer. "He said he wanted to talk to you."

I looked at her, but her own eyes were lowered toward Joshua.

"He says he's going to try to talk me into being in the movie," she said. "I told him he could talk about anything he wanted to, as long as he paid for lunch."

She raised her dark eyes and looked at me. "You don't mind, do you? If you mind, I won't do it."

"I don't mind," I lied.

The next morning, Joshua and I were on the road minutes after Zee had driven off to work. At the head of our long, sandy driveway, she had gone right, toward Oak Bluffs, and we went left. It was early, so the dreaded A & P traffic jam had not yet formed, and we got through Edgartown with no problems and went on south to Katama.

Joshua was being grumpy, and I couldn't talk him out of it, so it was a whiny ride all the way to Katama, where I got the Toyota into four-wheel drive and turned east onto Norton's Point Beach. When I reminded Josh of the No Sniveling sign above our kitchen door, he only sniveled more.

"Fussing won't help our fishing any," I said.

He spit out his pacifier and cried.

"Look," I said, "it's a beautiful day. You've had breakfast, your diaper is clean, we're going to have the beach to ourselves, and the fish are going to be there waiting for us. What more can you want?" I found the pacifier and returned it to him. "Here's your plug, kid."

He wouldn't take it, and kept crying.

Demi-crisis.

I pulled off the jeep track, parked, and hauled him out of his car seat. Soaked pants. Good grief. I got him dried and powdered and into a new diaper. Still he cried. I put him on my shoulder and walked him down to the surf, patting him on the back. He burped a fair-sized burp. Aha! The old piss-in-your-pants-and-then-need-to-burp syndrome, eh? I should have guessed.

I hauled him around so I could see his face. He smiled weakly. What a guy. I put him back in the car seat, gave him his plug, and we went on.

To our right, the Atlantic Ocean slapped against the sand, and to our left Katama Bay reached up toward Edgartown. Ahead, parked off to one side of the track, was a white pickup. When we came up to it, I saw that it was empty. I also saw a DEP logo on its door. Somewhere nearby, no doubt, some plover-loving official was snooping around in hopes of finding a reason to close down the beach again next year.

I didn't see anyone who belonged to the pickup. Maybe the driver had gone for a morning swim and had drowned. Or maybe some other unpleasant thing had happened to him. Or her. EPA types came in all genders, and one sex was as bad as the other.

"Now, don't get all worked up just because of one government truck," I said to Joshua. "Just keep your mind on bluefish."

Joshua said he'd try to restrain himself, and we drove on.

The bluefish were waiting for us at Wasque Point, and there was only one other Jeep ahead of us. It belonged to John Skye and had contained the whole Skye family: John, Mattie, and the twins, Jill and Jen. They were all catching fish. A lovely sight.

I pulled alongside the Jeep, got Joshua set up in his lounge chair, so he could be part of the action, and took my eleven-foot graphite rod off the roof rack.

Mattie Skye came up from the surf with a nice six-pounder as I headed down to make my cast.

"They're here," she said. Then she beamed at Joshua, the way women do when they see babies. "Hi, Joshua!"

Joshua gave her his big smile and said hi.

I made two casts and got nothing.

"Gee, J.W.," said one of the twins, pulling in a fish, "I can't understand what you're doing wrong. Here, do you want to land this fish? I can get another one."

I could never tell one twin from the other. "No satire, please," I said. "The trouble with the younger generation is that it doesn't have any respect for its elders."

She landed her fish just as I made my third cast. As the lure hit the water, a fish hit the lure, and I felt that old familiar thrill that never changed no matter how many fish I caught. The rod bent as I set the hook, and the line sang as the fish ran with it. I got him turned and began to bring him in, hauling back, then reeling down and hauling back again.

He was a jumper, and went high into the air, tossing and thrashing. But I kept the line just tight enough, and he couldn't throw the hook. He jumped again and then again, and I heard myself laugh with delight at his beauty and strength. Then he was in the surf, still thrashing, and then I had him on the beach.

I brought him up to Joshua, who eyed him with approval. Nice fish, Dad.

It's good to have a kid who appreciates his father.

The twins seemed equally interested in Joshua and fishing, and divided their time between the surf and Joshua's lounge chair. I did the same, so the lad was never lonesome even though the fish hung around until the tide slacked off and the rip flattened out. By that time, I had a dozen nice six- to eight-pounders in my box and was feeling very fine.

I put the rod on the roof rack and got out my stainless steel thermos and Joshua's bottle. Coffee for me and milk for him. Good stuff to sip once the fish were gone.

John and Mattie came over to the Land Cruiser.

Mattie, whose dashing first husband had, years before, driven his motorcycle at a high rate of speed into a large tree, leaving her a young widow with twin daughters, had found a new and good life with John for herself and her girls. John, in turn, doted on all three of them, and they had become a happy family.

"Well," John now said. "I think we have enough blues for the time being. What an August! This is the way fishing is supposed to be."

True. Between the four of them, they had over twice as many fish as I did. "What are you going to do with all of them?" I asked.

"The same as you. We'll give some away, fillet the ones we keep, freeze some, and smoke the rest."

That was, indeed, what I was going to do. I knew half a dozen people in Edgartown who loved eating bluefish but who, for one reason or another, couldn't catch their own. I routinely took fish to them when I caught a few. John and Mattie Skye, like most surf casters I knew, had similar acquaintances to whom they gave fish. It was a rare bluefish that went to waste on Martha's Vineyard, and mine never did, since I had a commercial license and had markets for any fish I caught and didn't want for myself or my friends.

"I see that the DEP is eyeballing the beach again," said John, who was not above rubbing a little salt in my well-known sores.

"You're mean, John Skye," laughed his wife.

"I saw their pickup when I came by," I said, hearing the only half-feigned sourness in my voice. "But I didn't see any people. I'm kind of hoping that a flock of giant plovers swooped down and carried them away where they will never be seen again."

"I take it that you didn't bother attending Lawrence Ingalls's talk with the Marshall Lea Foundation. They gave him a standing O."

"I met him earlier in the day. We didn't chat long, and I didn't go listen to his speech."

"We did," said Mattie. "We thought he was pretty good."

"I think he's a fanatic. Hitler was a good speaker, too, remember?"

"Tsk, tsk. No Nazi comparisons, please."
She grinned.

"That was his pickup you passed on the beach. We saw him there when we came by. He's a dedicated public employee, up at dawn and out on the job. Your tax dollars at work, my boy!" John matched his wife's grin.

"Why is it that only the jerks are dedicated?" I asked. "Why can't they be lazy slobs like everybody else?"

The distant *whump-whump* sound of a helicopter entered my consciousness. I looked north and saw a dot in the sky growing larger. A helo, sure enough, loafing down East Beach, flying low.

It arrived and circled over us, filling the air with sound. We could see that a passenger was aiming a camcorder at us, and we all waved. The camcorder person waved back, then the helo went slowly on to the west, following Norton's Point Beach.

I recognized the logo on the side of the plane as being that of the company I'd hired for Drew Mondry. Apparently the pilot and photographer were doing a little Vineyard scouting of their own as they flew to meet Mondry and me at the airport.

I looked at my watch. "Hey, I gotta go."

I told the Skyes about my job as tour guide

while I packed Joshua and his gear into the Land Cruiser.

"No kidding!" exclaimed one of the twins, who were helping get Joshua squared away. "You've been working with the movie guys? Say, any chance they need some extras?"

"You'll be back in school when they start shooting," said her mother.

"I'll cut classes!" said the twin.

"Me, too!" said her sister.

"We could be twins," said the first twin, hooking arms with the other one. "We could wear the same clothes and do our hair the same way. I'm sure they'll want us!" She looked at me. "You'll put in a good word for us, won't you, J.W., friend of our childhood, father of our very favorite baby boy, fisherman par excellence?"

She smiled the loving smile.

Where do girls learn these things? Is there a secret school somewhere that only girls know about where they're taught the smiles and fluttering eyelashes and all the other winsome stuff?

I narrowed my eyes. "As I recall, it wasn't long ago that you were making sarcastic comments about my fishing abilities. Remember that 'you want to land mine?' stuff? I do. I don't think the movies need any wise-guy girls working for them."

Twin One clutched her throat and staggered back. "That wasn't me! That was her!" She pointed at her sister. "I'm the good twin!"

"She's lying!" exclaimed Twin Two. "She's the evil twin! No one would want to hire *her*, but I know they'd want to hire *me!*" She did the eyelash bit.

I got into the Land Cruiser, and they both rushed up as I closed the door.

"Please! Pretty please!" They clasped their hands as if in prayer.

"If I find out they need two clowns, I'll mention you," I said. I looked over their heads at their parents. "Are teenage sons as bad as teenage daughters? Do I have this to look forward to in fifteen years?"

"We don't have any teenage sons," said Mattie, "but I imagine they're just as wacky."

"Great." I rolled my eyes and drove away while Joshua, tired from the morning's fishing, decided to take a nap.

Coming off the Wasque Reservation onto Norton's Point Beach, I could see the DEP pickup still parked where it had been. Loathsome Lawrence was still at work, apparently, although I didn't spot him moving around anywhere.

When I came alongside the pickup, I saw why.

He was lying on the ground in front of the truck, staring at the sky. There was blood on his shirt and some trickling from his mouth.

I stopped and went to him. I touched his throat. No pulse. I lay my head on his chest. No heartbeat. I put my hand on his forehead. Still warm. I looked both ways along the beach. Far to the west, a vehicle was disappearing from view as it reached the paved road at Katama.

I put my mouth to his and tried to get air into him. I could fill his lungs and empty them, but it did no good. I switched and worked on his chest, trying to get a heartbeat. Nothing.

I got off my knees and went to the Land Cruiser. From under the front seat I got out the phone I'd never used before, and called 911. Then I went back to work on Lawrence Ingalls, even though I knew it was a waste of time and energy.

Finally, I stopped. I had blood on my hands and face and clothes.

The Skyes had never come by, which probably meant they'd gone home via the On Time ferry.

I walked down to the surf and washed my hands and face, then went back to the Land Cruiser and made another call, this one to the airport with a message for Drew Mondry: I wouldn't be flying with him this morning; something had come up.

By then I could hear the sirens coming down toward Katama, and not too much later four-wheel-drive police vehicles from the sheriff's department and Edgartown appeared off to the west and came down the beach.

They stopped, strung out on the two-track roadway used by ORVs. The sheriff was there with some deputies, the chief was there with some Edgartown cops, Doc Boone and some medics were there, and Corporal Dominic Agganis of the state police was there, along with the island's newest state trooper, Officer Olive Otero, the two of them having bummed a ride down with the sheriff.

There are ten different police forces on Martha's Vineyard, and Lawrence Ingalls's death had brought representatives of three of them here. We might not have order on the island, but we had plenty of law.

Doc Boone confirmed the obvious: Lawrence Ingalls was dead. He then hazarded a guess that the gunshot wound to his chest had done the job.

Several of the cops and deputies, under the supervision of Dom Agganis, spread out, moving cautiously over the sand, looking for whatever they could find that might be enlightening. While they did that, I told my tale to the chief, the sheriff, and Olive Otero.

They listened and scribbled an occasional note. When I was done, Olive Otero said, "If you worked on him like you say, how come your hands aren't bloody? He's got blood all over his face and chest."

"I told you. I washed my hands and face."

"Oh, yeah. You still got it on your clothes, though."

"That's right. I decided to take them home and wash them there."

"And you saw another vehicle leaving the beach after you found the body?"

"That's right."

"But you couldn't tell what it was or anything like that? Make, maybe? Or color?"

"It was too far away. It was darkish. I only saw it for a second."

"You know this dead guy?" asked the sheriff.

"I know who he is. His name's Lawrence Ingalls."

"How'd you know that?"

"I was introduced to him."

"When was that?"

"Day before yesterday. Up in Gay Head."

"Oh, yeah?" said Otero, making a note. "Met him just day before yesterday, eh?"

"That's right."

"And you never met him before that?"

"No."

"And today you met him here."

"I didn't meet him. I found him."

"You didn't meet him when you drove out to go fishing?"

"No. I saw the pickup here, but I didn't see him or anybody else."

"Was the other vehicle here at that time? The one you say you saw when you found the body?"

"No."

The sheriff looked at me. "You don't happen to have a gun with you, do you?"

I felt a coldness. Anger is often the product of fear, they say. "Search me," I said, spreading my arms. "Search the truck."

"Maybe we should search the ocean there, too," said Otero, pointing at the surf. "Out as far as a man can throw a pistol, maybe."

"While you're at it, you should dig up the whole beach," I said, hearing the fury in my voice. "I've been alone down here for quite a while. I could have buried it anywhere."

"Now, take it easy, J.W.," said the chief.

"It's just that I read the letters to the editor and listen to the gossip," said Otero, looking at me. "You may never have met this Ingalls guy before day before yesterday, but you never made any secret about what you thought of him. And now he's dead, and you say you found him still warm. That's some-

117

thing people are going to talk about."

"I'm a stupid guy," I said, leaning toward her. "I always stick around after I kill somebody, and I always do something dumb like calling the cops so they'll know it was me that did the deed!"

None of them seemed impressed by my satire.

"Motive and opportunity," said Otero. "You have both."

"So did somebody else!"

"Maybe. Tell me about when you met Ingalls day before yesterday. It's funny that you met him then and he's dead today. Didn't you two get along?"

I had the feeling of a man being handed a shovel to dig his own grave.

"You don't seem to have a very high opinion about what I have to say, so ask Joe Begay," I said. "He was there."

"I will. Anybody else there?"

"A guy named Drew Mondry and a woman named Beth. She was with Ingalls. I don't know her last name."

"Anybody else?"

"No."

The sheriff eyed me. "I'd like to hear your version first, J.W."

Terrific. But if our places had been reversed, I'd have wanted the same thing.

So I told them what had happened on the Gay Head beach.

They listened and took notes, and when I was through I didn't have to guess about who their prime suspect was.

— 10 —

Joshua was smelling bad when we got home just before noon, so I got him cleaned up first, then took care of the fish I had left. I was feeling chilled and nervous, almost as though I were actually guilty of killing Ingalls. No wonder people failed lie detector tests. I could imagine what Beth whatever-her-name-was would tell Otero and the sheriff when they questioned her about the incident in Gay Head.

All my bitching about Loathsome Lawrence was coming back to haunt me. More evidence that all too often our brains are out in the south forty while our mouths are right here. Fate loves a jest, as they say, and what's more ironic than to be scalded by our own hot air?

I wondered if Zack Delwood's loud mouth had caught Olive Otero's ear as well as mine had, and if she and the other minions of the law were checking out his whereabouts this morning, or that of the other hundreds of islanders who had made no bones about their hostile feelings toward Ingalls. Unlike most of the bitchers, however, Zack not only had a big mouth but also had big muscles and a violent streak that had, on more than one occasion, wreaked havoc on lesser men. He liked his reputation as a tough guy and seemed to me to be just the sort of character who might have kacked Lawrence Ingalls. Zack and I were not friends, nor seemed destined to be, but I hoped he wasn't the one. I didn't want it to be anyone I knew.

I thought Joshua was looking a bit sleepy, so I carried him around until I was sure of it, then put him to bed. He gave me a last heavy-lidded look and drifted away.

Unlike his innocent Land of Nod, mine still had Cains in it, causing trouble.

I recognized an old, familiar enemy: self-pity. I was wallowing in it. The No Sniveling sign above the kitchen door was there for a reason. I needed the reminder more often than I should. I willed my whining away. It wandered off, but stayed in sight, not wanting to entirely leave.

Disgusting. I turned my back on it. It might still be there, but I didn't have to look at it.

I also didn't have to live with being on the short list of murder suspects. Whatever trouble I might be in was of my own making, in part, at least, and I couldn't really fault the cops for their suspicions, but it wasn't the sort of interest I wanted from the law. The question was: what could or should I do about it, if anything?

During my brief career in the army, I met a widely traveled guy who had lived an adventurous life, the latest chapter of which was being sent with me to Southeast Asia. He told me that whenever he was down to his last dollar and had no idea about how to extract himself from whatever challenging circumstance he was then in, he would find a bar, buy a beer, and sit there until he had things figured out. And, he said, things did always get figured out. He'd get to talking with the bartender, maybe, or to some other customer, and before long he'd meet someone who could help find a job to earn travel money, or would take him over the next border, or would introduce him to a woman who would take him under her wing until he was on his feet again.

I had envied him his far-roaming escapades, for I had traveled nowhere in my then seventeen years, and I'd laughed at his tales and said he must be the original happy wanderer.

I can still remember his face when he replied. It was a sad face, with ironic eyes and an almost bitter mouth.

"Kid, I've known a thousand guys just like me, and there isn't a happy wanderer in the bunch. Every one of them would trade all they've done for a home and family. Hell, just being in the army with you and these other guys is better than the life I've led so far."

At the time I'd found that hard to believe, but later, after I'd lost track of him and after my brief participation in the war over there, and still later, after my first wife had left me and I'd left the Boston PD, I knew he was right.

Still, the beer idea was a sound one, so I got a Sam Adams out of the fridge, popped the cap, and sat down to think things over.

Alas, no helpful person sat down beside me to show me the way out of my trouble, so I was obliged to work it out alone. I was still at it two beers later when the phone rang.

It was Drew Mondry. I looked at my watch in surprise. It was early afternoon. I had been brooding for longer than I'd imagined.

"Sorry I missed the flight," I said to Mondry. "There was a problem down on South Beach that tied me up."

"That's okay," he said. "They had a guy with a camcorder on board, and between him and his camcorder and me and my camera, I have a good record of where we went and what we saw, even though I don't know what we were looking at. I got a copy of the video, and I want you to go over the shots we took and tell me what we were seeing. A few places look like possible locations, and I'd like to have you take me there so I can have a look at them from ground level. Can you do that?"

"Sure."

"Can we get together tomorrow morning? The film should be ready by then. Have you got a VCR?"

"We do."

"Can we look at the video there? That way you won't have to haul your son over here to my room."

And you can spend some time in Zee's house, I thought. Did he know that she would be working, or did he imagine that she'd be at home?

"Sure," I said. "But we only have an itty-bitty TV. If you need a big screen, we'll have to go somewhere else."

"All we need is a screen big enough for you to identify a half-dozen sites for me. I took stills of the same sites, and we'll have those, too."

"We can give it a try."

"Great. I'll see you in the morning. Nine-ish? I've got to go now. I have some calls to make to the Coast." He hung up.

The Coast. I'd often heard the Pacific Coast referred to as the Coast, but I'd never heard the Atlantic called that. Why not? Was there some sort of cultural bias at work here? Some pro-Pacific sentiment of some kind? Was it, perhaps, a verbal legacy from frontier times when the West Coast was ahead of you, as opposed to the East Coast, which was behind you?

On the other hand, there's the tale of the arch New Englander who observed that California was a nice enough place but was too far from the ocean. There was certainly a little pro-Atlantic Ocean bias there.

Or maybe the Coast was a term you used for whatever coast you weren't on at the moment. When you were east, the Coast was the West Coast; when you were west, it was the East Coast. Or maybe the identity of the coast in question was always determined by an accompanying phrase such as "back to" or "out to." You went "out to" the West Coast, but "back to" the East Coast. If we had a north coast, would we go "up to" that one? Or if we had a south coast, would we go "down to" that one?

We did have a south coast, come to think of it. On the Gulf. Did Mississippians and Alabamians say they were going "down to" the coast? Or, to think yet again, did Ohioans go

125

"up to" their coast? Or were Great Lake coasts somehow immune from these matters?

I heard Joshua stirring around after his good, long, and no doubt water-soaked nap, and went in to change him.

"Well," said Zee, home after work, out of her uniform, and holding her happy son on her lap. "How has your day been, cub?"

Joshua told her what he'd been up to, and she listened and nodded and made noises indicating her interest in his narrative.

I'd already told her about my day, but the only thing she hadn't already known was the part about the Wasque fishing and the call from Drew Mondry. She knew about Ingalls's death because they'd brought his body to the hospital before transporting it off-island so the medical examiner on the mainland could take it into his care, and she'd gotten most of the finding-the-corpse story from Tony D'Agostine, sergeant of the Edgartown police, who had arrived with the body. Tony, who like most police officers had rarely been involved with murder, had been glad to talk about it.

The violent demise of the late Lawrence Ingalls was, in fact, already a hot topic of conversation on the island and off, the tale having been leaked early and often by various individuals who knew or thought they knew

126

something about the discovery of the body.

And mine was a name being increasingly bandied about. I'd gotten a call from Quinn, up in Boston, who wanted my version of the story for the *Globe*. I gave it to him because he was an old friend from my cop days. Another caller from the rival *Herald* got a shorter account. Murder on Martha's Vineyard was big news in Boston, apparently, being the sort of Evil in Eden story that captured the public fancy. After the *Herald* call, I'd taken the phone off the hook.

Now it was back on, but we'd agreed that I wasn't home and that Zee didn't know when I'd be back.

"Joshua thinks we need to have an answering machine," said his mother. "One of those that you can let answer while you listen to hear who's calling and then answer yourself if you want to." She bounced him on her knee and gave him a kiss. "Don't you, Joshua, you cutie?"

Joshua the cutie burbled and drooled, indicating that he did think so. Zee and he beamed at each other.

I wasn't as sure as Joshua. As far as I knew, we were the only house in the United States without an answering machine, and I took a certain amount of reverse snobbish pride in that. On the other hand, it *would* be nice to know who was calling so I could decide whether to answer or not. I was rapidly discovering that I did not like being in media spotlights. So much for a career in TV or the movies. Drew Mondry might think that Zee had what it took for the silver screen, but he wouldn't get anywhere with me even if he asked me.

Which he'd had plenty of opportunity to do, but hadn't so far.

Maybe he'd intuitively sensed that I'd refuse.

Or maybe there was some other reason.

Looks? Personality? Hmmmmm.

After Joshua ate, and was rolling around on his blanket on the floor, watched with careful interest by Oliver Underfoot and Velcro, who stayed just out of his reach, I fixed his parents vodka martinis. Two green olives for me, two black ones for Zee. I put out a plate of crackers, cheddar, and smoked bluefish, and Zee and I nibbled and sipped and watched our family members watching us and other things visible only to babies and cats.

"I don't like you being a suspect," said Zee. "Even if you didn't do it, people will always wonder, and some of them will think you did do it even when they catch the real killer."

"This could touch you, too," I said to Zee.

"The people who work with you may start to treat you differently."

"None of my friends will. None of my real friends. I don't care what the others think or do." She made a fist. "If they say anything about you, though, I'll punch out their lights!"

I had never heard her say such a thing before, and was slightly shocked. I put my arm around her. "No, don't punch anybody's lights out. I appreciate the offer, though."

"They'd better not say a thing!" said Zee.

"It doesn't make any difference what they say," I said.

"They'd better catch this guy quick," said Zee. "The longer it takes, the worse it will be. The problem is that there are too many suspects."

True, but he had his defenders. I met one of them the next day in the parking lot of the A & P.

Early morning is the only time to shop at the A & P during the summer. There's no traffic jam getting in and out of the parking lot, and there aren't any lines at the cash registers. Of course some of the stuff you might want to buy hasn't been put out on the shelves yet, but that's a small price to pay for a quick entrance and a quick exit. Joshua and I had arrived just after the doors had opened, and now we were heading out again, pushing our carriage.

The woman named Beth was waiting for us. Later I guessed that she must have been going to our house to find me, but had spotted us and followed us to town, waiting for her chance. She found it when I put Joshua in his car seat and started loading the groceries into the back of the Land Cruiser. I heard her voice from behind me.

"You killer! You wouldn't leave him alone, would you?"

I turned and saw her. She was pointing an old-fashioned revolver at me. Her face was filled with pain. Beyond her, the guy who collects the carts in the parking lot and takes them back to the store looked at her, looked again, and ran into the store. Another customer came out and pushed her cart right by us, seeing nothing.

"I didn't kill him," I said in a distant-sounding voice. I moved myself away from the Land Cruiser, getting Joshua out of the line of fire. "I found him dead. I tried to revive him."

"Liar! Don't move another step!"

"My son's in the truck," I said, still moving. "I don't want you hitting him by mistake."

Her eyes flicked to the old Toyota, and I inched nearer.

"And there are other people who might get hurt," I said. "That lady there . . ."

She suddenly saw the woman with the shopping cart, off to my left, trying to get her car door open, still unaware of any drama.

She hesitated and I pointed to my right. "And there's that little girl." I was on my toes. I raised my voice. "Stay away, honey! Don't come any closer!"

Beth looked to her left, trying to see the girl who wasn't there, and I ran at the gun.

I caught her gun arm and brought her wrist down across my rising knee. The pistol flew out of her hand. She screamed like an animal and stabbed at my eyes with her other hand. I pushed her away and we both went for the gun. She was quicker, but as she swept it up, I hit her behind the ear with a hard fist and she went down and out on the pavement. I picked up the pistol.

The woman shopper had finally noticed us, and was staring open-mouthed. Then her face grew furious.

"Beast!" she cried. "Wife beater!" She looked beyond me. "Call the police! I saw it all! I'll testify in court, you misogynist! You won't get away with this!"

Misogynist? I'd always fancied myself a philogynist.

I turned and saw a small crowd at the door

of the store. As I looked at them, one of them dashed inside.

Not too much later I heard the sirens coming. I checked Beth. She seemed to be breathing normally. I leaned against the Land Cruiser and waited.

— 11 —

I was sitting in the chief's office with sleepy Joshua on my lap. The pistol lay on his desk in a plastic Baggie.

The chief looked at it, and reached for his pipe and tobacco. "I wouldn't have been surprised if some woman or maybe her husband had taken a shot at you back in your bachelor days, when you were running wild with the ladies. Now that you're a married man and all settled down and like that, I thought that the only woman who might shoot you would be Zee. I didn't think it would be Beth Harper."

"Ha, ha. Very funny. This crackpot thinks I kacked Lawrence Ingalls. I would appreciate it if you'd sit down and have a talk with her and tell her that I didn't do it. I don't want her trying this again. She might kill me next time!"

"I'll have a talk with her."

"Good."

"But I won't tell her you didn't do it,

because I don't know whether you did it or not."

"Gosh, thanks again."

He stuffed tobacco into his pipe. "Don't get all huffy. I'll tell her that I'm pretty sure you didn't do it, and that'll be the truth because not even you are dumb enough to kill a guy then call the cops to come and find you there."

Killers at the scene actually call the cops pretty often, of course, but it's usually after domestic violence or a killing between friends, when the survivor really doesn't know what else to do and hasn't any other place to go. Murders like this one, way out in the boonies, are usually different. These killers generally like to get away if they can manage it.

"You use your grandfatherly charm," I said. "And don't give her gun back to her."

"If she decides to shoot you," he said, "she'll find another gun. You really have a sweet effect on the people you meet. Five minutes after you're introduced to Ingalls, he dukes it out with you, and now this woman you barely met two days ago pulls a gun."

"Where'd she get the six-shooter, by the way?"

"Well, now, it seems that it was Ingalls's weapon. He had a permit for it, all legal and everything. She got it out of his house up in Chilmark before she came looking for you. He'd had a place up there for a couple of years. Might explain why he had such strong feelings about enforcing the environmental laws on the island. Hell, the Marshall Lea people practically have him canonized."

The Marshall Lea people. The No Foundation. Not my favorite conservation group. Naturally, they'd have been big Ingalls fans.

"I'm not much of a believer in saints," I said. "And I never heard of one who needed a pistol permit."

"Which may help explain why you have yours," said the chief. He got up. "Let's go outside so I can stoke this furnace."

The chief's office had its own outside door, which allowed him to escape his smokeless office and indulge in his tobacco habit when the craving came to him. Although a reformed pipe smoker myself, I envied his briars nevertheless, and often thought of taking up the habit again.

We went out and he lit up with his trusty old Zippo lighter. I took a quick sniff of the fumes (lovely!), then carried Joshua upwind.

"A lot of people shoot on this island," said the chief. "Maybe Ingalls shot targets."

I knew many of the island hunters and targeteers. "I never heard of him doing that,"

I said. "But I'll ask Manny Fonseca. If Ingalls was a shooter, Manny will know."

The chief nodded. Manny Fonseca was not only Zee's shooting instructor and Edgartown's most dedicated gun aficionado, but he had personally customized the .45 Zee was shooting. He had a basement shop in his house filled with shooting paraphernalia and literature, he was NRA all the way, he bought and sold weapons as fast as he could get his hands on them, and he knew every other shooter on the island.

"On the other hand," said the chief, "Ingalls's permit was in his wallet, and it reads that it was for all lawful purposes, so maybe he had some other reason for wanting it."

In Massachusetts, you have to say why you want your pistol permit. You can say you want it for target shooting, or for protection of person and property, or for other reasons. Wanting it for all lawful purposes is the most comprehensive reason, and allows you to carry just about whenever you want to. My permit and Zee's were for all lawful purposes, even though Zee usually only carried her little Beretta .380 and/or her new .45 to and from target ranges and pistol competitions, and I rarely carried my old police .38 at all.

"Maybe he thought somebody didn't like him," I said.

"If so, he was right. Somebody didn't," said the chief. "But when he needed his gat, he didn't have it."

Such is often the case. Having a weapon to defend yourself, an idea strongly supported by the NRA and guys like Manny Fonseca, usually doesn't do you any good. Typically, you don't have it when you need it, or it gets stolen out of your house, or you get shot with your own gun. Even cops, who are well trained with weapons, are often killed or wounded with their own sidearms. Guns are dangerous things.

I rocked Joshua gently back and forth, and he slept on. "I know a lot of people who didn't like Ingalls," I said, "but I don't know of any who were mad enough to shoot him."

"Some people think you were." The chief puffed his pipe.

"Come on!"

"Or maybe Zack Delwood."

I left that one alone.

"Hey," said the chief, "look at it from the outside. Whoever offed him apparently did it on the spur of the moment, taking advantage of a random opportunity. Who could have known that he'd be down there on the beach? And nobody could have known that there wouldn't be any other people around, so nobody could have planned to kill him there. It was just a chance meeting that the killer took advantage of.

"And you fit the bill. One day you and him punch each other up in Gay Head. Two days later he's alone and alive on South Beach when the Skyes go by. At Wasque, you tell John Skye that you saw his truck but not him. Nobody else comes driving by Wasque. You drive back along the beach. You say you found him dead, but maybe you find him alive and the two of you go at it again and you do him in. Probably it's an accident, but maybe not. You panic and put in a call for the cops. No wonder Olive Otero has you in her sights."

"And the sheriff, too. Don't forget about him."

"Well, maybe him not so much, although there is an election coming up. But Olive Otero for certain."

I rocked Joshua. "Yeah. I just happened to have a pistol with me that nobody's ever seen me with, and afterward I toss it out in the ocean. Sure."

"Maybe it was his pistol and you used it on him. Maybe you were struggling for the gun and it went off."

"Maybe the moon is green cheese. If I used

his pistol and threw it into the ocean, what's it doing lying there on your desk?"

He removed the pipe from his mouth and admired it. "What a keen thinker you are. Look, there's not enough to nail you for this, but there's enough to keep a lot of noses to the ground, sniffing at your heels."

"Including yours."

He nodded. "Naturally including mine. This is my town. You and I may be friends, but that doesn't mean I'm going to stop doing my job. I'm going to have my detectives looking wherever they have to look."

"Yeah, well, I can understand that." I could, too.

"There's another thing . . ."

"What?"

"Since it's an ongoing investigation, I've told my people to keep what they find out to themselves. I'm afraid you're out of the loop. It won't do for a suspect to know everything the police are doing."

He stuck his pipe in his mouth and looked at me.

A suspect. Of course I was a suspect, but the word made me angry, although I knew it shouldn't. "You won't tell me anything, but you won't mind me spilling my guts to you," I snapped.

"Won't mind at all," he said, nodding.

"You can talk to us any time you want. Right now, for instance. You have anything you want to say?"

Joshua, perhaps feeling the tension in the air, moaned and got one eye partly open.

"I do have something to say," I said, keeping my voice low so as to lull Joshua back to sleep. "I won't miss Ingalls, but I didn't kill him. I figure that vehicle I saw off to the west probably belonged to whoever did it, because I came from the east and didn't see anybody that direction. You find the guy in the vehicle, and you'll find the shooter."

"If there was a vehicle," said the chief calmly.

"There was a vehicle!"

"That's one of the things we'll be checking out."

His cool voice was in sharp contrast to my hot one.

"While you're checking, check Ingalls's background," I said. "Victims have stories, too. Maybe his will tell you who did him in, and why."

"That's being done."

"And what have you found?"

"Like I just told you, it's an ongoing investigation. No news yet to report to the public. When we've got something to say, you'll get it the same time as everybody else. No sooner."

Joshua's eyes were fluttering and he was making noises. He then produced a familiar fragrance.

Terrific. His diapers were in the Land Cruiser, which was parked in back of the station.

"I gotta go," I said, turning in that direction.

"Maybe you should get yourself a lawyer," said the chief as I walked away. "And if you see Moonbeam, tell him I want to see him."

I paused. "Moonbeam? Why Moonbeam?"

"Because Moonbeam worked for Ingalls, and nobody's seen him since the killing."

So I wasn't the only suspect, it seemed. "I haven't seen Moonbeam," I said.

"Well, if you do, tell him I'd appreciate it if he'd come by the station for a chat. Same goes for Zack Delwood."

"Moonbeam, Zack, and I don't socialize much," I said, and headed outside.

At the Land Cruiser, I changed Joshua and gave him his plug, and he seemed content as he watched me with his bright eyes.

A lawyer. I didn't know any lawyers. At least I didn't know any lawyers that I wanted to know.

I put Joshua into his car seat and drove home. As I unloaded him into his crib, put his dirty diapers to soak, and washed out his bottles, I was glad that he took up so much time, because it gave me something to do while I thought about my situation. I had never been a murder suspect before, and I didn't like it.

I wondered who would know a good lawyer that I could afford. I wondered if there was such a thing as a good lawyer I could afford. The lawyers I'd read about made more in an hour than I was likely to make in a day or even a week.

I switched gears and thought about Lawrence Ingalls. Unless the chief was right and he had been killed by a random murderer who just happened to be passing by on South Beach, somebody had deliberately followed him and killed him.

I needed to know more about him. I could start with Beth Harper, who had been so incensed by Ingalls's death that she had hunted me down with malice aforethought. It was a pretty extreme act for someone who had only been his assistant, since assistants don't usually go around avenging their bosses.

Where was she now? In jail, awaiting arraignment for assault or attempted murder or whatever? Out on bail?

I called the jail. Beth Harper was there. I said I'd be right down.

But before I could get Joshua and his gear

ready for departure, the phone rang. It was Drew Mondry, who sounded more cheerful than anyone should.

"Hey," he said. "I'm looking for locations for some interior shots. A big old house of some kind, and a large study or library. One of the leads in the film is a scholar. The brains behind the big treasure hunt. I need a house he's living in and a room that looks like where he does his work. You know: lots of books, a desk piled with papers, maps on the walls, an old Persian rug on the floor. That sort of thing. You know of any place like that?"

He had described John Skye's house so well, he might have been standing in John's library. I thought of the twins and their antics on the beach that morning.

"I do know a place like that," I said. "There might be a couple of problems for you to solve, but I'll take you there."

"Great." He paused. "Say, let me talk to Zee for a minute."

I may have paused, myself. "She isn't here," I said. "She's working."

"Oh. Well, it isn't important."

"You want to leave a message?"

"No, no." He hesitated, then: "Well, I'll see you in the morning."

"I'll be here."

"Great." The phone buzzed in my ear. I looked at it, hung it up, gathered Joshua and his traveling gear, and drove down to the county jail.

The Dukes County jail is in downtown Edgartown, across the street from Cannonball Park. Unless you're paying attention, you might not even know it's a jail, since it looks pretty much like an ordinary house until you go around back and see the police vehicles and the caged exercise areas.

Inside are a foyer, an office, and several cells, mostly used to house drunks overnight or hold people without bail money until they can go before a judge at the courthouse down the street.

For several years now, one of the Vineyard's sustained arguments has been whether or not Dukes County should have a new, modern jail.

Proponents of this idea, led by the sheriff, point out that the current jail is too old and too small and should be more centrally located on the island, out by the airport, for example, so up-island cops could more easily get their prisoners behind bars, and so those sometimes noisy and feisty prisoners would be farther away from the busy streets of Edgartown, thus decreasing the level of danger to the community.

Opponents, led by the sheriff's oldest and most steadfast political enemy, say the jail isn't too old or too small, and that if a new one is built it will cost a fortune and pretty soon the county will be getting a bunch of imported, off-island jailbirds as prisoners, thus raising the level of danger to the community.

Proponents say this is nonsense. Opponents say it isn't.

So it goes. And probably will keep right on going, since Edgartown, a village dependent on tourists, nevertheless took forty-five years to build public toilets for its tour bus traffic.

Meanwhile, the old jail, built over a hundred years ago, does its duty as best it can. Part of its duty today was keeping Beth Harper locked up until she was either bailed out or otherwise released or sent elsewhere.

I pushed the button at the locked visitors' door and after a bit the buzzer buzzed and Joshua and I went into the little foyer. Clyde Duarte, the ever mild, noncombative jail keeper, was in the doorway of his small office. Behind him were a paper-stocked desk and several TV screens showing various parts of the building. "Hi, J.W.," said Clyde. "How are things?"

"Things could be worse. I want to talk with Beth Harper."

Clyde raised a brow. "I heard she tried to take a shot at you. You sure you want to see her?" He looked at Joshua, who was staring around at his very first jail. "Your new boy, eh? Doesn't look a bit like you, I'm glad to say." He grinned. He had four children at home and another on the way.

How many times was I going to hear how lucky Josh was not to look like me? "Yeah, I want to see her," I said.

"Well, I'll find out if she wants to see you." He started toward the cells.

"Tell her I'm considering dropping all charges," I said.

"That should get her attention," said Clyde. "I'll be right back."

There's a room where lawyers can meet privately with their clients. Clyde took me there, then went to get Beth Harper. I took one of the chairs and put Joshua in my lap. Clyde came in with Beth and pointed her to another chair. She sat down.

"You need me, let me know," he said, and went back to his office.

Beth Harper nervously rubbed her wrists, which possibly had been cuffed not long

147

before. Her face was sullen, and she looked pale in spite of her tan. Her voice was jerky. She spat out short sentences.

"What do you want? I know my rights. I don't have to say anything. My lawyer is on his way."

I got up. "Okay. See you later. In court." I went to the door.

"Wait," she said. "Wait." I turned and looked at her. Her eyes met mine, then fell away. Her hands rubbed each other. "That man said you might drop all charges."

"That's right. But it depends on what you tell me."

"How can I trust you? You killed Larry! Even if I tell you what you want to know, you might not drop the charges at all!"

I went back to my chair and sat down. Joshua stared around the room. I put my eyes on Beth Harper's face.

"The first thing is, I didn't kill Ingalls. I found him already dead."

"You're lying! You said you'd get even with him! I heard you!"

People often remember what they want to remember or what they think they should have seen or heard, which is why eyewitnesses are often of so little help in criminal cases.

"No," I said, "you heard him say that to

me. There were two other people there, Joe Begay and Drew Mondry. You ask them who started that fight and who threatened who."

"I don't believe you! You hated him! All you damned fishermen hated him!"

"You don't have to believe me. Talk with Joe Begay and Drew Mondry."

"How am I going to talk with them? I'm in jail, for God's sake!"

"Your lawyer's coming, remember? You'll be out of here in no time. You can talk with them then."

She stared at the floor.

I tried combining the stick and the carrot. "The second thing is this," I said. "No one saw Ingalls get killed, but a lot of people saw you point that gun at me. That means that you're the one who's in real trouble. But if I don't press charges, most of that trouble will go away."

Those hands of hers rubbed each other and massaged her wrists. "What do you want from me?"

"Information. You may know something that will help me find out who really shot your boss."

"I already know who did that."

"No, you don't. Why did you decide to kill me?"

She stared at the floor. "It was stupid. I know that."

"People don't usually go around avenging their bosses."

Her eyes lifted and flared at me. "We were going to be married! Soon!" She started sobbing.

I waited until it passed. "So you were engaged. I'm sorry. He was quite a bit older than you are, wasn't he?"

"He was forty-five. So what? It didn't make any difference. We loved each other!" More sobs.

I looked down at Joshua, who smiled up at me, unaware of human tragedy. When the sobs stopped, I said, "Where'd you get the gun?"

"It was his. I went up to his house and got it."

"Why did he have a gun?"

"I don't know. I don't know anything about guns."

And a good thing, too, else I'd probably not be sitting here.

"How'd you know where it was?"

"We were engaged. I've been in his house. He kept it in a drawer by the bed."

Terrific. The first place a burglar would look. Like most people, Ingalls might have been smart about some things, but he had been dumb about others. Most of us are like that: good and bad, smart and stupid, dark and light.

"Tell me about Ingalls."

She brushed at her face with her hands. "What do you mean? What about him? What do you want to know?"

I didn't really know what I wanted to know. I said, "He probably got killed by somebody who knew him. Did he have any enemies?"

"Yes! You and all those fishermen!"

I had to admit that I'd walked into that one. "I mean besides me and all those fishermen. Anyone at work, maybe?"

She lifted her chin. "Larry was very well respected by his colleagues. Everyone admired him."

That was probably not the case, since no one is immune from the petty and not-so-petty bickerings, envies, and rivalries that occur in almost all organizations. Even Jesus had a betrayer, after all. But Beth Harper, in her grief, probably believed what she was saying.

"Anyone in his family, then, or his social circle?"

Her words came in a rush, like angry water. "How dare you mention his family! They're wonderful people. Larry didn't have to work, you know. He had plenty of money. He worked for the environment because he loved it! He could have stayed up there in Hamilton and played polo like everybody else, but he didn't. And he wasn't just a biologist, you know. He was an Orientalist, too. He could have kept taking those trips to India and Indonesia every year, and been a scholar, but he didn't. Instead, he stopped doing that and stayed right here in Massachusetts, so he could work for the Department of Environmental Protection. He loved this island most of all; that's why he built a house here! Everyone loved him!"

"Not quite everyone."

"What a filthy thing to say! You're disgusting!"

I felt a little dot of anger. "Keep in mind that I'm also the guy who can drop charges against you. Tell me about his friends. Start with the ones up in Hamilton. That was his hometown, I take it."

She may have noticed my irritation because she unknotted her fists, took a breath or two, and told me next to nothing about Ingalls's Hamilton friends. They were polo players, riders to the hounds, yachtsmen, investment brokers, lawyers, the North Shore rich who lived in Hamilton and Wenham, Manchester and Prides Crossing, Beverly Farms and Marblehead.

They were prep school, Ivy League, and old-Boston-firms types; Beth seemed to know that about them and not much more. Ingalls, unlike most of them, had taken a different professional path and gone to work for the DEP.

Lawrence Ingalls, halo wearer.

"How about his Boston friends, then? And the people he worked with there."

She knew these people better, for his working colleagues were hers as well, and she had come to know his friends.

"I used to see him in his office when I first went to work for the department. He and some of the rest of us would go out to a local pub after work sometimes, and that's where we got to know each other. He split his time between Beacon Hill and the field, and he was good in both places. We were all really focused on our work. It was almost like a revolutionary call. When we joked about it, we called ourselves the Greenies, and said that our plans to seize control were almost complete; that all we needed now was some capital."

The Greenies.

"And what did all the wives and husbands think about what their spouses were doing? Were there any romances that broke up marriages?"

She brushed back her hair. "Maybe that happened. But I didn't do anything like that, and neither did Larry. He wasn't married, and he didn't have a steady girl."

"He never put any moves on anyone else's woman?"

"No! He didn't do things like that."

"Because if he did, the woman's man might hold a grudge. It wouldn't be the first time."

"There was nothing like that. Larry dated some of the single girls, but he wasn't a womanizer. He was a bachelor, and work took up all his time. He wore himself out working, in fact, and had to get clear away from it on his vacations, so he could get some rest. He was still taking his holidays in the Far East when I first knew him. Then for a few years he took them down in the Caribbean, and then he built his house in Chilmark and would come down here and not tell anyone where he was. All of the rest of us were in on the conspiracy. None of us would say where he was. When he came back, he'd be full of zip again, and ready to go.

"No, he wasn't involved with any women at work or even in Boston, as far as I know. Until he and I started going out, that is."

"Had he ever been married?"

She paused. "A long time back, when he was still in college. I think they were both just too young. He never really talked about it."

"How about his friends here on the island?"

"He had a lot of them. The Marshall Lea Foundation people, your friend Joe Begay, his neighbors. He got a lot of kids interested in the environment. Their parents, too, sometimes . . ."

Tears welled up in her eyes once more. They streamed down her cheeks. She stopped talking and stared through me at some image I could not see.

I put Joshua on my shoulder and got up.

"I'll drop all charges," I said. "Maybe they'll try to get you on disturbing the peace or something like that, but they can't nail you for heavy-duty stuff unless I go along with them, and I won't."

She was still looking into space. "I don't know how anyone could have done it," she said in a watery voice. "Everybody loved him."

— 13 —

At home, I put Joshua in his crib and told him to go to sleep, and to my surprise, he did. What a guy.

Then I called Joe Begay.

"Are you calling from your cell?" he asked. "Is this your one phone call? I heard about what happened to Larry Ingalls."

I gave him the details.

When I was done, he said, "I can see why the fuzz like you for the job. Opportunity, motive, the works."

Everybody's a comedian. "Well, I didn't do the job."

"I believe you. But if you didn't, who did? Besides Zack Delwood and a thousand other people who hated Ingalls's guts, who's as good a suspect as you?"

"I thought I'd better try to find out, just in case the law likes me so much that it doesn't look anywhere else. There's an election coming up next year, and the sheriff is planning on running again. He can use a good conviction."

"You sound a little cynical, J.W., like you don't have a lot of faith in the judicial system."

As a matter of fact, while I'd been a cop in Boston I'd seen too many bad guys walk out of too many courtrooms to have total confidence in either cops or courts. Half the time it was the cops' fault that the accused walked. Eager to solve a case, the police would grab the most likely suspect and go for the gold with him rather than pursuing other possible perps. And when the prosecution's case was weak, as it often was, the suspect, almost always "known to the police" but not necessarily guilty of this particular crime, would be back on the streets almost before the cops were.

The sheriff of Dukes County was not a hanging sheriff by any means, but a conviction in a murder case certainly wouldn't hurt his political cause; and it might do wonders for Olive Otero's career.

I told Begay about my visit with Beth Harper. He listened, then said, "Are you sure you want her out there walking around?"

"No, but I'll have an eye out for her next time. I think it was just a one-time thing. I think sitting in that cell may have given her second thoughts about being a gun moll."

Begay gave a small grunt. "Your insights

157

into women aren't the keenest in the world."

True enough. "Hogwash," I said. "I landed Zee, didn't I?"

"A fluke, just like Toni marrying me. Well, what can I do for you? You didn't call just to bring me up to date on this business."

"Like I say, I want to find out who done it, so people will get off my back. I don't like having cops watching me all of the time."

"Nobody's been watching you, J.W. Don't be paranoid."

"You know what I mean. Knowing that somebody with a badge has it in his head that you might be a danger to society."

And he did know what I meant. He was, I suspected, another one of those retired or supposedly retired operatives whose Vineyard addresses lead some to refer to the island as Spook Haven. One thing I knew Begay could still do was get information. In this case, he might have it firsthand.

"Ingalls had a house somewhere up Chilmark," I said. "I'd like to take a look at it. Do you know where it is?"

There was a short pause on the other end of the line. Then he said, "Just in case anybody ever asks me, I don't think I want to know any more about your plans, but I can tell you where the house is."

And he did. Ingalls's place was at the end of

one of those long dirt drives that lead off North Road. As Begay described it, I realized that I knew the road.

"Say, isn't that the road where Moonbeam lives?"

"How do you know where Moonbeam lives? I didn't know you two were pals."

"We aren't. We were trading scallops for a pig. A couple of years ago. I had the scallops and he had the pig. He raises pigs and slaughters them, in case you didn't know."

"I didn't know, but I'm not surprised."

Moonbeam was thought by some to be the Vineyard's answer to the Snopes. His house was falling down, his wife was haggard and fiercely protective of their many children, his outbuildings were disintegrating, and his yard was full of the broken, rusty, rotting items that you see wherever you encounter the homes of the rural poor, who rarely throw anything completely away, just in case they might need it sometime.

Moonbeam kept chickens and pigs and an occasional sheep, and what he didn't sell or barter, he ate. There was a roughly fenced garden behind his house, in which his wife grew potatoes, beans, and whatever else she could protect from the weeds no one else in the family would help her pull. And behind that was a still incompletely filled trench in

159

which a sewer line led back to a septic system still uncovered years after it had been installed.

But Moonbeam could slaughter a pig as well as anybody, and that was all I had required. I'd cooked a lot of sate and other porcine delights that winter.

According to Joe Begay, Lawrence Ingalls's island house was at the far end of the drive that first led past Moonbeam's place.

Finding the house would be no problem, but since the Berubes had sharp eyes to go with their dim wits, my visit would not be a secret, and the illegal entry that I was contemplating would have to be done leaving no clue that I'd gone in. Bad enough that it would be known that I'd gone to the house at all, but on the other hand, what could anyone make of that, other than that I was nosy?

I thanked Joe Begay for the information.

"Look," he said, "I wasn't what you'd call a close friend of Larry Ingalls, but I knew him and had respect for the work he did for the DEP, and I want to know who killed him. So, if you need a Tonto, let me know."

Joe Begay was part Navajo and part Hopi and, he'd once told me, probably part whoever else had passed through Arizona in the last four hundred years; but he didn't strike me as any kind of Tonto.

"If things get complicated," I said, "*you* get to be the Lone Ranger and *I'll* be Tonto."

"Keep in touch, Kemo Sabe."

I looked at my watch. Now seemed as good a time as any. I'd be back before Zee got home.

I put my yard sale–purchased lock picks in my pocket. I was sorry that Eddie the Wire wasn't coming along to give me pointers I might need, but I was getting better with the picks and hoped that I'd be up to the task alone.

Joshua was gone, gone, gone. I packed a bag for him, then wrapped him in his blanket and put him into his car seat, still sleeping. I wondered if I was the first would-be house-breaker to take a baby along with him when he went to work. Joshua was getting an early introduction into the life of crime. I almost, but not quite, felt guilty, and definitely decided not to tell Zee about my excursion.

Chilmark is arguably the loveliest township on Martha's Vineyard. It has the island's highest hills, is bounded by the Atlantic on the south, by Vineyard Sound on the north, and by Gay Head on the west, and it hosts the only nude beach on the island (reason enough for some people to live in no other town). It has three roads leading east to west: South Road, Middle Road, and North Road.

Middle Road is the prettiest, but all three wind past farms, old houses, and stone fences, and all three have narrow, sandy lanes leading off through the trees to houses where people who like their privacy live. The lane leading to Moonbeam's disintegrating home and outbuildings, and then on to Ingalls's house, looked no different than any other, but was identifiable by the ramshackle Berube mailbox that fronted it.

I turned onto the lane and passed through the trees and undergrowth until the rubble of Moonbeam's few acres began to appear: two abandoned cars, long since stripped of anything useful; an aging backhoe by the sewer line (which had some fresh fill in it; *quel* surprise! Had Moonbeam actually been doing some work at home before taking off for parts unknown?); a broken plow from ancient days; a shapeless lump of cloth, stuffing, and springs that had once been a mattress; rusty buckets and tubs, full of holes and dents; unidentifiable objects and pieces of paper lodged in bushes and trees; the wretched refuse of a lifetime of poverty. Moonbeam had no need of the community dump. He lived amid his own. I wondered if the chief had ever caught up with him.

I passed his house, which was slowly settling into the earth, and waved at Connie

Berube, who straightened from tending to her latest baby, and stared at my passing truck. Here and there in the yard, others of her children stood and gazed at my truck as well, all of them beautiful, all of them empty-eyed. Somehow they had all inherited their mother's one-time loveliness and their father's dull mind. Exquisite and delicate, their faces betrayed no sign of intellect. They were born to fail, to be victims. Only some kind fate could save them, and such fortune seemed unlikely.

Moonbeam's pickup was not there, but Connie's newish, blueish Subaru sedan was parked in the yard. In spite of their poverty, Moonbeam and his wife had pretty good wheels. A crooked antenna on the top of his house indicated that they also had TV. Cars and the tube; the necessities of modern living. Moonbeam's until the bank repossessed them, at least. I wondered how he got financing, but let the idea go since no one understands less about money than I do, and I've given up trying to learn, convinced that my lack of money sense is akin to tone deafness or color blindness, that there is no hope for me, and that I'm wasting my time trying to make it otherwise. I grasp the barter system, but I leave all more sophisticated financial theory and practice to the experts, who, I suspect, don't really understand such things, either. No wonder they call economics the dismal science.

The light blue eyes in those delicately boned faces followed me until the lane turned and I drove out of their sight. A quarter of a mile farther on, I came to the end of the road and to Ingalls's house. I stopped and got out, understanding for the first time just how much money Ingalls's family must have. For this was not a house built on the salary of a state biologist.

It was a big place, set high on a hill, overlooking Vineyard Sound and the Elizabeth Islands. A sandy walk led down to a private beach where a Sailfish was pulled up above the high-tide line. There was a veranda on the ocean side of the house, a small barn in back that served as a two-car garage, and seemed to have a guest apartment on the second floor. Comfortable old lawn furniture sat in the shade of large trees beside a flower garden. The house was new, but with its traditional weathered-cedar shingles and gray trim, it looked like it had always been there.

I knocked on the door, then walked around the house calling hellos. No one appeared. I went back to the barn and knocked on the side door there. No one. I went to the back door of the house and knocked. Then I walked down to the beach and looked in both directions. No one. I went back to the rear of the house, looked around in the guilty way people do when they're about to, say, urinate behind a tree, and got out my lock picks.

Lawrence Ingalls's house was better than most, but his locks weren't, and I was inside pretty fast, hoping that I wasn't setting off any silent alarms in the Chilmark police station. I shut the door behind me and looked around.

What was I looking for? I wasn't sure. Anything that might tell me who might have disliked Ingalls enough to shoot him. I doubted that I'd find any such thing, but like the jazz man said, "One never knows, do one?"

I was in a fair-sized mud room off the kitchen. It was neat and clean, with comfortable benches where you could sit down to take off your boots before going into the house. There were a couple of closets for coats and hats. I looked inside of them and found rain gear, work gloves, a couple of summer jackets, and some Bean boots.

I went into the kitchen. It was big and well laid out, the sort of kitchen I'd love to have. It was so clean that I wondered if Ingalls actually used it. I looked in the cabinets and in the big pantry and found the normal kitchen stuff: dishes, pots and pans, utensils, canned foods, flour, sugar, salt, a few spices, and such.

The fridge held milk and salad makings, a couple of beers, cans of soft drinks, several candy bars, and a half-full bottle of white wine. The freezer was mostly full of ice cream in several shapes and forms: on sticks, in sandwiches, and in bulk. Ingalls had apparently had a sweet tooth. There were also a couple of frozen pizzas in there with the ice cream. He'd been a snacker, too.

I went into the big combined dining and living room. There was a huge new television set against one wall, but the rest of the furniture was old and comfortable-looking. Rich people, they say, never *buy* furniture, they *have* furniture. When one of them gets another house, they fill it with furniture they already have somewhere else. Ingalls's furniture was that kind. The room's decor was Oriental in part, with statuary, wall hangings, and artifacts from India and points east, reflecting Ingalls's interest in that part of the world.

The television set was placed on a cabinet beside a VCR. Inside the cabinet were dozens of videotapes, mostly of adventure films and children's movies. Many had titles I didn't recognize. There were also travel films, mostly about the Far East, and unopened boxes of video film. On a bottom shelf was a camcorder, another popular electronic item for which I somehow had never found a need, although I could see how one could be both useful and a lot of fun. Now that we had Joshua, maybe we should get one and record his childhood, so he'd have a record later on.

Or maybe not. I put the question in my Ask Zee file.

I went into what was a den or library. The walls held many filled bookshelves and there was a large desk. On its top were a computer, a printer, and what I guessed was a fax machine. Books and papers were stacked on both sides of the machines. Against one wall was a line of wooden file cabinets. A lovely, highly erotic Indian painting hung between two windows that looked out over Vineyard Sound.

I went to the desk and fingered through the papers. It was all environmental stuff: brochures, letters, memos, notes. The books were books about ecology, trees, animals, tides, waste management, aquafilters, birds.

I tugged at the drawers of the desk. Locked. Hmmmmm.

I went to the file cabinets and tried them. Locked again.

Hmmmmm, again.

I went to the bookcases. Some of the

shelves were filled with books about environmental issues. Others held travel books, particularly about the East. Some of them were old. Older than Lawrence Ingalls, certainly. But other shelves held different material. Here and there I spotted a title I knew, because when I'd been in the Boston PD, I'd met a fellow who had quite a collection of such stuff. Ingalls had the *Kama Sutra* of Vatsyayana, and the *Gulistan of Sa'di*, and a copy of *Chin Ping Mei*. I browsed further and found a copy of *The Perfumed Garden of Sheikh Nefzaoui*. This classic erotica was mixed with more modern, generally less attractively illustrated books on the same subjects.

I have no fault to find with people for whom such writings and artwork are interesting, although I personally find real women, Zee in particular, more sensual and erotic than images or verbal descriptions of lovers and sex.

Still, the books and illustrations did cause me to pause and consider the locked drawers of the desk and cabinets.

I got out my lock picks and started toward the desk.

As I did, I heard a car drive into the yard.

Fear and guilt lend us wings. I was out the back door and locking it behind me before the car came to a halt. As I heard the car's engine stop, I walked around to the front of the house, hands in my pockets.

I recognized the car as the one I'd seen in Moonbeam's yard. The driver was Connie Berube. She was frowning, arms crossed in front of her, hands clutching opposite elbows. I ignored her and went right to the Land Cruiser, where I checked on Joshua. Tired Josh was still snoozing.

"What are you doing up here?" asked Connie Berube, glancing around as if she expected to spot some vandalism I might have performed.

I made a sweeping gesture, encompassing the whole property. "I wanted to talk to who-ever's here, but nobody's home. I've looked on the beach and out back. Nobody."

She stared at me with suspicious eyes. "Ain't nobody here, mister." The suspicious eyes narrowed. "Do I know you?"

It seemed a little late for subterfuge. "J. W. Jackson," I said. "We met a couple of years ago. I traded some scallops for a pig. You may remember."

She thought about that, then nodded. "I remember." Her eyes were pale blue and there was a furtive, challenging quality to them. I thought that anyone living with Moonbeam would need to become feral to survive. I wondered where she'd come from, and how Moonbeam had persuaded her to marry him and produce that hoard of lovely, empty children.

"Mr. Ingalls is dead," she now said. "You hear what happened?"

"I heard. I thought maybe he had some folks I could talk to."

"No folks here. Police say there's some live up in Massachusetts some place that're coming down, but they're not here yet. They got to come back from Europe or Africa or one of those places, I guess." She nodded toward the house. "I cleaned for him and kept an eye on the place when he was gone. Last time I seen him, he said he was going to work down on the beach. Huh. Guess that's where they found him."

"How long did you work for him?" I asked.

She studied me. "Since just after he built

this place. I did the house and Moon did the yard. Brought in some money we could use. Guess that'll all stop now." Her face was finely boned, and I could see where her children had gotten their beauty.

I looked at her car.

"He must have paid pretty well," I said.

"None of your business what he paid," she said, her frown deepening. "Whatever it was, we earned it. Right now you probably got better things to do than wait for his kin to show up."

"When are they coming?"

"I don't know. They're off somewhere, like I said, and they got to come back over the ocean before they can come down here."

"It looks like you and Moonbeam took good care of things here. Maybe Ingalls's people will hire you to keep on doing what you're doing now. I hear they've got the money to do it if they decide to. You ever see a woman named Beth Harper up here?"

She nodded toward the driveway. "Time for you to be moving along, mister. Cops told me to keep an eye on the place like usual till Mr. Ingalls's family shows up."

"You ever see Beth Harper up here?"

Her hands tightened on her elbows. "I don't snoop in other people's business, mister. You take yourself along, now."

171

"She and Ingalls were going to get married. And she must have a key to the house," I said. "This morning she tried to take a shot at me with Ingalls's pistol. The one he kept in the cabinet beside his bed. She must have come up here last night or this morning to get it, and you must have seen her."

"You get going, mister. Right now. Else I call the police."

"She must have been up here quite a lot. You ever see that pistol of his? You cleaned his house; you must have seen the pistol."

"I never seen no pistol! I clean and dust, but I don't snoop! You've had your chance, mister. I'm calling the cops!" She turned to her car.

I held up both hands. "No need. I'm on my way. Maybe I'll see you again."

She stared at me and said nothing. I got into the Land Cruiser and drove down the long sandy lane to North Road. She followed me as far as her own hovel.

What a sentry she was. Better than a dog, or a goose, or any of the other guardians people kept around their houses. If Ingalls had valued his privacy and property, she was worth whatever he paid her.

It was certain that she knew Beth Harper, and almost certain that she had seen Beth come up to Ingalls's house when Beth had gotten the pistol. The fact that she hadn't interfered with Beth's pistol-retrieving expedition meant that Beth was a regular visitor, not a stranger like me, and indirectly reinforced Beth's claim that she and Ingalls had been engaged or were at least more than boss and underling.

Joshua yawned and began to stir. I headed down east, toward Edgartown. At home, I changed Josh's diaper yet again. How many years of diaper changing did I have in front of me, I wondered; how many tons of diapers would I wash and dry and fold and then wash again and dry and fold again before Josh caught on to using the pot? I'd read of people who trained their cats to use the toilet. Maybe I should use cat-training methods on Josh. Maybe I could train Oliver Underfoot and Velcro at the same time.

Maybe not.

I got Josh clean and sweet smelling just before Zee came through the door.

We kissed; she hugged Josh and went to the bedroom to shed her uniform. When she reappeared, wearing shorts and an out-of-season Christmas T-shirt that said, "Just say HO," I handed her her ice-cold Luksusowa martini. Motherhood had changed her, though. Instead of putting her feet up and savoring her drink as she once would have done, she sipped the drink, set it aside, and got down on the floor with her son. He gurgled at her, obviously pleased. She baby-talked back at him in spite of our agreement that we were always going to talk to him using adult tones and words.

Is there a more universal image of humanity than that of mother and child? I sat back with my own martini and munched cheese, smoked bluefish, and crackers while I watched them. I didn't blame her for wanting to be with him. After all, I'd enjoyed his company all day; now it was her turn. The cats came in through their flap in the door and took in the scene with a glance. They went into the kitchen for a quick snack, then came out and joined me as I observed my family. I was happy.

Later, though, when Zee was sleeping, curled against me, as warm and sweet as our son in his better moments, I thought again of the death of Lawrence Ingalls and my business with Drew Mondry. They were intrusions into the life I preferred to live, and I wished they were gone. But of course they weren't gone. Our lives are never free of intrusions. Maybe they consist of intrusions, and our planned lives are only intervals between the interruptions.

The next morning, shortly after Zee went

off to work, Intrusion Number One, Drew Mondry, drove into the yard.

The first thing he said was "I don't know quite how to say this, J.W., but I think you should know that a couple of detectives looked me up yesterday and asked me about what happened up there in Gay Head between you and that guy Ingalls who got killed on the beach."

He was uneasy, perhaps wondering if he were talking to a killer.

I nodded. "I gave them your name."

"That's what they said. I told them that Ingalls started the fight, and what happened after that. What people said and everything."

"Good."

"They never said whether they believed me or not."

"They never do. Don't worry about it. I'm sorry you're even involved."

He looked relieved. "I don't mind being involved. I just hope that I haven't gotten you into any trouble."

"None. You've probably helped, if anything. Besides, I'm not sure I'm in any trouble."

"Good, good." He shook his head. "Hell of a thing. I meet him one day, and two days later he's been murdered. The real thing is nothing like the movies, I can tell you that."

That was for sure. I changed the subject. "Did you bring the video?"

He turned back to the Range Rover. "Here it is." He handed me a videotape, apparently glad to be talking about his work instead of Ingalls's death. "I've seen the Chappy beaches, so we'll skip the first part of the film. But I want you to identify some of the other places, so you can take me to them later. A few look like possible locations, but I won't know until I see them from the ground."

We went inside, where Joshua was in his crib, considering the world with his big eyes. He and Drew Mondry exchanged good-mornings as I put the tape into our VCR, then Mondry and I sat on the couch and looked at the film. As always, the island was lovely and fascinating from the air, the perspective from a plane exaggerating its shape and dimensions until it looked to be a completely different place than that portrayed on maps.

The helicopter had taken off from the air-port, then had circumnavigated the island, flying west along the beach to Gay Head, then back along the north shore to West Chop, then southeast over East Chop all the way to Edgartown, where it turned inland and flew over the center of the island, working its way west once again to Gay Head, then back, at last, to the airport.

176

I identified the various great ponds on the south shore, and named the cliffs and beaches, including Lucy Vincent Beach, where the nude sunbathers waved at the helicopter as it passed over them. I pointed out the compound that once had been owned by the widow of a president, good fishing spots, and some of the sites we'd already visited by car.

Coming back along the north shore, I spotted Lawrence Ingalls's house and ID'd the ruins of the old brick works, along with the many points, ponds, and the houses of some of the Vineyard's more celebrated citizens. One of these belonged to Beverly Sills, who no longer sang, but whose tape of selections from *La Traviata* so often had given me great joy and made me pleased to have her share my island. Some day I was going to get together with Beverly, Pavarotti, Willie Nelson, and Emmylou Harris, and the five of us would cut a tape of my favorite C and W and opera songs. It would be a sure hit.

We flew over the chops and then over Sengekontacket Pond, where I pointed out our house; then, as we went inland, I showed Mondry various sites, including the farm that belonged to John Skye, which Mondry immediately identified as one of the places he'd like to visit, especially after I told him of the big library inside the house. The new high school addition looked huge, and the roads of the many housing developments, some completed, many not, wound like snakes or worms through the trees.

Mondry wanted to visit certain places for reasons that eluded me, since to my unprofessional eye the sites he selected seemed no more, and sometimes less, interesting than others. He made real notes and I made mental ones until the film ended as the helicopter returned to earth.

I rewound the film and handed it to him. He seemed pleased with our hour together. "You can take me to the places we talked about?"

"Most of them. A couple might be hard to get to because I don't know the right roads to get us there. Besides, we may run into some locked gates. That one little stretch of beach you liked belongs to the Marshall Lea Foundation, and they don't like to have cars on their property."

"Maybe I can call and get permission."

"Tell them there might be some money in it for them, and maybe they'll let us in. Outfits like that always need more money than they have." What an irony it would be if my advice brought the Marshall Lea people more money so they could buy more land that they

178

wouldn't let anybody use.

I once read of a town that was politically divided between two groups known as the Asphalts and the Greens, the Asphalts being pro-development and the Greens being conservationists, who favored open spaces and no Wal-Marts. Before all this plover to-do, I'd have categorized myself as more Vineyard Green than Vineyard Asphalt, but the more suspicious I became of guys like Lawrence Ingalls and outfits like the Marshall Lea Foundation, the less that seemed to be the case. What to do, O Lord?

"Let's have a look at the places we can get to," said Mondry. "I'll try to get permission for the other spots later. Maybe we won't even need to do that, if we're lucky today."

"Why not?" I got Joshua and his gear ready for travel, and we went off in Drew's Range Rover.

He was, he explained, looking for locations for the treasure the film's eighteenth-century pirates had supposedly buried and for which the modern characters were looking. For this, a beach with, say, some cliffs as background would be good. He also needed a house where the brains behind the efforts of the modern treasure hunters would be living, something with good exteriors and some space for planned action scenes in front of it.

And he needed the large library he'd spoken of, where those brains would be symbolized by books, a computer, tables of papers, and piles of charts.

I drove to two beach possibilities, and played with Joshua while Mondry walked about taking notes and shooting stills of the locations. Then we drove to John Skye's house.

Bonanza!

Mondry knew instantly that this was the spot for exterior shots of the needed house.

Mattie Skye came out as we went up to the door. I introduced her to Mondry.

"Ah," said Mattie, giving him her lovely smile. "J.W. said he was working for you."

"Drew, here, is looking at possible locations," I said. "I thought this might be a place he could use."

"And it looks terrific!" said Mondry. "What a lovely old farm!"

Mattie's brows lifted. "What are you talking about, J.W.?"

I told her. She was fascinated. "You mean you might shoot some scenes right here in our yard?"

"Only with your permission and only if you allow us to compensate you for the inconvenience we'll be causing you," said Mondry. "You might get a kick out of us being here,

180

but I assure you that it'll be a pain in the neck, too."

"Maybe not," I said. "According to the grapevine, you guys won't begin shooting till after Labor Day, and by then Mattie and John and the twins will be back in Weststock."

"Whoa, now." Mattie grinned. "It's true that John has to be back at work then, and that the girls have to be back in school, but I don't have to be anywhere. I can stay right here and watch my house be immortalized!"

Mondry eyed her appreciatively. "That might be even better. Maybe we can use you as an extra. I'm trying to get J.W.'s wife to do that. Maybe if you'll do it, she will, too!"

"I'll speak to Zee," said Mattie. "But I warn you, Mr. Mondry, if you use me and not my daughters, you may have a war on your hands!"

Mondry smiled diplomatically. "I'll be delighted to consider them, Mrs. Skye. If they're half as lovely as their mother, I'm sure we can use them."

Slick Drew. Ever the charmer.

"I want to show him John's library, too," I said. "Is the master at work?"

"He won't mind being interrupted, I'm sure. He's been slaving away all morning, and he'll be glad to have an excuse to stop. Come on in." She led Drew Mondry into the house.

181

"My husband," she said, "is writing the definitive interpretation of *Gawain and the Green Knight*. He's been at it forever."

"Ah," said Mondry.

John didn't mind being interrupted, and willingly pushed himself away from his desk.

After introductions, he waved a hand at his papers and his computer. "You know *Gawain*, Mr. Mondry? No? Well, you're not alone. I've been studying him for forty years and I barely know him myself!"

Mondry was sweeping the room with his eyes, taking in the walls of books, the huge desk, the ancient Oriental carpet, the charts of the Vineyard and the south coast of New England, and the rusty fencing mask mounted on a wall over triangulated foil, sabre, and épée, testimony to John's long-ago undergraduate fencing career.

"This is it!" he said, nodding. "Perfect! This is Neville Black's library!"

— 15 —

Neville Black, it turned out, was the scholar of dubious morality whose expertise in the matter of pirate gold had led the motley crew of treasure hunters to the Vineyard in the script of the movie.

"Ah," said John Skye. "A scholar of dubious morality, eh? Not a rare sort of bird at all. Every college has its share of them!"

John was fiftyish, tall and balding and unconcerned about the small potbelly he was carrying around with him. Emergency rations in case of atomic attack, he said. He was a professor of medieval literature at Weststock College, and a notable scholar, although you'd never know it from talking to him. Rather, he was inclined to make light of academia and the pettiness and pretentiousness of its citizens, including himself. Teaching esoteric subjects such as his own, he was fond of saying, was the closest thing there was to not working at all, since very few people could tell whether you were doing anything worthwhile (or anything at all, for that matter), and all you had to do to earn a reputation was show up and look alternately vague and intent. The groves of academe flourished, he said, because of the great amount of manure spread by their inhabitants.

But I'd seen his books in the library of my old alma mater, Northeastern University, and in the other libraries where I'd studied while chasing an education and being a Boston cop, so I knew he had more of a reputation than he claimed. If he didn't take himself very seriously, other people did.

Now I looked down at Joshua, who was nestled in the chest pack I'd rigged so I could carry him and still have both hands free for important things like fishing. "Your mom and I got married outside in the yard," I said. "Did you know that?"

He hadn't known, he said, but he did now.

Drew Mondry was walking around the room, snapping pictures and nodding.

"Ah, the silver screen! You'll be a famous at last," I said to John.

"Or my library will be, at least," said John. "I can bask in the reflected glory."

"The tour buses will stop here, and people wearing polyester will get out and take pictures of your house. You can make them pay a fee to see inside."

"I'll be able to retire and send the twins to private schools."

"We'll travel during the off season," said Mattie. "I'll have a maid all year, and somebody who does nothing else but clean the bathrooms and wash windows."

Behind us, a door opened and the twins came in from wherever they'd been. The barn, probably, working on something having to do with their horses.

"Hi, J.W.," said Jen or Jill. "Hi, there, Joshua." She and her sister came up and smiled at Joshua, who stared back.

"You're very thoughtful today," said the twin.

He agreed that he was.

Drew Mondry was looking at the twins, who were a pretty pair. I introduced them to one another. "These are the two problems I was telling you about," I said to Mondry. "They come with the house, unfortunately, and they vant to be stars."

"Oh!" said a twin, staring at Mondry. "You're the movie guy!"

Mondry produced his charm. "I'm the movie guy. And you're the famous twins I've heard so much about."

The famous twins gave me quick glances, wondering what I had been saying about them. I wondered, too, since I couldn't remember saying much of anything.

"We want to be in your movie!" said one of them, looking back at Mondry and getting right to the point.

"We think it would be lots of fun!" said the other.

"It can be fun," said Mondry. "I don't do casting, but I know the people who do. I think they might want to use you. You and your mother and maybe your father, too." He smiled at John and Mattie. "Especially if we use your house for a location."

"Oh, Daddy!" cried a twin. "You'll let them use the house, won't you? You wouldn't deny your children the opportunity to be movie stars, would you? You wouldn't either, would you, Mom?"

Daddy and Mom looked at each other.

"Now, don't push your parents so hard," said Mondry diplomatically. "This is a big decision. When a movie company comes in for location shots, it takes over the whole place. Not everybody wants to put up with it." Then he flashed his California smile. "Say, would you kids like to take me out and show me around the place? I'd like to look at that barn, too, while I'm here. You have horses there, from the looks of it. I'd like to see them. Maybe we can get them in the movie, too."

Maybe I'll make both you and your horses into stars. Words to win the hearts of teenage girls. Drew was a real smoothie. I watched the twins lead him to the barn and wondered if he waved the big screen in front of every good-looking woman he met, or just in front of those I knew.

"Well, what do you think?" asked John, looking at his wife.

"I think it would be fun!" said normally practical Mattie, with a big grin. Like daughters, like mother.

"Done, then!" said John. "If they want to use the place, they can do it. And if they can use you and the girls as extras, that's even better."

So far, I was the only one I knew who hadn't been offered a job as an extra. Was it because my classic good looks might be resented by the male star? I looked down at Joshua, who looked back up at me. "What do you think?" I asked him.

That might be it, he replied gravely.

I'd read several stories about the movie-to-be in both the *Gazette* and the *Vineyard Times*, but couldn't recall the casting, so I asked.

"Who's going to be in this movie, anyway?"

Mattie knew. "Kevin Turner and Kate Ballinger and Martin Paisley."

187

Their names had been in the local papers all summer, but I could only see the woman in my mind. She was one of those actresses who was really beautiful but could look less than that if her role required it.

"Kevin Turner is the new swashbuckler," said Mattie, observing my blank face, "and Martin Paisley is the Dracula guy."

"I thought that was Bela Lugosi."

"There've been a lot of Draculas since Bela Lugosi! Martin Paisley is the latest one. He played Chopin, too. In *Blood and Ivory*. Maybe you remember him in that movie."

"I heard it was terrible."

"It was terrible, but he was good. So pale and wan that he just broke your heart."

"He didn't break my heart," said John. "It was a very sappy movie. Jeez, drops of blood on the piano keys, already. He was a pretty fair Dracula, though. Not as good as Bela, of course."

Of course not. They got Frankenstein's monster right the first time, too. A classic is a classic is a classic, and they should leave them alone.

"Kevin is the famous womanizer," said Mattie. "On and off screen. A trail of broken hearts. They say he's the new Errol Flynn! I can hardly wait to meet him!"

"Swords and daggers and heaving bosoms,"

said John. "He won't win any Oscars, but he can swash and buckle with the best of them. Of course, he should never try to remake *Robin Hood* or *Captain Blood* or *They Died With Their Boots On*. The original Flynn did them as well as they can be done."

More classics. Hollywood's golden age.

"Flynn was the reason I went to Weststock for my undergraduate work, you know," said John. "I refused to attend a college where I couldn't take up fencing. I planned on becoming the world's champion. And it was all because of Flynn movies and Fairbanks movies. I found out that Weststock had a fencing team, and that was good enough for me. I got my degree in English, but I actually took a multiple major in foil, épée, and saber. I was pretty good, too, but naturally not as good as Flynn or Fairbanks. They never lost." He looked up at the weapons and mask on the wall. "That was a long time ago."

"But the blood still runs hot!" said Mattie, grabbing him in both arms. "My hero!"

John grinned a jaunty grin, twirled an imaginary mustache, and made a couple of parries and thrusts with a pointed finger.

"Ha! Take that, you villain! You're safe, my lady. The evil baron will trouble you no more!"

They kissed.

Ah, romance! I was glad to see that it never died.

Drew Mondry and the twins came back into the house on the best of terms, having charmed one another to the fullest extent of their considerable abilities.

"Well, folks, what do you say?" asked Mondry. "Your place looks like a perfect location. I'd like to make a deal with you, if I can. There'll be some money in it, of course."

"And there'll be us!" exclaimed a twin. "That'll be part of the deal!"

"If I can talk the casting director into it," corrected Mondry.

"Try! You can do it!" cried the other twin. "Daddy, Mom, our lives will be ruined forever if you don't let them use our house!"

"Well, we certainly don't want your lives ruined," said her mother.

Hands were shaken, twinish sounds of happiness were heard, good-byes were finally accomplished, and Mondry and I drove away.

"Quite a family," said Mondry.

"Indeed."

"The girls are terrific. My daughter is just a little younger."

"They want to be stars, for sure."

"Well, I can probably get them into some background shots, at least. Being a star isn't what people think. You have to want it to put up with the grief."

"How'd you get into the business?"

He waved a hand. "I'm a pretty good-looking guy, and I acted a little in high school, so I played around with the bug. Went out to Hollywood and made the rounds. Got an agent. Supported myself any way I could. Made some commercials. Wore out my shoes. Found out that my face wouldn't do it for me and that I didn't want it bad enough, I didn't have the fire in the belly. But I liked the business, so I stayed on the fringe. Then I got the big break I needed." He glanced at me with a smile. "I met a girl and married her.

"She had a brother who had the fire I didn't have. He got big, and because I was married to his sister, I got jobs I probably wouldn't have gotten otherwise. Don't get me wrong; I'm good at what I do. But there are a thousand other people who can probably do it just as well. The difference is they never married Kevin Turner's sister."

"You're married to Kevin Turner's sister? The same Kevin Turner who's going to be in this movie? Lady-killer Kevin?"

"That's right. Kevin is Emily's little brother, and I work on all of his pictures. I work on others, too, and I think I can make it now even if he retires or goes into a monastery or something; fat chance of that, but I probably wouldn't be in the business at all if it wasn't for him making sure I got my foot in the door."

Real life is odder than any fiction, as many have observed.

"I don't think I'll be around watching them make this movie," I said, "so tell me what they'll be doing here on the island."

"Well, I've seen the script, so I know what they think it's going to be about, although that may change before they're through. It's a rare movie that ends up the way it was originally planned."

"So I've heard."

"The idea here is to tell two stories at the same time: the original pirate story about burying the treasure back in the eighteenth century, and the modern story about treasure hunters trying to find it. The plan is to flip back and forth between the stories, with the same actors playing roles in both centuries. Kevin, for example, is going to be the eighteenth-century pirate who buries the treasure, and a twentieth-century descendant of his who, a couple of hundred years later, comes to the Vineyard to find it. Kate Ballinger plays the pirate's woman and Kevin's modern mistress, and Martin Paisley will play the modern scholar who researches the treasure story and the eighteenth-century

192

man of letters who was the brains behind the original pirate raid that got them the treasure."

"It sounds like they've got a script that will let your brother-in-law swing on ropes and have sword fights and drive fast cars, too, while he makes lots of love to the ladies."

"You bet. And maybe that's all it'll be. On the other hand, it could be a pretty good movie, with the modern characters learning something about themselves and their own lives as they find out more about the pirates."

"Where's your money laid down?"

"Only my bookie knows."

I looked at my watch. "You have time to do some reading about real pirates on the Vineyard?"

He brightened. "Yes. That might be useful."

So I took him down to the Vineyard Museum, one of the island's treasures, and we went into the library.

— 16 —

The library of the Martha's Vineyard Museum includes a lot of island treasure stories. I brought books to Drew Mondry, and he began to read.

In the August 14, 1811, edition of the *Baltimore Whig*, there is a memorandum from the Port of Philadelphia that includes the following report by Captain Dagget of the brig *Fox*:

About the 20th of July last, was found in the surf, on the south side of Martha's Vineyard, by an inhabitant, an open boat, the tracks of three men and the appearance of something they had been dragging after them, was traced over the sand till it was lost on the upland, the same day, in the vicinity of the place, three men apparently foreigners, applied to a boatman, to put them on the main, he carried them to New-Bedford, the men said they had been cast away — they had a large sum of money with them. On the 2nd inst. near where the boat was found, the leg of a man was discovered sticking out of the sand: the jury of inquest being called, he was dug out and found to be a man with his throat cut, and a knife lying by him; had been dead too long to ascertain whether old or young; had on a pair of canvas trowsers and short blue jacket.

Twelve years later, on January 18, 1823, Miss Hannah Smith made this entry in her journal:

We are informed today that the people of Edgartown have been exploring and digging Chilmark beach in quest of gold, which they suppose was buried there eleven years ago by four pirates that landed there and murdered one of their crew.

One of the pirates had lately been convicted when on his deathbed in New York, and confessed the treacherous act. He confessed that they hove their captain and mate overboard, robbed the vessel of all gold and silver, scuttled and sank her, and escaped in the boat which they left on Chilmark beach.

He confessed, likewise, that after knocking the man down three times they cut his throat because he stood out in a violent manner and would not join them in their wickedness, and declared that he would not have anything to do with their money.

Likewise that when they landed they thought themselves on Long Island and they were about to make their escape to New York with their booty swung across a pole on their shoulders. But the fog clearing up, they found their mistake, buried their booty on the beach, and hired George West to carry them immediately to New Bedford, for fear they might be detected. Captain West said at the time that on their passage the pirates fell a-quarreling about their passage money, and he dare not speak nor stir for fear they would throw him overboard, for they had the appearance of murder in their visage.

A third report about these particular pirates and their buried hoard has it that one day, years after Captain West had ferried his scary passengers to New Bedford, two strangers arrived on foot at a house on Squibnocket Beach and asked to stay there for a few days, explaining that they were naturalists interested in marine curiosities. Oddly, these naturalists preferred to make their studies at night, and two or three days later hired a wagon in Holmes Hole, which they did not return until the next day, after which they departed the island, never to be seen again. Local residents later found a hole some twelve feet across in a marsh, and concluded that it lay on what might have been a bearing range for buried treasure.

So the bad guys (a couple of them, at least) apparently escaped with the loot. Not for the first time, or the last, as any cop can tell you.

"I like it," said Mondry. "Maybe we can bury somebody with the treasure in our film."

I brought him more books telling stories of other Vineyard treasures: the tale of the kettle in the sandbank beside North Road, where a single gold coin remained after the kettle disappeared; the tale of the lady who buried her money and valuables near Beck's Pond to save them from the British during the Revolutionary War, but who could never find the cache again; and the tale of the old pirate who, on his deathbed, told of a trove buried "where two brooks empty into Vineyard Sound," but which later searchers could never find.

We read about the three treasure hunters

who dug at midnight by a large rock near Tarpaulin Cove. They had just struck a buried chest with their shovels when the earth opened and nearly swallowed one unfortunate chap, who was barely saved by his friends. Uncanny noises were heard, and the three fled, never to return.

Other rocks figured prominently in other Vineyard treasure stories. There was the mysterious Money Rock north of Indian Hill, and a flat rock on the old Mayhew Luce farm, beneath which, it was said, pirates were fond of hiding their loot. And of course there was Moonbeam's tale of the Blue Rock of Chappaquiddick, where the farmer witnessed murder on the beach.

Good stuff, all of it. Admittedly, Joshua went to sleep while Mondry and I were reading, but what does a kid know about the important things in life?

"Great," said Mondry, pushing away the last tale and looking around at the book-filled shelves of Vineyard history and lore. "This is some kind of place. If we need to do any research about the island, I know the place to come."

True. Libraries are the real treasures in most towns, full of riches and people who'll help you find them. Some librarians look very severe, but I suspect that most of them are born romantics, who really believe that there is no frigate like a book to take us lands away, nor any coursers like a page of prancing poetry.

We left the library and I walked Mondry past the great lighthouse lens and through the other museum buildings.

"Dynamite," said astute Drew. The more I was with him, the less I found to dislike. Rats.

We got back in the Range Rover, where he ruined my gentle mood. "Well," he said, "about all I have left to do here before I head back to L.A. is take your wife out, and try to talk her into working on this film. I don't think I've ever seen anyone who photographs better."

I felt that green feeling.

"How do you know she photographs well?" I knew she did, because I had lots of pictures of her, but how did Mondry know?

Because he had pictures of her, too. Ones he'd taken when we'd all gone scouting the island together. While he'd been photographing the locations that interested him, he'd also taken snaps of Zee and Joshua and even me. He showed them to me now.

Zee glowed at us from the photos, most of which she clearly never knew were being taken. She was smiling at Joshua, pointing to something she thought Mondry should note, grinning at me, talking with Toni Begay, looking out over the Gay Head cliffs.

Being Zee.

"Your wife is a fine person," said Mondry. "But she's also a very great beauty. And her personality jumps out of these photos. I really think she's got what it takes to be in films."

"You can make your case to her," I said. "Then she can decide."

"I know you've said you don't mind. I hope that's really true."

"It's true," I lied.

"Good." He looked again at the photos. "God, she is really something. You must be really proud of her."

Pride has always perplexed me. I felt it when looking at Zee or Joshua, but never knew why, since what I saw in them had nothing to do with any accomplishment of mine. And I distrusted the feeling when it came from anything I was or did; those times, it struck me as nonsensical. But then, most of the deadly sins are just forms of silliness and stupidity. I should know, being intimate with all of them, including, especially right now, jealousy and covetousness.

"She's something, all right," I said. I looked down at my son. "You think so, too, don't you, Josh?"

Josh agreed, even though he didn't wake up to say so.

At our house, Mondry shook my hand, thanked me for everything, and asked me to tell Zee that he'd call her about seven.

I said I'd do that, and he said he'd send me a check for my work. Then he smiled at Joshua, and drove away, and I went into the house to fix supper.

That evening, right on schedule, he did call and Zee said, sure, she'd meet him for lunch tomorrow before he caught an afternoon plane to Boston on his first hop back to California.

"You really don't mind my doing this?" she asked when she hung up.

Everybody was asking me that. "Not a bit. I could probably get used to being married to a movie star with an income in the millions." I put an arm around her waist and pulled her to me. She wrapped her arms around my neck.

"I have an idea," she said, smiling.

But just then Joshua woke up and began to babble and whine. Zee shook her head, unwound herself from me, and headed for his room. "You know," she said over her shoulder, "it's a wonder people ever get a chance to have another kid after they've had the first one. There's no more privacy!"

201

It was a familiar observation, and she was right; but somehow a lot of parents managed to avoid single-child families. I suspected we might, too.

The next day's *Vineyard Gazette* had the latest dope on the killing. The *Gazette* is properly famous for its idiosyncratic prose style and its total focus on the Vineyard and nothing else. If half the world were destroyed by a giant meteor, the *Gazette* would report the fact only if some islander happened to be involved. Normally the *Gazette* underplays tales of violence and evil island doings, preferring to extol the positive aspects of Vineyard living, but this edition made much of Ingalls's death because he had been in the center of the Norton's Point wrangle, because the *Gazette* was unabashedly pro-environmentalist in both its editorial policies and its story selections, and because murders were, in fact, a rarity on the island.

The front-page story included my role as discoverer of Ingalls's body, and was based on police reports, as near as I could tell. I was described as a well-known island fisherman. Later, I was also identified as an outspoken critic of the DEP's decision to close Norton's Point.

I learned that an autopsy had revealed that Ingalls had died as a result of a single gunshot wound to the chest, that the gun had been fired from fairly close range, and that the weapon, not yet found by the police, was probably a .38 or a nine-millimeter.

I suspected that my old police .38 and Zee's little Beretta 84F and her new .45 would soon bring the police to my door with a warrant that would allow them to take the guns away for test firing. That was all right with me, since I was sure none of them was the murder weapon.

I read on and learned about Ingalls's aristocratic North Shore background, his Ivy League education, his interest in the East, his commitment to the environment, and, finally, the fact that due to his love of the Vineyard, he was going to be buried on the island. The funeral was scheduled for Monday. His parents, who had been traveling in Europe, were already on the island, staying in Ingalls's house in Chilmark. Other relatives, friends, and business associates were gathering from various parts of the United States. I didn't think that many people would show up at my funeral.

The police were busy with their investigation and were asking for assistance from anyone who had information that might help solve the crime.

I put down the paper and took Joshua out

into the yard. I sat him under an umbrella so the sun wouldn't eat him, then spent an hour in the garden pulling weeds while I thought things over. Weeding is good for that. Your hands do one kind of work and your brain can do another. In this case, my hands were doing the better job of the two.

Out beyond Sengekontacket Pond, the August People were abundant. Cars lined the road on the barrier beach, and on their far side were bright umbrellas in the sand. There were brighter kites in the air, and colorful Windsurfer sails moved back and forth on the blue water just beyond the beach. Overhead, the pale blue summer arched high above wheeling gulls, and the hot summer sun beat down.

I wondered how many of the people over there knew or cared about the death of Lawrence Ingalls. More than are usually aware of the deaths of strangers, I guessed, for a killing in Eden is worthy of a comfortable chat with your neighbor on the next beach towel. I wondered if any of them had put me on their suspect lists and if, indeed, there were any other names on those lists.

The sun climbed higher and Joshua's umbrella shadow moved off him. I cleaned myself off in the outdoor shower and took Joshua in for lunch. Somewhere Zee and

Drew Mondry would soon be getting together for a lunch of their own. Tarzan and Jane. Val and a black-haired Aleta.

What lovely woman would say no to an offer to appear in a motion picture? And was there any reason for Zee to do so? I could think of none at all.

After lunch, while I was mowing the grass, an Edgartown cruiser came down the driveway. The chief got out. I was sweating and was glad to take a break. I shut off the mower, picked up Joshua from under his umbrella, and walked over to the car.

"I've been expecting you," I said.

"I figured you might be. I didn't bother getting a warrant. I gonna need one?"

"No, you don't need one. Come on in."

He followed me into the house. In the kitchen, I passed Joshua to him. "Hold this guy," I said.

The chief was a grandpa, and used to kids. He and Joshua eyed each other.

"I'll say one thing for you, laddie," said the chief. "You don't look a thing like your dad."

I got Zee's Beretta, her .45, and my Smith & Wesson out of the gun cabinet and brought them back to the kitchen.

"These what you want?"

"That's them. You got any other handguns

205

I don't know about?"

"Nope."

"Well, the forty-five is the wrong caliber, but I'll take it along, too."

I found a paper bag and put the pistols into it. "Here." Traded the bag for Joshua, who seemed glad to be back in familiar arms.

The chief looked almost embarrassed. "I know these aren't the weapons, but we have to check them out."

"I know. But get Zee's forty-five back as quick as you can. Manny Fonseca's got her lined up for another shooting contest on the mainland, and she's going to need lots of practice."

"It shouldn't take long, but I'll have to keep the guns until the tests come back."

"I know."

He turned toward the door, then hesitated and turned back. "I know you didn't do it, but you're a suspect anyway. You understand?"

"Do what you have to do," I said.

"Yeah." He started out of the house, then paused. "Oh, something you maybe should know. I got hold of Zack Delwood and asked him some questions. He was a bit put out at you."

"Zack's put out at somebody all the time."

"Yeah, but this time he's really irked."

"Why?"

"He figures you're the one who steered me to him about this killing. Put him on the suspect list, as it were."

A pox on Zack Delwood. "Where'd he get that idea?"

"You and him have always ruffled each other's feathers, so maybe he's just been looking for a reason to pound on you. I told him that you didn't finger him, but being the kind of guy he is, he figures I'm lying." He shook his head. "When I talked to Zack, I thought maybe he might have done Ingalls in, but later I talked to Iowa and Walter and they told me Zack was fishing beside them up at the Jetties when Ingalls got himself shot. If I can track Zack down again, I'll tell him he's off the suspect list, but meanwhile keep an eye out for him. He may try to put his fist through your face."

Terrific. First Ingalls takes a swing at me, then Beth Harper tries to shoot me, and now Zack Delwood was after my head. Being innocent was dangerous business.

When Zee got home that evening, she told me that she'd agreed to try out for a role in the movie. She said that Drew Mondry had caught an afternoon plane to Boston, on his way back to California, and that he thanked me for everything and looked forward to seeing me soon.

"You'll be a star," I said, handing her her ice-cold Luksusowa martini. "You'll light up the night."

— 17 —

On Monday it was raining, making the sad business of a funeral even sadder. Zee had the day off, and preferred to stay at home with Joshua instead of going out into the drizzle to attend the memorial service for somebody she'd only seen once in her life. I had more motive than she did, so I sat in the back row of the church during the funeral and tried to look inconspicuous, certain that the mourners would prefer that a suspect in the case not attend the rites.

There were a lot of people there, steaming and dripping, and I recognized some of them. Beth Harper was sitting with people I took to be Lawrence Ingalls's family: an elderly woman and man I presumed were his mother and father, and a couple of fortyish couples I guessed were his siblings and their spouses. Another woman seemed to be with the group yet somehow not part of it, and I wondered who she was. A cousin? A friend of the family? I couldn't guess.

I recognized several members of the Marshall Lea Foundation, including Jud Wilber, the president, and Dina Witherspoon, the secretary. Somewhat to my surprise, I also saw Joe and Toni Begay, with Hanna on Toni's lap. And to my greater surprise, I saw Connie Berube. Beneath her wet raincoat, Connie was wearing a dark dress that looked, even to my unpracticed eyes, quite a bit out of date. She stared expressionlessly at the minister, who was evoking the mercy of his God on behalf of Lawrence Ingalls's soul.

Officer Olive Otero of the state police was wearing civvies, and sitting not too far from me, eyeing the crowd. On the other side of the room Tony D'Agostine, one of Edgartown's finest, was doing the same. I thought there were probably another two or three representatives of law and order in the crowd, too, since it is a truism that killers sometimes come to the funerals of their victims, or visited their graves over the following months and even years. I was sure that none of the police had overlooked me with their roving eyes.

When the minister finished commending the soul of the deceased to the Almighty, I slipped out ahead of the crowd, drove up to the Chilmark cemetery through the summer rain, and found a parking place before the funeral procession arrived.

The gravestone of a famous TV and movie celebrity, dead from, what else? an overdose of illegal chemicals, adorns the entrance to the cemetery. Originally, the grave lay elsewhere on the grounds, but when the feet of hoards of pilgrims to the holy site threatened to wear a highway through the graveyard and do damage to the memorials of its other residents, smart Chilmarkers moved the star's stone to the very gate of the cemetery. It is now the first gravestone you see, and there, ever since, fans have adorned the site with beer cans, joints, needles, flowers, and other memorabilia associated with their hero's fast and eventful life. The gravestone is the second most popular tourist site on the Vineyard, being nosed out only by the bridge on Chappaquiddick.

People are curious animals, as many members of the same odd group have observed.

I stood beneath a tree some distance from the dark and soggy rectangle into which Ingalls's coffin would be lowered, and watched the graveside rituals. People stood under umbrellas or with their collars turned up, and the rain came down, not too hard, but steadily, a soaking rain, the kind gardeners love to have for their plants. But today they were planting Lawrence Ingalls, who didn't need the moisture and would never need anything again, in fact. He had come to the end of needing or wanting and was now due to be recycled into something other than he had been as mortal man.

The energy that had taken the shape of the human being he had been would not be lost, but it would take a new form: first, as food for the living things that eat us in our graves; then, probably, as food for whatever eats the things that eat us, for everything that lives eats and is eaten; then, further along the food chain, perhaps as fertilizer for some yet to be born blade of grass, and later as heat, or light, or new life, or some other earthly or celestial substance or power or potency. It would change, but it wouldn't be lost, for energy is never lost.

Under trees and umbrellas, some not too far from me, the police who had been at the church still watched the mourners, having come out into the rain to do their duty and maybe spot somebody who didn't really belong there or who was acting oddly.

I couldn't see anyone who seemed to fit that bill better than I did.

I waited until the service was over before leaving. As I walked to the Land Cruiser, Tony D'Agostine came alongside me. His raincoat and rain hat were shiny and trickling water.

"Hell of a day for a funeral, J.W."

"The dead don't mind what kind of day it is."

"I'd like it to be sunny when they put me under," said Tony. "I want people to be happy and to have a party with plenty of beer. I don't want a sad bunch in the rain, like here today. Saw you in church."

"And I saw you. And Olive Otero. And Joe Begay. I guess he was there for the same reason the Marshall Lea bunch was. Environmentalists all."

"What were you doing there, anyway?"

"Same as you, Tony. I wanted to see who showed up. I didn't expect to see Moonbeam's wife."

"I guess she kept house for Ingalls. They were his nearest neighbors."

"Who was the extra woman with the family? The one with reddish hair."

"Ah. That was Ingalls's ex. Woman named Barbara Singleton. She came down with his folks."

I gave that some thought. "His ex? She seemed pretty close to the family."

"Yeah. Seems a little odd, maybe, but sometimes when a couple splits up, the parents hang on to both of them. Sometimes, even, Mom and Dad like the ex in-law better than they like their own kid."

True. "You think Ingalls's parents liked her better than him?"

Tony brushed water from his mustache. "Don't put words in my mouth, J.W. Size of this funeral, he had a lot of friends."

"He had at least one enemy."

"Olive Otero thinks she knows who it was. You."

We got to the Land Cruiser. I said, "The only time I saw him alive, we didn't get along. But somebody else killed him."

"Speaking of which," said Tony, turning his back to the wind, "they've been running tests on those weapons of yours." There was a restrained excitement in his voice.

"And?"

"And none of your pistols fired the round that killed Ingalls."

Even though I'd known that must be true, I felt an unexpected feeling of relief. Being innocent doesn't free you from the fear of guilt. With the relief came a bit of the anger that children feel when they've been falsely accused. I kept it out of my voice.

"When can we get them back? Zee's supposed to be practicing for a meet."

Tony's voice was eager. He had something to say. "You'll have to talk to the chief about that. I know you're not surprised about your own weapons being clean, but we tested another one and came up golden. The thirty-eight you took off Beth Harper."

That was interesting. I looked at Tony. "Ingalls was shot with that gun?"

Tony nodded. "No doubt about it."

"That was Ingalls's own gun. Beth Harper got it out of his house before she came hunting me."

He nodded. "That's what she says, anyway. The gun did belong to him. There's no doubt about that. His father identified it as one he gave Ingalls years ago, along with some others. Rifles and shotguns and the like. Family heirlooms of some kind. Belonged to a great-uncle who hunted elephants, or something like that." Tony squinted at me through the rain. "Another thing. There's only two sets of prints on the gun. Yours and Beth Harper's. What do you make of that?"

What did I make of that? I made that my prints were on the murder weapon. "What do I make of it? I make that Beth Harper's are there because she tried to shoot me, and mine are there because I took the gun away from her. What do you make of it?"

He shrugged. "I don't make nothing of it, but Olive Otero likes it a lot. She thinks it ties you tighter to the killing, and she'd like to make an arrest pretty soon." He pulled back a sleeve and glanced at his watch. "I gotta be going. I ain't supposed to hobnob with criminals."

He smiled slightly, waved, and walked away.

Fifty yards down the road, Officer Olive Otero was leaning against her unmarked car, watching me, I got into the Land Cruiser and drove past her out of the cemetery. Having Olive Otero suspicious of me didn't make me feel good, but having Tony behaving like a friend did, especially since I didn't think that Tony would be acting that way without the tacit approval of the chief. If it turned out that I was guilty or there was enough evidence to arrest me, the chief would do it; but until then he was cutting me some unofficial slack by keeping me informed of what was going on.

Olive Otero apparently was not so inclined. I wondered if Dom Agganis, the other state cop on the island, shared her suspicion. Dom and I had had a few testy moments, but we'd also gone fishing together, so it was hard to tell where he stood. He'd be fair, whatever happened, and that would have to satisfy me for now.

The funeral procession had broken up. Some cars had turned toward West Tisbury, and others had headed up-island. I, recognized the last of the latter as Joe Begay's big Dodge 4 x 4, and followed after it.

At Beetlebung Corner, some cars turned toward Menemsha and North Road, but Joe Begay's took a left and pulled into the parking lot in front of the Chilmark store. I pulled in beside him. Toni was in the passenger seat and Hanna was in her car seat. Joe got out and went up onto the covered porch. I waved at his wife and child, and climbed the steps and joined him.

"Saw you tailing me," he said. "Will it ruin my reputation to be seen in public with a suspected killer?"

"If you think so, I'll just keep walking."

"Nah. Stick around. That article in the paper put your name on a lot of lips, though."

"Yeah. 'Deadly enemy of victim claims to have discovered corpse.' Great."

"Well, they didn't exactly go that far."

"No, not exactly."

The summer rain fell steadily, drumming softly on the roof. August rains like this one were lovely and pleasant, life givers, friends, washing away the stains of everyday living and making things bright and glowing and new. Other rains were cold and cruel, like enemies, or like ourselves sometimes. Or like whoever killed Lawrence Ingalls.

I told Joe Begay what Tony D'Agostine had told me about the murder weapon, then went on: "The thing is that the only prints on the gun were mine and Beth Harper's. Why weren't there any of Ingalls's prints on it?"

"Probably because he cleaned his weapons after using them," said Begay. "Some people do, you know."

"Beth Harper says he kept the gun in his bedside table. You think he would have wiped off every one of his fingerprints before putting it there? If it was me, I might clean the weapon after using it, but I'd never bother wiping the grips when I put it away."

"Not everybody's a slob, J.W."

"Don't give me a hard time. Would you have wiped the gun clean before putting it away beside your bed?"

"I don't keep a gun beside my bed. I don't need one. I don't have as many enemies as some people, I guess."

Actually, I thought that Joe Begay had probably collected more than one enemy during the twenty years he'd worked for whoever it was he had worked for doing whatever it was he did wherever it was he did it.

I gave him a sour look. "Okay, you don't keep a gun in your bedside table. But if you did, would you wipe off every fingerprint before you put it there?"

"No. But maybe Ingalls did."

"I can't see that, but somebody wiped the gun."

218

"Maybe Beth Harper did it."

"Why would she do a thing like that? She got her own prints all over it when she came after me."

"Too many maybes for me, kid."

"Did you ever go up to his house?"

"Couple of times. Cocktail parties with the Marshall Lea crowd. You were conspicuous in your absence."

"He ever show you around the place? You know, upstairs, downstairs, and all around the town?"

"Yeah. I got the grand tour once, at least. It's quite a house, and Larry was proud of it."

"He ever show you his guns?"

"His guns?" Begay frowned.

"Yeah. He got some guns from his father. Old rifles and whatnot that belonged to some ancestor. The pistol was part of the package. He ever show you the rest of the stuff?"

Begay stared at the rain for a while. Then he said, "Well, there were old rifles mounted over some fireplaces. Huge things. Elephant guns used to belong to some big-game hunter in the family, he said. One was a seven hundred Gibbs. Double barrels. Looked like a cannon."

I felt a little thrill. "How do you know it was a seven hundred Gibbs?"

"Because he told me so. Took it down and

219

let me hold it. Weighed a ton. Kill an elephant for sure, or maybe even a tank. I never saw anything like it."

"And then he put it back."

He nodded. "That's right. Ah, I see what you mean. If he didn't mind getting his prints and mine on a fine old rifle like that, why would he have bothered to wipe off a pistol he kept right there by his bed?"

"Yeah. And if he didn't wipe off the gun, who did? And why?"

"I don't know the who," said Begay, "but the why's easy. Whoever shot Ingalls wiped off the pistol so his prints wouldn't be on it, and put the gun back where it belonged."

"Just in case anybody ever thought it might be the murder weapon."

Begay nodded again. "Not a likely thing, really. If Beth Harper hadn't decided to kack you, why would anybody have tied that gun to the Ingalls shooting?"

"Well, it's tied now. I think I'm going to need some help. Are you interested in the job?"

He looked at me. "Make me an offer I can't refuse."

"No problem: a six-pack of the beer of your choice."

"Done," said Joe Begay, putting out his wide brown hand and taking mine. "What do

220

you have in mind, boss?"

"The child is father of the man," I said. "I want to know all about your late friend Larry Ingalls."

"I'll make what they call discreet inquiries," said Begay. "You want to know anything in particular?"

"I want to know everything."

"Oh, that."

"That."

"I'll be in touch." He walked through the rain to the Dodge and drove away.

— 18 —

It was just after noon when Joe Begay left the Chilmark store, so I bought one of the good sandwiches they sell there and a bottle of water, there being no beer for sale in dry Chilmark. Only Edgartown and Oak Bluffs sell booze on the Blessed Isle, which is why the island's bar fights all take place in those towns. You can only have bar fights where there are bars.

Having no saloons in their towns doesn't, of course, mean that up-island rowdies don't have drunken brawls; it just means that they have to travel to Edgartown and Oak Bluffs to find their fights, or, after making whiskey runs down-island and back, punch each other out in the privacy of their own homes.

Since there was no booze for sale at the Chilmark store, there were also no fights there that day. All diners, including me, sipped nonalcoholic beverages and were at peace. We munched and looked out at the falling rain, and at the shimmering green glow it gave to the grass and leaves.

The glamour of the scene and the memory of Lawrence Ingalls's death and burial blended in my mind, and made me conscious, once again, of the paradoxical grandeur that is life, and of the ephemeral opportunity we have to walk through it. But I am no poet, nor was meant to be, and could find no images or phrases to capture meaning from my thoughts, so I let them go, finished my meal, and drove to Edgartown to see Manny Fonseca.

Martha's Vineyard doesn't have one general-use weather system, good for the whole island, but a number of separate little ones having little to do with one another. It is never surprising, for instance, to find on the same day thick fog at Katama, bright sun in Oak Bluffs, and rain squalls in West Tisbury. Thus it was that I drove out of the rain as I passed the airport and found myself under blue skies when I reached Edgartown. All weather is local, just like politics.

Manny's carpentry shop was on Fuller Street. It was there that I found him, in a room sweet with the smells of wood, oils, and stains. He was working on a custom cabinet of some kind. Being barely better than a two-by-four carpenter myself, I marveled, as usual, at the quality of his work.

Manny had magic hands.

He saw me and turned off the table saw he was using. "Hey, J.W., I hear you found that poor bastard on the beach. Potted with a thirty-eight, eh? No loss, if you ask me."

John Donne would probably have disagreed, but Manny wasn't John Donne. Manny was one of the Vineyarders who had been mad at Lawrence Ingalls for the last several years. In Manny's case, it was because he considered Ingalls to be a pointy-headed liberal, who, like all pointy-headed liberals, was always trying to ban guns or close off land to hunters, of whom Manny was one. Manny considered the Marshall Lea Foundation to be a hotbed of such people, and was at least theoretically happy every time something bad happened to anyone like Ingalls.

"Not just any thirty-eight," I said, "but a particular one. The police have it. It belonged to Ingalls."

Manny's brows lifted. "No kidding?"

"No kidding. But keep the information to yourself. It's confidential."

Manny nodded. "Sure. Ingalls's own gun, eh? Well, isn't that something . . ." His voice trailed off as he thought about it. I could almost see the gears turning in his head.

"It's something, all right," I said, "and it's why I came to see you. You know about everybody who shoots on this island. Do you know if Ingalls did any shooting? Hunting or target shooting or anything like that?"

Manny snorted. "Never heard of it, if he did. Figure I would have heard, him being the popular fellow he was." Manny's irony was pretty heavy-handed. "Course," he added, "he could have, maybe, had some private shooting range I don't know nothing about. That could be." He shook his head. "But somebody would have seen him if he was at any of the regular places. And word would have got around, 'cause most of the guys who shoot would have had their ears up if they'd heard he was shooting, because of all that liberal crap about banning guns and all."

I had never heard Ingalls say one thing or another about guns and hunting, so I passed on that one. All I'd ever hated him for was closing Norton's Point Beach.

"He's got a couple of elephant guns in his house," I said. "You hear anything about them?"

"Elephant guns? You mean them big old five-hundred-caliber or six-hundred-caliber rifles they used to use? He's got some of them in his house?" Manny's fascination with guns instantly overcame his dislike for Ingalls and his kind. "Say, I wouldn't mind having a look at weapons like that. You don't see too many of them around these days. You think there's any way I could get to see them?"

"You could ask his relatives, I guess. So you don't know anything about any of Ingalls's guns, and you never heard anything about him shooting any of them?"

"Nah. Say, now, about me seeing those rifles. You know who I could talk to? I sure would like to have a look at them."

But I couldn't help Manny out, and took my leave, wondering if I'd learned anything useful. As I went out the door, Manny called after me: "Tell Zee to get in touch. We got that meet coming up in October, and she needs to get in some practice."

"I'll have her call you."

Zee and I, who probably did more target shooting than most people, kept our pistols locked away when we weren't using them, but Lawrence Ingalls had kept his .38 in his bedside table. I knew that a lot of people probably did that, for real or imagined reasons. What had Ingalls's reason been?

I guessed that the chief might be downtown, so I turned down main and, sure enough, saw him standing in front of the Bickerton & Ripley bookstore, Edgartown's best, keeping his eye on Main Street. The investigation of Lawrence Ingalls's murder in no way meant that the police could curtail their normal activities. It just added to them. The chief was making sure that traffic was flowing; that no one was being killed when the bicyclists ignored the No Bicycles sign farther up the street, and that they shared the narrow street with the cars, which always won the encounters between them; that the meter maids and the summer rent-a-cops were doing their duties; and that the tourists who filled the sidewalks were on reasonably good behavior.

Things were going so smoothly that after I miraculously found a parking place on Summer Street and walked back to him, he didn't even mention moving to Nova Scotia for the summer, which he had been threatening to do for as long as I'd known him. It was a popular notion among Vineyarders that Nova Scotia was now what the Vineyard had been twenty or thirty years ago, back in the good old days before all these tourists started coming down. A lot of people besides the chief swore they were going to move up there, but I never knew anybody who actually did.

"What are you doing here?" he asked as I came up and stood beside him. "You're married to the prettiest woman on the island, and you have that nice, quiet place up there in the woods, and here you are downtown."

"I wouldn't want this to get around," I said,

227

"but I actually came to see you."

"I mix with riffraff all the time," said the chief, "so nobody'll be surprised to see us together. What do you want?"

"Manny Fonseca wants Zee to start practicing for a meet in October, so she needs her gun back."

The chief, like lots of cops, is always looking at things, even while he's talking to you. Now his eyes were roaming up and down the street, just in case something might happen that he should know about.

"Tony D'Agostine tells me he ran into you up in Chilmark."

"Yeah."

"Well, things being what they are, you can have your weapons back any time you want 'em. They're at the station. Go by and pick 'em up."

"I don't need a magic piece of paper?"

"I didn't need one to get 'em from you; you don't need one to get 'em from us."

"Fine. You ever search Lawrence Ingalls's house?"

"No. It's not in my town."

"I just thought that maybe if some of you minions of law and order searched the house, you might find something that would give you a slant on who might have shot Ingalls."

He watched the street. "Gosh! You're a

keen thinker, J.W. Why, I'll bet not a single law officer in Massachusetts would have thought of such a thing."

"Does that mean that Dom Agganis or somebody has been up there and looked the place over?"

"It might mean that. But if Dom found anything interesting, he didn't tell me."

"Well, learning that Ingalls's pistol is the murder weapon might change his mind, don't you think? The pistol was in the house until somebody shot Ingalls with it, then put it back. If I was a cop, which thank God I'm not, I think I'd go back to the house and look some more."

"You're not the only one who thanks God you're not a cop. But I think you're right. I think that Dom or Olive Otero or some other detectives might go back up there. I don't think any of the family would mind, even if they were there, which they won't be."

Really? "I thought they were all staying there. Mom, Dad, the brothers and sisters and everybody."

He shook his head. "Nope. They'll all be leaving tomorrow morning, the way I hear it. Busy people, and no real point in their hanging around. The ex-wife will be staying down and looking after things for them till the will is read and everybody knows who stands where. I don't think she'll mind having cops come in to look around some more, especially if they've got a warrant."

The ex-wife. Barbara Singleton. Was she a curious choice for a caretaker, or a logical one, since everyone else in the family had places to go and things to do? I thought of the Old Masters, and how, about suffering, they were never wrong; how nothing stops for pain or death.

I said, "Joe Begay tells me that Ingalls has some old elephant guns hanging over his fireplaces, and that he let Joe handle one before putting it back."

"So?"

"So Ingalls didn't care if there were fingerprints all over his elephant guns, but his pistol was wiped clean before Beth Harper and I handled it."

That brought his eyes from the street. He looked at me. "Of course, that person could be her or you. But it wasn't her because Beth Harper was with a bunch of Marshall Lea people when Ingalls bought it, and it wasn't you because you say it wasn't and of course you'd never lie about a thing like that."

"I went up to Ingalls's house last Wednesday, but nobody was there. Connie Berube lives on Ingalls's road. Ask her if I was ever up there before that or since. She's got eyes like a hawk, and so do those kids of hers. Somebody would have seen me if I'd gone up there and gotten the gun, then taken it back again after I shot Ingalls. And I already know that Beth Harper didn't shoot him, either."

"Oh, yeah? How come you're giving her a clean bill of health? She tried to shoot you, remember?"

"That's why. If she'd shot Ingalls, why would she try to shoot me for shooting him? Doesn't make any sense."

"People I meet don't always act sensible," said the chief. "Well, I see that my man down there at the four corners has got himself a little traffic jam. See you later."

"You find Moonbeam yet?"

The chief gave me an expressionless look. "No."

He walked down toward the backed-up cars.

I stared at nothing for a while, then walked to the Land Cruiser and drove back to Manny Fonseca's place.

"Hey, Manny," I said. "I think maybe I know a way you can get a look at those elephant guns. Can you shake free from work if I call you tomorrow?"

Does a lawyer feel a keen moral duty to take any case that will make him rich? Will the psychologist he hires testify to anything the lawyer wants? Will the sun rise in the east and set in the west? Of course Manny could shake free from work.

I told him I'd be in touch, and drove to the police station to pick up the family pistols.

One thing was pretty certain: I was no longer the only star suspect in the case. I was sharing that billing with Moonbeam Berube.

As I came outside, I met an ex-suspect. Zack Delwood. He stood beside my truck, big fists clenched. "You're the one pointed the finger at me, ain't you? You did Ingalls in, but you sicced the cops on me! You and them is as thick as thieves!" He hunched his big shoulders and came at me. "I'm going to teach you to keep your mouth off me!"

I stepped away. "The chief's talked to Iowa and Walter. He knows you were with them when Ingalls got killed. And I never pointed the finger at you."

"You're a liar." He lumbered toward me as I backed away.

A fight right in front of the police station. Just what I needed.

I put my hand into the paper bag. "Let me show you something, Zack." I gave him a glimpse of the pistols. He stopped. "I don't feel like mixing it up with you," I said. "Go home."

He glared. "You won't always have a gun,

you son of a bitch. I'll see you again."

He spat on the ground and walked away. I got into the Toyota, waited till my pulse stopped pounding, and drove home.

— 19 —

The next day the up-island clouds were gone and the whole island was under summer sun once again. Squalling Joshua made sure we were up early. Too early, in fact, for anything but family endeavors. I realized that I was glad of that, since of late my family hadn't spent much daylight time together.

Zee was scheduled to start working the evening shift later in the week. The evening and graveyard shifts weren't as hard as the day shift because fewer tourists rode mopeds at night and there were, consequently, fewer moped accidents for the police to mop up and the emergency ward to repair. The only problem with these shifts from our point of view was that I was sometimes asleep when Zee got home or I was getting up as she was going to sleep. Today, however, we were both home and awake, so after cleaning, calming, and feeding noisy, starving Joshua, we loaded up the Land Cruiser and took a morning outing to the far Chappy beaches, where no one but fishermen could intrude upon us. I felt good as we drove away from civilization.

We parked on East Beach, just north of the Yellow Shovel. The Yellow Shovel was a site whose code name was known only to us and Al Prada, who'd once found a child's yellow plastic shovel there and had, after adding it to his vast and ever-growing collection of kids' shovels found on the beach, made a cast and landed an unexpected bluefish. As he was pulling in his umpteenth fish, still all alone, Zee and I had happened by and joined him. It's said that company doubles joy and halves sorrow, and so it was that we'd all had a fine time sharing the mini-blitz, and that afterward the spot was known to us cognoscenti as the Yellow Shovel. Over the years we'd caught other bluefish there, and now we were there with Joshua.

Nantucket Sound rolled east from us, and fishing boats were passing, headed to the Wasque rips and beyond. The air was warm and the sky was high and blue. We laid out the old bedspread we use as a beach blanket, put Joshua's portable playpen beside the bedspread, put him in it, and set up an umbrella to keep him from too much sun.

"Ah," said Zee, stripping down to her wee bikini, "just what the doctor ordered." She stretched her brown self out on the blanket.

"Nice bod," I said, leering, as I peeled down to my own bathing suit.

"Come down here and say that, if you dare."

I dared.

After a while, a 4 x 4 came along from Wasque, headed toward Cape Pogue. We untangled before it got to us. Iowa was driving and Walter was beside him. They were two guys who almost lived on the beach. They waved and kept driving. We waved back.

"These constant interruptions are destroying our marriage," said Zee. "Go catch us a fish." She lay back and closed her eyes.

I got to my feet and looked down at her. No wonder Drew Mondry wanted her in his movie. Botticelli would have wanted her in his, if they'd had them in his day.

I looked at Joshua, who took his attention off his own feet, which were waving in the air, to look back. "You're in charge," I said.

I got my rod off the roof rack, walked down the beach a little way, and made my cast. No bluefish took my good Roberts plug. I cast again. Again, no bluefish. I cast again. Still no bluefish.

I fished for half an hour and caught nothing. Back at the bedspread, Zee kept a partially shut eye on Joshua, who was back to keeping his own eyes on his fascinating feet. I fished some more. One of the nicest things about fishing is that you don't have to catch fish to have fun. If you just want fish, you can get them easier and cheaper at the A & P.

Another thing about fishing when there are no fish is that you can look around at the scenery, feel the breeze, and, if you like, think about something else. I thought about my plans for later in the day.

When I walked back to the truck, Zee was changing a diaper.

"What is it about this kid?" she asked. "I'm sure he didn't inherit this habit from me. He must have gotten it from you."

"All us manly men are full of that stuff," I said.

"How could I have forgotten? I knew that. Every woman knows that." She picked up powdered, sweet-smelling Joshua and touched her finger to his nose. "When the girls start hanging around you in a few years, I'm going to tell them all about this diaper business. What do you think of that?"

Shameless Joshua smiled up at her and said he thought it was a good idea.

We lay down on the bedspread and let the August sun improve our tans. Things were good, the way they were supposed to be. I turned off my brain and was happy lying there, shoulder to shoulder, hip to hip, beside warm, brown-skinned Zee.

But life wears a Janus face; like the two-faced god, it tenders as many endings as beginnings, and offers portals that lead to both light and darkness. So after the sun reached its zenith and we finished lunch, it was time to leave the lovely, lonely beach and head back to a more cluttered, less pristine reality. We packed up and headed home.

As we passed Wasque Point and its eternal fishermen, and went west on Norton's Point Beach, past the dozens of parked 4 x 4's and the hundreds of people soaking up the August sun, I told Zee what I planned to do.

"Do you really need to get into the house?" she asked. "Won't it look suspicious, especially to that new state cop?"

"Otero can't get much more suspicious," I said. "And I do want to get into the house. Maybe something in Ingalls's past got him killed, and maybe there's something in the house that will give me a clue."

"I don't like it," she said.

I pulled out onto the pavement at Katama and shifted into two-wheel drive. "It's not illegal and it's not dangerous," I said.

"I still don't like it," said Zee, her jaw seeming to become harder. "I don't want that

238

Otero woman to have another reason for squinting her eyes at you!"

Had Olive Otero really been squinting at me? I looked at Joshua, who was in his mother's lap.

"What do you think, Josh?" I asked. "Should I go or not?"

Smart Joshua, recognizing a no-win situation when he was in one, said nothing.

"There," I said to Zee. "He agrees with me."

"He does not."

"Anyway, Moonbeam has Olive Otero's attention now; I don't. So there's nothing to worry about."

We drove away from the kite-filled beach sky, past the walkers and cyclists on the bike path beside the road, through lovely Edgartown with its white and gray-shingled houses and gardens of bright flowers, and on to our house in the woods, down at the end of our long, sandy driveway. There we unpacked the mountain of gear you need to have whenever you travel with a baby, and I made my phone calls.

First to Lawrence Ingalls's house. A woman answered.

"My name's Fonseca," I said. "I'm calling to express my condolences. I was working and couldn't get to the funeral."

She had a detached-sounding voice. "Thank you. I'm Barbara Singleton. I'm afraid that all the family members have left the island, but if you'll give me your name again, I'll be glad to let them know of your call."

"Thanks. Like I say, my name is Manuel Fonseca. I talked to Larry just last week, and I was supposed to come up there to the house today. But then this terrible thing happened . . ." I let my voice trail off.

"You're right. It has been terrible. We're all very distressed."

Actually, I didn't think Barbara Singleton sounded too distressed at all. I tried to make sure that I did. Not too distressed, mind you; just distressed enough.

"Yeah," I said. "Look, Mrs. Singleton, I know this is the worst possible time to be calling, but Larry and me were working on a little business deal, and I'm afraid that if I don't tell somebody about it, I may lose out."

There was a pause. Then, "I'm afraid I don't understand, Mr. Fonseca. What business deal?"

"It ain't a big one, maybe, but it means something to me. It's them guns of his. I buy, sell, and collect weapons, and Larry told me about them big-game rifles he's got. Said he might be interested in selling them to me. I

240

was supposed to come up and look at them today, and if I was interested we could maybe make a deal."

Barbara Singleton's voice was cool. "I really don't think this is the time for such —"

I interrupted and talked fast. "Now, I understand that I can't just come up there and make a deal with you, Mrs. Singleton, or probably with anybody else, either, until the will gets read and the family decides what they're going to do with the estate and all. But Larry and me did talk about them rifles and I'd sure hate to lose out on at least having a look at them while they're still there. That's all I want to do, Mrs. Singleton, just get a look at them before some dealer or auction house or whatever maybe takes them off some place and sells them when I can't be there. I sure would appreciate it, Mrs. Singleton, if I could come up there this afternoon like Larry and me planned I should do. I ain't gonna take nothing or buy nothing. All I want to do is look at them rifles so later, when things settle out, I can bid on 'em or buy 'em from the family. I sure would appreciate that chance, Mrs. Singleton. And you don't have to worry about me being some kind of con artist or crook, Mrs. Singleton. Just call the Edgartown police if you want to, and they'll vouch for me. You ain't taking any chances having me up there, I'll tell you for sure. And I won't be there long, neither. Just long enough to take a quick look at them rifles."

I thought my Manny Fonseca imitation had gone on long enough, maybe too long, so I shut up.

There was a silence at the other end of the line. Then, to my relief, Barbara Singleton said, "Well, if you and Larry talked about this, I guess it'll be all right. You can look at the rifles, but of course you can't buy them or take them or anything like that. When can I expect you?"

"I'll be up there in an hour. Thanks a lot!"

Zee and Joshua eyed me from the kitchen door. "Isn't it against the law to pretend to be somebody else?" asked Zee, frowning.

I felt a smug smile on my face. "As a matter of fact, it isn't. Anybody can say they're any-body. You could claim to be Greta Garbo or Eleanor Roosevelt or the Virgin Mary and it wouldn't be illegal unless you were using the name for unlawful purposes."

"Isn't that what you're doing?"

"No. Nothing illegal is going to happen. Trust me."

"I just don't want you to get into trouble," she said. "And don't quote Zorba to me." She looked down at Joshua. "I don't want your dad to be a jailbird, that's all."

Joshua thought that one over, but didn't say a word.

I called Manny Fonseca, told him we were supposed to be in Chilmark in an hour, and asked him to pick me up on the way and to drive his truck.

Ten minutes later, his truck came down the driveway and turned around. I got in and we headed up-island. Manny was happy.

"So you talked 'em into letting me see them rifles, eh? Good work."

I told him how I'd done it, and he slapped his hand against the steering wheel. "Couldn't have done it better myself, by God!"

"You just remember that you're the one who called her," I said. "I'm only a friend who came along for the ride. Call me J.W. and leave off the Jackson. She might not fancy having me there if she knows who I am."

"You got it," said Manny. He put a hand to his hip and shoved the pistol on his belt into a more comfortable spot. Manny always went heeled. Because, as he said, you just never know.

It was true that you just never know, but I wasn't so sure that having a pistol in your pocket would take care of the unexpected very often. I apparently lived a much less dangerous life than did Manny or other

243

gun-toters who needed to constantly bear arms, for my problems were usually better met by other means. Of course, showing my bag of guns to Zack Delwood had stopped him, and if Lawrence Ingalls's pistol had been in his own pocket instead of in somebody else's, things might have worked out better for him. So Manny wasn't completely wrong; you really didn't ever know.

— 20 —

When we turned off North Road, Manny said, "Hey. This is Moonbeam Berube's driveway. I been here before, but not for a long time. You know Moonbeam?"

"Who doesn't know Moonbeam? I see him on the beach and I traded some scallops to him once, for a pig."

"Old Moonbeam looks like he's got some pig in him, himself. You think it's true what they say about him? That he's the way he is because ever since the first Berube landed on the island, nobody but kin would marry anybody in the family?"

I'd heard that story, of course, and others like it. The most famous tradition of incest on the island was the subject of the well-known nineteenth-century investigation of deaf or partially deaf people up-island whose use of sign language caught the attention of scholars and resulted in a printed study of their hearing impairment and its causes.

"There are a lot of Berubes on this island,"

I said, "and I don't think most of them are even related to Moonbeam. Besides, Moonbeam didn't marry any of his kin. Connie Berube's from someplace on the mainland."

"I heard that story about him getting her out of a Kentucky whorehouse," said Manny. "Maybe she's off-island kin. You know she's called the cops on him, don't you? Got a couple of restraining orders to keep him from beating up the kids, but always took him back afterward."

Martha's Vineyard is famous for beauty and its wealthy and well-known visitors and landowners. Its movie stars, politicians, writers, artists, and other celebrities have attracted thousands of less famous people to its shores. In the imaginations of its visitors and in the descriptions of the island in travel guides, the Vineyard is a fairyland of lovely vistas, yacht-filled harbors, quaint and beautiful villages, and golden sands. What few visitors apparently know is that the island's year-round population, the one still there after the summer people have gone home, is one of the poorest in Massachusetts, and that from this poverty comes all of the domestic violence, crimes, stupidities, and drug and alcohol problems associated with long-term economic deprivation. On the island, as in all small communities, certain people always know about these darker realities. School-teachers, doctors and nurses, social workers, ministers and rabbis, and the police know, because their work puts them in contact with poverty's consequences: beaten children and wives, lying parents and children, drunken adults and teenagers, incest, drug-dealing illiterates, whole lineages whose members have always been in one sort of trouble or another from generation to generation. As the chief once said to me, "If two or three families would move off this island, I'd only have half as much work to do." It was a phrase that could have been said by the police in any small town.

Like Manny, I read the weekly records of court proceedings in the local papers and knew that Moonbeam had appeared there on occasion. Once, in fact, he'd been sent away to a mainland brig, but I couldn't remember why. He wasn't the only islander who had spent a few months in the calaboose and come back again with his reputation no worse than it had been before.

We passed Moonbeam's place and noted that the backhoe and other clutter was about where it had been before. His pale-skinned, fine-boned children watched us pass, showing no expression on their faces.

"Look like their ma," said Manny, as

Connie appeared from the far side of the disintegrating house, put a protective hand on the shoulder of her nearest child, and stared at us.

Their bones were hers, but their eyes were not. Hers were not empty of emotion as were those of her children, or dull and hooded like those of her husband. Connie's eyes were tired, maybe, but also fierce and bright. Looking back, I watched her watching us until the road turned and I could no longer see her.

"You ever seen these guns we're going to look at?" asked Manny.

"No," I lied. Why complicate things unnecessarily?

We pulled up in front of the house and got out. To the north, between us and the Elizabeth Islands, sailboats were moving across the blue water of Vineyard Sound, and a trawler was headed toward Block Island and points west.

"Pretty," said Manny, who, like most hunters and other outdoor types, had an eye for nature's beauties. But scenery was not his interest at the moment; big-game rifles were. He started toward the house, with me in his wake. As we got to the steps, the door opened and Barbara Singleton stepped out onto the roofed entranceway.

248

"I'm Barbara Singleton," she said. "You must be Mr. Fonseca."

"Yes, ma'am. Manny Fonseca. Nice of you to let us come by, what with the funeral being just yesterday and all."

"That's quite all right." She looked past him at me.

I'd already put on a smile. "Just a friend along for the ride," I said. "Hope you don't mind."

"This here's J.W.," said Manny. "An old pal. I'm teaching his wife how to shoot."

"Zee's the gunner in our family," I said, grinning. "I'm lucky to hit a barn from the inside. Sorry about Mr. Ingalls."

"Thank you." She stepped back and held open the door. "Come in, Mr. Fonseca."

"Call me Manny, ma'am. I won't take up much of your time."

"And I'm just plain J.W," I said, as we stepped through the door.

"This way, please." Barbara Singleton led the way into the large living area. She seemed to be about forty years old. Her skin and hair were smooth and clean, and she walked with the step of youth. She paused and gestured at the fireplace. "There are two rifles there above the mantel, as you can see. There's another fireplace in the master bedroom upstairs and a third in the basement. There are other rifles hanging above them, as well. Please look at these two first, and then I'll show you the others."

I glanced at Manny and could almost see the drool on his chin as he looked at the rifles on their pegs. To me they seemed to be fairly normal, if rather old-fashioned, looking guns, but clearly they were more to him.

"Thank you, ma'am," he said, and went toward the fireplace as though toward an altar.

Barbara Singleton stepped aside and gestured. "You, too, Mr. . . ."

"J.W., Mrs. Singleton, just J.W. But, no, I'm not particularly interested in guns. Manny's the one with that bug. I'm more interested in fishing rods." I looked around the room. It looked the same as the last time I'd seen it. "Nice place you got here."

"It is nice, but it's not my place, Mr. . . . J.W. It belonged to my ex-husband." There was a wedding ring on her finger. She caught my glance at it, and added: "I'm a widow."

"Oh." I nodded, then frowned, then smiled, then frowned again.

She took a breath. "I'm afraid I've made things more confusing than need be. I was once married to Mr. Ingalls, who owned this house. Later, I remarried. My second husband died two years ago." A small smile played across her face. "Thus, you see, I am a widow, but not the widow of Lawrence Ingalls, the man who owned this house. He was my ex-husband."

"Ah."

We stood there for a moment and watched Manny take down the first of the rifles and begin to examine it. I saw now that it was a double-barreled gun. Manny handled it lovingly.

In a quiet voice, I said, "I have a badge in my wallet, Mrs. Singleton. I'll show it to you, if you want, but I'm not here officially. I just bummed a ride with Manny in hopes you'd be able to answer some questions about Mr. Ingalls while Manny looks at those rifles."

I actually did have my old Boston PD shield with me, but she didn't ask to see it. Instead, she gave me a tired look and said, "I'm sure I can't tell you anything I haven't already told the other officers who've been here, and I couldn't tell them much at all. Larry and I were divorced almost twenty years ago, and I know very little about his life since then."

"You may know something and not even know you do. You've remained close to his family, and it's clear that they trust you to serve their interests here at the house until the estate is settled. The relationship between you and the family is a little unusual, you'll have to admit. In the years since your divorce, you must have at least heard family conversations about your ex-husband's activities."

"I'm afraid I've heard very little. Charles and Ethyl are sensitive people, and don't discuss Larry's life when I'm with them. They know how much the divorce distressed me." She touched a hand to her head and smoothed an already smooth strand of yellow-brown hair.

We watched Manny replace the first rifle on its pegs and take down the second. It was like watching Galahad achieve the Grail.

I said, "You must have married Mr. Ingalls when you were very young, Mrs. Singleton. And you couldn't have been married long, if it's been twenty years since your divorce. What went wrong?"

She watched Manny. "That's not your business, Mr. . . . ."

"Call me J.W. Everybody does. I know it's not my business, Mrs. Singleton, but it might help me understand Lawrence Ingalls. Some people change a lot between when they're young and when they're older, but other people don't. If you can tell me what went wrong between you, maybe I'll get some information that'll help me figure out who might have killed him. You would like to know who did it, wouldn't you?"

She crossed her arms beneath her breasts, the way some women do when they're getting stubborn. "Maybe it wasn't anything wrong with him. Maybe it was something wrong with me. I don't want to talk about it."

Why so great a no? "I doubt if it was something wrong with you, Mrs. Singleton. You married again and had a happy life, didn't you?"

After a moment, she said, "Until Jack Singleton died, yes. But what does that prove? Larry and I just had bad chemistry, that's all. Jack and I were compatible."

I thought of my own first marriage and how it had gone wrong even though it wasn't anyone's fault, and how my new marriage with Zee was so different.

"Your first parents-in-law didn't think there was anything wrong with you, Mrs. Singleton. They've remained your friends and protectors. Was Lawrence Ingalls cruel to you? Did he bully you? Was he unfaithful? What sort of man was he?"

Her voice was suddenly sharp. "What do you know about what Charles and Ethyl think about me? You don't know anything!"

Manny had returned the second rifle to its pegs and was now coming back to us, so I said nothing.

"Wonderful old weapons," he said, his

253

voice filled with excitement. "You know what you got there, ma'am? You got a matched pair of Holland and Rigby five hundred double express guns! I've read about 'em, but I never thought I'd ever see the real thing! You got a real treasure there, ma'am!"

His enthusiasm was infectious enough to thaw the ice that seemed to be forming in Barbara Singleton's soul. "I'm sure I don't know what a Holland and whatever even is, Mr. Fonseca, but there are more rifles upstairs and others in the basement. Would you like to see them now?"

"Does a bear sh—!" Manny caught himself just in time, and instead exclaimed, "Yes, ma'am. I surely would!"

We went upstairs to the master bedroom. In addition to the huge bed, side tables, and dressers, it, like the study below, held book-shelves, a desk, and file cabinets. There was a walk-in closet with mirrored doors, a large TV set against the wall opposite the foot of the bed, and a fireplace faced with two com-fortable chairs. Above the fireplace hung two more old rifles. An open door revealed a dressing room, which, in turn, led to a private bathroom, complete with bidet. All in all, the suite was almost as big as my whole house.

Manny went right to the guns, while I looked at everything else, including the books in the bookcases. More books on the environment and the Orient, and more classic and contemporary erotica. Some books on Mexico and the Caribbean. I went and stood beside Barbara Singleton. She gave me a cold look.

I gestured at the bookshelves and said, "I don't want to annoy you, Mrs. Singleton, and I'm sorry if I've already done that, because I need your help. Anything you can tell me about your ex-husband might be important. For instance, did you ever go off to China or wherever it was that he used to go when he was younger? I know he had a great interest in that part of the world."

Her face paled and hardened even more. "I'm not going to discuss my marriage with Larry. I think that you should wait for your friend out in your car."

I hesitated, then nodded. "I'm sorry to have offended you, Mrs. Singleton. That was not my intention. I'll find my own way out."

She gave me a stiff nod, and I left the room. At the foot of the stairs I looked back. She wasn't there, watching me, so I went into the study.

— 21 —

The file cabinets and the desk drawers were still locked. I took a fast look at the bookshelves. The same books appeared to be there. Maybe that meant the same stuff was still in the locked drawers. I studied the room, taking in Oriental vases in crannies between bookshelves, and a dancing Siva on a pedestal beside a window. Since Ingalls had locks, it meant he had keys. He'd probably carried them with him when he was alive, but now that he was dead, where would they be?

Odds on, they were somewhere in the house, probably still on his key ring, since it made no sense for them to have been taken elsewhere. Barbara Singleton knew where they were, for sure, but she wasn't ever going to give them to me.

I peeked into and under the Chinese vases, but found no keys. Ditto for under the Siva and the papers and books on the desk.

I heard footsteps and voices on the stairs and flattened myself against the wall behind the open study door. Barbara Singleton and Manny went down other stairs into the basement.

I went back to the desk and cabinets and studied the locks. Like most locks, these were simple and would only serve as deterrents to honest people. They would pose no problems to anyone who really wanted to open them. Having assured myself of this, I slipped out the front door into the yard and waited for Manny.

When he appeared, thanking Barbara Singleton again and again for having been given the incredible privilege of examining the rifles, I was in the truck, listening to the C and W station in Rhode Island. Garth was singing about a guy who had done his loving woman wrong and was sorry he'd ever let it happen. It was classic Garth, and I was almost sorry for the guy he sang about. But not quite. I didn't think Garth was either, really.

"What happened to you?" asked Manny, climbing into the driver's seat. But before I could tell him I'd just gone out for some air, he rushed on: "Whatever, you missed a sight you'll probably never see again! You know what that Ingalls fella had there, just hanging out in plain sight? I'll tell you! Besides them matched Holland and Rigbys, he had himself a Rodda four-bore! Them guns is rare! And

257

hangin' right with it was one of them four-bore Greeners with them side safeties! Holy cow! Both of them rifles in the same room!"

"No kidding?" I said, never having heard of any of those apparently famous weapons.

"No kidding!" said Manny. "And that ain't all. Down in the basement there's a six hundred Nitro Express and a .577 Snyder single shot! My gosh! I told that woman that she should lock them weapons away someplace safe, 'cause they're worth a lot of money, yes siree!" He shook his head, grinning at the memory of all that beauty. "J.W., I owe you one, for sure. Hadn't been for you, I would have missed 'em and never even known about it!"

"Glad it was worth the trip for you," I said. "You think you can afford to bid on any of those guns if they come up for sale?"

Manny put his teeth over his lower lip while he did some calculating. Then he tilted his head to one side. "Maybe one of 'em. Not the Holland and Rigbys, for sure; they'd never split them up. And not that Rodda four-bore. The Greener, maybe, or the Nitro, or maybe the Snyder. But I dunno. Lot of money any way you cut it. I'd love to have 'em all, but any one of 'em would be terrific. Terrific just to see 'em, matter of fact."

We passed Moonbeam's house and I felt the eyes of his pale children and their fierce mother follow us out of sight. Then we drove on down to Edgartown, Manny waxing lyric about the rifles, me making meaningless noises in reply while I wondered what was locked in Ingalls's desk and files, why Barbara Singleton didn't want to talk about her divorce, and why Charles and Ethyl Ingalls treated their ex-daughter-in-law with such respect and trust.

Zee and Joshua came out of the house when Manny took me home, and Manny couldn't resist telling her of the treasures he had found. Zee smiled and nodded and said that it must have been really exciting. Then the two of them agreed to meet down at the Rod and Gun Club the next afternoon and get in some pistol practice. Then Manny, still happy, drove away, and I took Joshua out of his mother's arms.

"Were the rifles really as wonderful as that?" asked Zee.

"They were to Manny. But if I'm going to ogle something, it won't be rifles, it'll be you." I leered at her accordingly as I told her about our expedition to Chilmark. When I was through, she said, "So you pretended to be a cop, eh? I don't think that was too smart. You could get in trouble."

"I didn't ever actually say I was."

"But you implied that you were."

"Imply, imshmy. All I did was ask her some questions, and she didn't answer most of them, anyway."

"You worry me sometimes, you know that? So what are you going to do now?"

"Make some phone calls."

"Who to?"

I looked at Joshua. "She means 'to whom,' but she's Portuguese, so she talks funny."

Zee had a sharp elbow. "Nobody says 'to whom' anymore. Who to?"

"To Quinn, for one," I said, rubbing my ribs. "To Joe Begay, for another."

Quinn owed me one for the interview I'd given him after Ingalls's murder. Besides, he considered himself to be Joshua's unofficial uncle. I dialed the *Globe* in Boston.

He picked up his phone on the first ring.

"Quinn here."

"And a good place for you to be," I said "The loose women of New England can use a few minutes of rest."

"J.W.! You've called about Zee deciding to leave you and come up here with Josh to live with me, right? Now, I know your nose is probably a little out of joint, but, face up to it, you were never meant to have a woman like her. So just put her on the phone so we can

260

arrange where to meet. I know she's anxious to get out of there."

"I think she's busy packing, but I'll have her call."

"Excellent. Naturally, you'll want to bestow a generous divorce settlement upon her, even though you know she's going to marry me."

"But of course."

"Fine. Now that that's settled, what do you want?"

I told him what had happened since last we'd spoken.

"I think you probably need a lawyer more than you need me," said Quinn. "I know this guy named Brady Coyne. He's not only a lawyer, he's a fisherman. He —"

"I don't need a lawyer," I said. "I want to know all I can about Lawrence Ingalls. What he was like as a kid, when he got married, whether he took his wife along on those trips he used to make to the Orient, where he went and what he did over there, what went wrong with his marriage, and what kind of guy he was in general. If he did anything odd or hung around with any dangerous types, I want to know that, too. Did he do drugs? Did he import them? Did he ever get anybody mad at him? That sort of stuff."

"Only that, eh? Well, if I drop everything

else that I'm supposed to be doing, I might be able to put a dent in that list in a couple of years."

But I could tell that his ears were up and his nose was already in the air, sniffing. Murder in Eden, mixed with big money and a possible scandal involving an old New England name made a brew with a heady aroma.

"I'll be glad to get anything you can give me," I said.

"I can give you one thing right now," said Quinn. "You can bet your last dollar, if you still have one, that Ingalls did some dope somewhere along the line. You and me and Bill Clinton are the only people between thirty and sixty who didn't."

"You'd better make that just you and Bill Clinton," I said.

"I guess we'd better make it just Bill Clinton," said Quinn. "I'll be in touch."

He rang off, and I called Joe Begay. His answering machine said that nobody was home but that I should leave a message after the beep. I told the post-beep silence that I'd called and would like to be called back.

I couldn't decide whether or not I liked answering machines. I knew I didn't like the big kind that companies had, which told you to punch this number for this, and that number for that, and, finally, to punch this last number if you wanted to talk to a genuine human being but after that, even, sometimes had still another list of numbers that supposedly would put you in contact with the particular human who could best tell you what you wanted to know but, after you punched that final number on your Touch-Tone phone, sometimes just thanked you for your patience with a click and a dial tone.

Like everyone else, I hated those answering machines, but the kinds that people had in their houses might not be so bad.

On the other hand, I couldn't think of any really good reason to have one, so I didn't. Was it my fate to be the last man to enter the twentieth century? The last to have an answering machine, the last to have a fax, the last to have a computer, even? I was a contender, at least.

I served flounder almondine, rice, and a garden salad for supper, and offered jug sauvignon blanc, the house white, with it. Delish, as might be expected.

As I was washing up the dishes afterward, the phone rang. It was Joe Begay. I asked him how things were going. He said slow. I brought him up to date on my adventures and asked him to try to find out about the same things that I'd asked Quinn to find out about. He said it would take time, but that he knew some people who might be able to get their hands on some information.

After I hung up, I thought some more about the truism that we usually get murdered by family members, friends, and acquaintances, and decided that while I was waiting for whatever Quinn and Joe Begay might come up with, I'd go visit some people who had at least worked fairly closely with Ingalls. They probably wouldn't want to talk to me, but that was nothing new. I'd met a lot of people like that lately.

Maybe it was my breath.

But if it was, Zee didn't mention it later, as we lay on top of the summer sheets and she pulled me to her, sending Ingalls, Begay, and everyone and everything else out of my mind.

— 22 —

The next day Joshua was grumpy. Nothing pleased him. He didn't like his milk, he didn't like being carried around, he didn't like not being carried around, he didn't like anything. Burping him didn't help; cuddling him didn't help; changing his diaper didn't help.

I took his temperature. It was maybe a bit high, but nothing serious.

He cried and whined and spit out his pacifier.

"Maybe I should stay home with him," said Zee, worried, even though she would have advised any other young mother not to be.

"No, I'll take care of him," I said.

"Maybe you'd better call Dr. Clanton," said Zee.

Dr. Clanton, old and gray and always a quieting influence on young parents, was our pediatrician, soon to retire to his gardening and painting. He knew from vast experience that babies, like bigger people, almost always got over whatever was bothering them without any help from anyone, but he knew, too, that parents needed to think something was being done for their offspring, so he always gave solemn advice such as "Well, he's going to be cranky and out of sorts for a while, but it's nothing serious. You should just make sure that he's comfortable and dry. And don't worry if he doesn't want to eat. It won't hurt him to go without food for a while, although you might offer to feed him every now and then in case he decides he's hungry. You can give him a little Tylenol, too. I think his fever will probably go down, but if it goes up very far, call me."

It was the equivalent of the take-two-aspirin-and-call-me-in-the-morning-that'll-be-fifty-dollars-please advice to adults that doctors know will usually cure their patients because we usually cure ourselves.

"I'll call the doctor if he gets any worse," I said to Zee, hoping I sounded confident that things were really okay with Joshua. I was caught in that common conflict between mind and emotion. My brain was saying what I knew Dr. Clanton would say, but my feelings were saying that Joshua was really awfully small and that maybe it was something serious.

"Dr. Clanton's retiring, you know," said

Zee, still worrying over her son. "We're going to have to get a new pediatrician in the fall."

"We can ask Dr. Clanton for a recommendation. I'm sure he'll point us at someone who's good."

"The new person is taking over his practice. A young doctor from off-island."

I decided not to point out that all Martha's Vineyard doctors are of necessity from off-island since the island has no medical school.

Instead, I said, "We can check him out, and maybe he'll do. It would be good to have one doctor for Joshua all the time he's growing up."

Joshua bawled, and Zee and I exchanged more uneasy looks.

"You go on to work," I said. "He's howling, but it doesn't sound like a really hurting howl; it sounds more like a mad howl or probably an uncomfortable howl. If he gets worse, I'll definitely call Dr. Clanton."

"Call me, too."

She didn't want to go, but she did, leaving me and Joshua alone.

Joshua cried and waved his arms and legs. I picked him up and walked around with him. He kept crying. I sang to him and he cried some more. I got a little liquid Tylenol and tried to get him to take it. He spit it out.

All morning long he whined and cried. Then, suddenly, he went to sleep, exhausted by his own tears, it seemed.

I felt his forehead. Still a bit of fever, I thought. It was clear that I wouldn't be going out to talk to anybody today. No wonder Holmes and Spade and Marlowe and Millhone and Carlyle never had kids. If they'd had them, they never would have gotten any detecting done.

I found a phone book and looked up some numbers, then made my first call. A cheerful feminine voice answered.

"Marshall Lea Foundation. How may I help you?"

You can tell me who hated Lawrence Ingalls, and why, I thought. But I said, "Jud Wilbur, please."

"Who shall I say is calling?"

"My name is Quinn. I'm calling from Boston, regarding the Ingalls case. I'm a reporter for the *Globe*."

"Oh." A short hesitation, then: "One moment, please. I'll see if he's in."

He was in, all right. Otherwise she would have told me so. The question was: would he want to talk to a Boston reporter? I heard the sound of a phone being lifted.

"This is Jud Wilbur. Mr. Quinn, is it?"

"That's right. I'm working on a story about the murder of Lawrence Ingalls, and I'm trying to talk with people who knew him well. Your name came up as president of the, let's see here, the Marshall Lea Foundation. I understand that Mr. Ingalls worked closely with the foundation, as an expert on environmental issues."

"That's correct. Larry was a fine man and a real friend of the earth. He had no official link to the foundation, but served as an advisor to us. His death was a great loss not only to us, but to everyone interested in preserving the environment."

"So I've gathered from other sources. What sort of man was he personally?"

The phone voice got cooler. "I'm afraid I don't know what you mean."

I assured him that the *Globe* was not the *National Enquirer*, and that I wasn't looking for anything scandalous, but that I was looking for the "real man" Ingalls had been. The lie fell easily off my tongue, and it occurred to me that I might have a future in advertising. Especially since the ice went out of Wilbur's voice.

"Well," he said, "I can tell you that he was a fine person. Generous with his time and talents, well liked by everyone here. He was very intelligent, strong willed, and on his toes at all

269

times. He wasn't one of those people who fall all over you, if you know what I mean, but he was always friendly. A very fine man, and one we'll miss."

"That's the sort of thing I'm after, Mr. Wilbur. Personal stuff like that. If I read you right, you're telling me that he was friendly, but not overfriendly. Is that right?"

Wilbur said he wasn't sure he wanted to say that Ingalls wasn't overfriendly. That phrase made Ingalls sound cold, and he wasn't cold at all. He was just not the exuberant type, if I understood what that meant.

"I think I can," I said. "He was friendly, but he didn't hang on people. Is that what you mean? That he was more reserved than exuberant."

"Yes, that's it. A very nice guy, but not the touchy-feely sort. Yes, that was Larry. What a loss."

"I'm sure. Well, you've been very helpful. Is there anyone there who seemed especially close to him? You know, anyone I could talk to who knew him really well, who might have broken through that reserve of his, and who could help me make a real person out of him for my readers?"

"Well, obviously one such person would be Beth Harper. I understand that they were engaged to be married."

"Great. Do you know how I can get in touch with her?"

"I think she's left the island. She worked as Larry's assistant for some time, as you may know. Perhaps you can get in touch with her at the Boston office of the Department of Environmental Protection."

"I'll do that." I pretended to look through my notes. "Another name I was given is Dina Witherspoon, who is, let me see now, your organization's vice president. Is she in?"

"She's more important than a vice president," said Wilbur with a laugh. "She's our secretary! An organization can run without a president or a vice president, but it can't run without a secretary!"

I gave a knowing chuckle. "It's the same in every organization, including mine, Mr. Wilbur."

"I'll punch you through to her, Mr. Quinn."

"Thanks," I said. "There's one thing more, Mr. Wilbur. I know it's unpleasant to talk about this, but do you know of any reason someone would have shot Lawrence Ingalls? Any reason at all?"

Wilber's voice was very controlled. "I have no idea at all, Mr. Quinn. But if I were investigating the crime, I'd be talking to some of the people who blamed Larry for closing down Norton's Point Beach. There was a lot of hatred there, as you may know."

Indeed I did. "Any hater in particular?"

He assumed the high moral ground. "I'm sorry. I'm in no position to make a particular accusation. I have no proof of any kind."

"How about something strictly off the record? A name I can check out, or a person I can talk to. Someone who might know more than others about what happened out there on the beach where they found Ingalls's body. Can you do that much?"

Wilbur was, of course, dying to tell. "Strictly off the record, then, there is one person you might want to investigate. A man named Jackson, who lives in Edgartown. He's a well-known rabble-rouser, and an enemy of everything Larry Ingalls stood for. He's also the man who claims he found Larry's body. You should investigate him, if you ask me!"

"Terrific. I really appreciate your help, Mr. Wilbur."

"You're very welcome. I don't want Larry's killer getting away with it, so I'll be pleased if anything I've told you will help find the person who did it. I'll switch you to Dina's desk now."

Maybe Joshua's crankiness was really a

blessing in disguise. If I'd gone to Marshall Lea headquarters with no way to hide my face and pass myself off as Quinn, I probably couldn't have gotten in to see either Wilbur or Witherspoon. The telephone was the right tool at the right time.

"This is Dina Witherspoon," said a husky voice on the phone. Her words re-created her in my memory. Dina Witherspoon was a beautiful woman. Tall, brown-haired, rich, intelligent, and devoted to environmentalism, she had long been the object of admiring masculine eyes, including my own. Next to Zee, I could think of no island woman who was more attractive.

Attractive, that is, except for her almost religious devotion to her great cause. Her burning passion for it made her less lovely to me, since I am deeply suspicious of all overly devoted people.

"My name is Quinn," I said. "I work for the *Boston Globe*. We're doing a story on Lawrence Ingalls. Your name came up as one who might give me some useful information about him. I'm trying to get some sense of him as a person. What sort of man he was, who might have wanted him dead, and why. I hope you can help me."

Her sepia-colored voice filled my ear. "He was a wonderful man, Mr. Quinn, maybe even a great man. He worked all of his life to save the environment, to save the earth. He was an inspiration to all of us here at the foundation, and will be missed more than I can say. He's irreplaceable."

"So Mr. Wilbur told me. What was he like as a person? Mr. Wilbur characterized him as friendly but a bit reserved. As a woman, how did you perceive him?"

"As a woman? As a woman, Mr. Quinn, I perceived him the same way any man would perceive him. I don't care for this 'as a woman' talk. It's sexist at best, and foolish at worst."

Land mine. I jumped back. "You're absolutely right," I said. "I apologize. But as one who worked closely with him, you must have developed a sense of his character. What was he like?"

"For one thing, Mr. Quinn, he never treated me or any of the other women here as anything but equals. He didn't put his hands on us or make sexist jokes or do any of that sort of thing. He didn't ask for dates, or stare at our legs or breasts. He was totally professional at all times. He was always friendly, but never tried to be intimate. He was a wonderful colleague. Bright, hardworking, dedicated. I never worked with a better person."

Saint Lawrence.

I said, "I understand he was engaged to a woman named Beth Harper. She may be the person who knew him best. I'd like to talk with her. Do you know where she is?"

The smoky voice said Beth might be in Boston, back at work there.

"I'll try to get in touch with her there. One last thing, Miss Witherspoon —"

"*Ms.* Witherspoon, Mr. Quinn."

Ye gods. "Ms. Witherspoon, then. Who were Ingalls's enemies? Everything I hear about the guy says he shouldn't have had any. But somebody killed him for some reason, and I could use some suggestions about where to start looking for that person and those reasons. Can you help me out at all? Just a name, maybe. Anything you can tell me, any direction you might point me."

"If you want to find the murderer," said Dina Witherspoon, "look at the people who hated him."

"At the ORV drivers who were mad because he closed off that section of South Beach?"

I could almost see her nod. "I imagine that most of them are just naive people who don't understand the importance of Larry's decision about that beach. But there are some crazies who are dangerous."

"Strictly off the record," I said. "Give me a name."

She gave me mine, just as Joshua woke up and began to cry.

What a day.

— 23 —

Joshua howled. I investigated. Aha! Diaper rash! Where had it come from? It hadn't been there before. I applied antidotes to Joshua's bottom and he seemed to feel better, even though he stayed whiny. In eighteen years I could send him away to college, but between now and then, he was in my hands for better or worse.

I took him outside and we checked the garden. New weeds had appeared. If we could figure a way to make weeds a cash crop, we'd be rich. I put Joshua in his foreman's chair under a parasol and went to work on my hands and knees. When I finished weeding the garden, I felt his brow. Not hot, not cold. Just right. We got into the Land Cruiser and drove to the Edgartown police station. There, I put him in the baby sling I used to carry him on my chest, and the two of us went in. The chief was in his office attacking a pile of papers stacked beside the computer on his desk.

"I should have invested in paper stock," he growled. "I'd be retired by now. You remember when computers were first the rage? Some of the gurus said that since everything could be done with electronics, offices could save a fortune on typing paper. Ha! We use more paper now than we did before. And so does everybody else. And the price of paper is going up every day!"

"Ah, for the good old days, eh?"

He sat back in his chair and shook his head. "Forget the good old days. I lived through them, and I wouldn't want them back."

I looked shocked. "What do you mean? You're always grousing about the traffic and the crowds being worse than ever. That sounds like nostalgia to me."

"Yeah, well, I could do with less of this damned paperwork, and a lot less traffic, but aside from that you can have the good old days, as far as I'm concerned. What brings you out of the woods?"

"Any news about the Ingalls case?"

"If there was, I wouldn't tell you. People would think we were in cahoots."

Zack Delwood already thought that.

I sat down. "By God, you're right. My reputation would be ruined."

"If I had your reputation, I'd want it ruined. Then I could rebuild from scratch and maybe get it right this time."

"Since you won't talk, I will," I said. And I told him most of what I'd seen and heard since last we'd spoken. I didn't tell him about my encounter with Zack Delwood or the lies I'd told, but I did go over my conversation with the folks at the Marshall Lea Foundation.

"I'm surprised," said the chief when I was through. "I'd have guessed that none of those people would give you the time of day. And here they treated you like an old friend. How do you figure that?"

"I attribute it to my sparkling personality."

"Sure. Anyway, I don't see that you've learned anything useful. Ingalls's friends all told you what a swell guy he was. Where does that get you?"

"Maybe nowhere, but maybe somewhere, if Joe Begay and Quinn come up with anything."

"If they do, let me know what it is."

"I'll tell you at least as much as you've just told me. What do you make of Ingalls's taste for erotic art and books?"

The chief shrugged. "I don't make anything of it. It's not everybody's cup of tea, but there's nothing unusual about it. In fact, it's pretty popular. And nothing new about it, either. If I remember right, there's whole

279

walls of such stuff in the ruins of Pompeii. And the old-time Greeks painted sex scenes on their pottery, too. Or maybe Ingalls was just a collector, like some people collect salt shakers."

I couldn't find anything wrong with his argument, so I asked him where Beth Harper was.

"I think she's up in Boston. Got out of town quick, just in case you changed your mind about not pressing charges against her, I imagine. She works for the DEP up there."

"Did you get a statement from her?"

"You mean about when she tried to shoot you? Of course. But once you dropped the charges, and we knew she didn't shoot Ingalls, we let her go."

"No, I mean about her relations with Ingalls."

"We asked her, but she was no help. She couldn't imagine him having any enemies. The guy must have had a halo, from what people say."

"I never saw it."

"I haven't seen any in my whole life. The people I meet in my line of work don't wear them. For that matter, neither do I."

Nor did I. "Find Moonbeam yet?"

He frowned. "No, but I want to."

"And I want something to eat."

Josh and I drove down through teeming Edgartown, and I wondered, not for the first time, why so many people were in town on such a fine day. Why weren't they at the beach, where any sensible person would be? Come to think of it, why weren't Josh and I out on the golden sands?

Parking places were scarce, but I found one on North Summer Street, and Joshua and I walked down to the Dock Street Coffee Shop for brunch. Joshua brought his own bottle, which nobody seemed to mind.

Over coffee and a Portuguese McMuffin, I listened to the latest gossip. There wasn't much that was new, except that Moonbeam Berube hadn't been seen in a while. The most popular theory was that Moonbeam and his wife were on the outs again, and Moonbeam was probably sleeping in his truck until things settled down. It wasn't the first time that Connie had thrown him out of the house. The last time had been when he'd sold her milk cow while she was shopping at the up-island market. Moonbeam, who didn't see very far into the future, and who had no attachment to animal, vegetable, or mineral, would sell anything, including other people's stuff, without a qualm, if it got him enough money to buy whatever it was he wanted at the moment. It had taken days for Connie to get over her fury about the cow, and she had only taken Moonbeam back after he got her a milk goat to replace it. There was some speculation about how long he'd be persona non grata this time, and general agreement that it was a good thing it was summertime, because a man living in a pickup could get mighty cold in the winter.

Nobody theorized that Moonbeam might be a killer on the run. Neither did I.

To my left, Pete Scorsese finished his meal and came past me, headed for the door. He paused and tapped my shoulder lightly with his big fist. "I know you didn't shoot that Ingalls guy," he said in a whisper that carried the length of the cafe. "But if you did, you made a lot of people happy." He winked and went on out the door.

Terrific. I looked down the row of seats to my right. Bill Perry, one of many ORV drivers who had long held the view that the world would be a better place without any Lawrence Ingalls, was sitting down there. He leaned forward and looked back at me. Then he lifted his coffee cup in a sort of salute and smiled at me. I stood up, and a silence fell over the room.

"Pete's right," I said. "I didn't shoot that Ingalls guy. Whoever did it is a murderer, and I hope they catch him quick."

I sat down again and the silence rang. It wasn't until I'd paid my bill and the door was closing behind me that the sound of voices again filled the cafe.

Joshua was feeling very well by the time Zee got home, but we decided that since he had had a bad day, taking him down to the Rod and Gun Club shooting range wasn't a good idea. Thus his mother, after changing into her shooting clothes, went down to the range by herself while Joshua and I stayed home. Together, he and I listened to the popping sounds of her and Manny Fonseca's pistols, as they blew holes in their targets for the better part of an hour.

When Zee came home, she was feeling good. She had shot well, apparently, and Manny had been satisfied with her work.

She, Joshua, and I went up onto the balcony, where Zee and I shared martinis and some pre-supper snacks.

"We're going to shoot again tomorrow," said Zee.

"Manny knows his pistols, so you should do as he says."

"I will. I'm getting better with the forty-five."

"You're going to play with the big boys, eh?"

She grinned. "Well, bigger ones than

283

before, I guess. There'll be some big girls there, too, according to Manny. I'll mostly be shooting against them."

"Maybe Josh and I will come along to be a cheering section."

She put Joshua in her lap. "That would be just fine."

I told her about my day.

"So Lawrence Ingalls was an angel, eh?" said Zee, when I was through.

"So it seems. Or so people say, anyway."

"But you don't think so. Do you think they were lying, or just wrong?"

She'd let her long black hair down, and I ran a hand through it. "Maybe both. Or maybe they didn't really know him. Or maybe they just don't want to bad-mouth the dead."

"You mean there might have been something that doesn't make any difference any longer, now that he's gone?"

"Yeah. I might feel the same way about somebody I knew or loved. I might do what they're doing: remember the good, and forget the bad. Bury the bad where it can't be found."

"But you're not going to let them do that, are you?"

I wound a thick strand of her hair around my hand and let it slip away again, remembering how, when she lay in bed with her hair spread on her pillow, her perfect face seemed to be at the center of a glowing black sun.

"Bill Perry and Pete Scorsese aren't the only guys who might actually believe I killed Ingalls. It's not a reputation I want to have, and I especially don't want people to think that you and Josh are a murderer's family."

"We're not. And I don't care what people think!"

But I cared.

"There's something else," she said. "I got a call from Drew. Apparently he tried here first, but the line was busy, so he called me at the hospital. He and some other people are coming down to the island early, to get some R and R before they start shooting the film."

Drew, eh? What a day I was having. "Great," I said. "When are they coming?"

"Next week. They just decided, so the papers don't even know about it yet. Guess who's coming!"

"Who?"

"Drew and Emily and their daughter, Carly, and Kevin Turner and Kate Ballinger! The stars themselves! Drew says he wants them to meet us! Isn't that exciting? Imagine, he wants us to meet Kevin Turner and Kate Ballinger!"

I'd met a few of the island's celebrities over the years, and though I'd found most of them to be no different than other people, meetimg more of them, including Kevin Turner and Kate Ballinger, was not high on my list of things I'd like to do.

"Great," I said.

"And there's something else . . ." Her voice had a tentative quality to it.

"What?" I turned toward her.

She was looking down at Joshua, and I had the sudden impression that she was doing it so she wouldn't have to look at me. "Drew wants me to fly out to Hollywood on Wednesday, to take some screen tests. He says I can come back here with them, when they come."

The evening sounds of birds, wind in the trees, and distant automobile engines filled my ears. I looked across the pond and took a sip of my martini. When I looked back at Zee, she was letting Joshua suck on her finger. He looked happier than anyone else in the family.

"What did you tell him?"

"I told him I'd talk to you, then let him know."

I took another sip. "What would you like to do, if you had your druthers?"

She clearly had anticipated my response. "I'd like to do what makes you happy."

Ah, so. I returned serve: "And I'd like to do what makes you happy."

She finally met my eyes. "I think we're going in circles here."

That's what you do when the injuns are about to ambush the wagon train. I stepped away from my feelings, and my mouth said, "I think you should go. I mean, after all, how many times do you get an offer like that? It should be fun. And Josh and I can bach it for a while just fine." I looked down at Joshua. "Can't we? We can do manly things without any women around to tell us how to behave."

Joshua's eyes were wide but noncommittal.

"Oh, I wouldn't leave Joshua," said Zee, almost with alarm. "I'd take him with me. In fact, you could come, too! We could all go together!"

"I doubt if that would fit into Drew's plans," said my voice before I could stop it.

She laughed a real laugh. "Oh, I don't think that he's planning to seduce me, if that's what you mean! He's not the professional-lover type. No, I'd have seen it in him by now if he was. And even if he did want me on the casting couch, I wouldn't be interested. You and Joshua are all the men I want in my life! I'd just like to see what a screen test's like and maybe see the inside of a studio and people making a movie while I'm there. Wouldn't you like to do that? Wouldn't you like to come, too?"

I put on a smile, and took Joshua from her lap to mine. "Not a chance! If I have to choose between Hollywood and Martha's Vineyard, I'll take the Vineyard every time! No, it'll be better if you go on out there by yourself, so you won't have to worry about the rest of us. You'll have a good time, and Joshua and I will be fine right here."

"You're sure?"

"I'm sure."

"Well, now I'm not sure I'm sure." She picked at some imaginary thread on the sleeve of her blouse. "Maybe I'll just stay home. They can give me a screen test when they get here, if they still want to."

I put my arm around her shoulder. "You go," I said. "And have a good time. You can use a break. And when you get back, we'll be waiting for you."

She gave me a long kiss. A little later she stood up. "It's getting cool," she said. "And it's time for the man-child to go to bed. Come on, Joshua."

She took him in her arms and went down the stairs.

I watched them disappear, and then looked back out over the pond. The evening seemed to be darker than it had been only minutes before.

— 24 —

I watched Zee's plane rise and head north to Boston, on the first leg of her flight to California. When it was out of sight, Joshua and I got into the Land Cruiser and went back home. It was an empty-feeling ride to an empty-feeling house.

Zee's good-bye kisses had been sweet, and her face had been bright with expectation, the way faces are when their owners are starting on adventures they expect to be happy ones.

"I'll be back in no time," she'd said. "And I'll tell you all about it when I get home. It'll be fun, I think. I'll even get to travel with some stars!"

"You'll be the star," I'd said, and she'd laughed.

"You and Joshua will be fine?"

"Absolutely."

"I'll phone you when I get there."

Everyone else had gone through the gate. "Go," I said, giving her a small push. "Have fun!"

And she was gone.

At home, Joshua and I were outside, weeding flowers, when the phone rang. It was too soon for it to be Zee's call from California, but it might be her, anyway. Maybe she'd changed her mind, and was calling from Boston. Or maybe she was calling from one of those telephones they have on airplanes these days. I got to the phone before it stopped ringing.

"Get with it, man," said Quinn's voice. "Buy yourself a goddamned answering machine like everybody else. Save yourself those mad runs from the yard!"

"City living is making you soft," I said, puffing. "You can't live without gadgets."

"Soft in the head, at least. Here's what I've got on Lawrence Ingalls."

What he had on Lawrence Ingalls was his birthdate, the names of the members of his family, which was the kind with old North Shore money, his education (Andover and Harvard, just like Dad), the dates of his marriage (right after his graduation) and his divorce (two years later), a list of the jobs he'd held (something to do with financing, briefly, in one of Dad's firms; in international banking, for a longer time, in one of Dad's banks; then steady employment for the state DEP, where he'd finally found his vocation).

"What about his private life?" I asked. "Friends, girls, all that travel to the Orient, that kind of stuff? What about his enemies?"

"Well, there was you, of course."

I went out to the porch with the portable phone, to keep an eye on Joshua. "Who else? What kind of a life did he lead?"

"Nobody at Dad's firms had a bad thing to say about him. No surprise there, of course, since who'd bad-mouth the boss's boy. And apparently, the truth was that he left those places just because he didn't take to the kind of work they did, and he had enough money so he could afford to quit. He found his spot in the environmental biz, and was good at it, according to my sources. A real go-getter. Smart and up on top of the latest information in the field. On the cutting edge, as they say. People he worked with think he was the cat's pajamas." Quinn could string clichés together with the best of them when he set his mind to it.

"No enemies?" I asked. "Nobody mad at him for any reason? Some guy who was envious? A jilted girlfriend? A jilted boyfriend, maybe?"

"You have a low mind, J.W. No, he apparently dated after the divorce, but nothing heavy ever came of it. Just friends, and like that. I guess women liked him and he liked them, but he never got thick with any of them, so there were never any bad feelings that I heard about. He wasn't interested in remarrying."

"Until Beth Harper." From the porch I could see that no eagle had swooped from the sky and snatched up Joshua. He seemed to be playing with his toes.

"I guess so," said Quinn. "But that's a recent thing. Nobody seemed to know much about it."

I was collecting zeros. "What about all that Oriental stuff? Where'd he go? Was he maybe smuggling dope or something? Did he get somebody mad at him that way?"

"You've been reading too many thrillers, my boy. No, our lad probably puffed a little weed and maybe dropped some acid or shot up with something just like a lot of people did back when he was in school, but he never was into anything heavy. Far as I know, he grew up to use the normal WASP drugs, just like Dad and the rest of us: alcohol, caffeine, and nicotine. What he was doing over in Asia was, first, following Dad's footsteps. The old man was in the service over there in the Big War, and went back afterward as a civilian doing business for his bank. When our boy Lawrence was working for the bank, he traveled for them over there, too. In fact, I think Dad went with him the first couple of times. Places like Indonesia and India and Singapore. I guess he liked the territory, because for a while after he left the bank, he went back on vacation almost every year. I understand he got to be some kind of an Oriental scholar, in fact."

"When did he stop? And why?"

"How should I know? I know he stopped, and started taking his vacations down in the Caribbean. And then he quit that and built himself a house on Martha's Vineyard a couple of years back. Since then, he's been down there when he wasn't working out of Boston. He apparently never took anybody with him when he went abroad, and all he ever said about it was the standard stuff: beaches and sight-seeing and like that."

"He never took his wife with him?"

"Nope. While they were married, he was traveling for the bank, on business. By the time he was going abroad on vacations, they were divorced. The only person who was ever over there with him was his old man, and that was only the first couple of trips. To introduce the kid to the right contacts, probably."

Hmmmmm. "What about his friends? Did he talk with them about his private life?"

Quinn said: "I asked about his friends. Everybody was his friend, sort of. The people he worked with, old school buddies he met again at reunions, and so forth. Aside from them, I don't know that he had any friends. He didn't seem to be the warm and cuddly type."

"Is cold the word?"

"No, not cold. Aloof? Cool? Formal? Something more like that. Just not the type who looked for a lot of friends, or needed them, like a lot of other people do. Got it from his old man, maybe. I hear he's the same way. Lots of casual friends, but no close ones. A bit of a loner. Hears the different drummer."

I ran all that through my brain and out the other side. Nothing. I tried a couple of last, wide shots. "The old man another Orientalist?"

"So I hear. Like father, like son."

"Did Lawrence become a scholar of the Caribbean, like he became a scholar of the Orient?"

"Not that I know of. I don't think he's a scholar of Martha's Vineyard, either, for that matter."

More nothing.

"Well, Sherlock," said Quinn, "who done it, and why?"

"The butler," I said. "In the conservatory with a rope. If you find out anything else, let me know. Forget the foreign travel part, and concentrate on the private-life-at-home part."

He gave a snort. "If I find out anything else, it'll be by accident. I don't have time to do this pro bono work for the likes of you. Unlike some people I could name, I've got a real job."

"Don't make me laugh," I said. "You're a journalist."

We rang off, and I went outside.

Joshua was still under his umbrella, taking in the sights: birds around the feeders, a branch moving in the wind, shadows dappling the lawn. His was a prettier world than mine. I wondered if he'd trade, but decided not to ask. He'd grow into mine soon enough; better if I tried to get into his.

I went back to weeding flowers. Out of the experiences I'd had before and after Ingalls's death, some sort of shape was beginning to form from the fragments of information I was getting. But parts of it were missing, and I couldn't make it out. Perhaps I had overlooked the parts. Or perhaps I'd not yet encountered them.

I weeded the hanging pots, and the flower boxes on the fence, and got to work on the ground beds. How long had it been since I'd first met Ingalls, on the beach in Gay Head? Only ten days. I thought about what I'd heard and seen since then, trying to remember everything. What did I know? Not a lot.

Then thoughts of Zee began to mix with those of Ingalls. Where was her plane now? What was she thinking about? What would she find waiting for her in California?

I remembered the Zen master who said to his confused student, "If you are confused, be confused. Do not be confused by confusion. Be totally confused!"

But I was not a Zen master, or even a good student, so I willed myself away from my confusion and tried to become only a weeder of flowers whose son was watching him as he weeded under a soft summer sky. But Zee and Ingalls continued to intrude upon the oneness I was trying to make of Joshua, the flowers and weeds, the sky, and myself, and I was still confused by confusion.

I was washing the supper dishes when Zee called from her Los Angeles hotel.

It had been a perfect flight, and she was tired but fine. Drew and Emily had met her at the airport. She was having dinner with them and tomorrow was getting a tour of a studio before getting ready for her screen test. L.A. was a huge place that went on for miles in every direction. There was supposedly a sign high in the Rocky Mountains of Colorado that said "Los Angeles City Limits"! How was Joshua? How was I? She missed us both, but would be home soon. She'd call again tomorrow. She loved us both.

I played with Joshua for a while, alternately watched and ignored by Oliver Underfoot and Velcro, who didn't seem to mind having been nudged out of their position as primary family pets by the newcomer who now occupied so much of their humans' attention.

When I thought the time was right, I walked with Joshua in my arms and softly sang "Wynken, Blynken and Nod" until his eyes were heavy, then I put him to bed. He fussed a bit, then quieted down. When I peeked the first time, he caught me in the act, having only faked being asleep. But the second time, he was off in the wooden shoe, sailing down that river of crystal light into the sea of dew.

The mountain would not come to Mohammed, so Mohammed went to the mountain. Since Joe Begay had not called me, I called him.

"I told you this would take some time," he said. "I don't have much yet. Just some dates and destinations from back in the seventies, when Larry was in Malaysia and Thailand and thereabouts."

"Quinn says his father was over there after World War Two, on banking business, and that when his kid was first in that trade, he took him over there to show him the way around."

"That'd be Carlson Bank and Trust. Pretty big outfit, but straight arrow, as far as I know."

"A lot of drugs come out of that area," I said. "A big international banking outfit might have a finger in that pie."

"I think I'd have heard about it if it did," said Begay casually, "but I'll double-check."

I wondered but didn't ask why he would have heard about it.

"I'd like to have you concentrate on Ingalls's foreign travel," I said. "I've asked Quinn to let that go and focus on his private life at home. That way, each of you only has to look at one thing, and afterward maybe I can put the two together, if there's anything to put together."

Begay heard something in my voice that I hadn't known was there.

"You think there is something, don't you?"

When he said that, I knew he was right. I did think that. It was almost a relief to realize it.

"Yes," I said. "I don't know what it is, but the past is prologue."

"What would we do without the Bard?" said Begay. "I'll talk to you later."

He rang off, and I got myself a Sam Adams

and took it out to the balcony, where I sat under the darkening sky and watched the lights glimmer from the far side of the sound. Above me, the Milky Way was a white road across the sky. As I looked up at it, more of old Bill's wisdom gave form to my thoughts: the fault lay not in our stars, but in ourselves. I drank some beer. It was cold and good, just like the night sky.

— 25 —

"It really is a tinsel town," said Zee two nights later. She was three thousand miles away, but sounded like she was just next door, where I wished she really was. "Everything's shine and glitter on one side and strictly business on the other. The people out here talk the talk and walk the walk, but when they go home, they mostly only think about the money. It's great! I'm having a terrific time!"

"How's the screen test coming along?"

"I've been made up, dressed up, dressed down, and I've read from a script. They've taken stills and movies and even tried to make me act. Everybody says nice things, but I'll tell you the truth: I don't think I've got what it takes. When I move around in front of all those people and cameras, I feel like I'm made out of wood. And when I try to read what they give me, I sound like an illiterate!" She laughed, and I felt happy. "I'm having fun, but I don't think we should sell the farm and move out here so I can have a career on the silver screen. I have met a couple of people who want to be my agent, though. Everything that moves out here has an agent, of course. But Emily — that's Drew's wife — gave me the right advice: I should enjoy everything, have a good time, and not take any of it seriously, especially what people say to me, because it's Hollywood, and everything is images. So that's what I've been doing."

"Good. Have you met any stars yet?"

"They pointed some out to me, in the commissary, but I haven't seen any close up. Or at least I don't think I have. I'm afraid that I'm really not very good at recognizing them, to tell you the truth. Maybe we should go to more movies or watch more TV after I get back, so I won't be such a hick."

Zee, the hick. "I'd think that all the glitter and glitz would make it hard for a star to keep both feet on the ground," I said.

"Stars aren't supposed to be on the ground," said Zee, faking primness. "They're supposed to be in the sky! That's why they call them stars! But really, Emily tells me that a lot of them are just ordinary people, even though a lot of others aren't."

"Isn't Kevin Turner her brother? Have you met him yet?"

"No, but I'm going to this weekend. Drew and Emily are throwing a party and Kevin is supposed to come. Right now, he's on the road, promoting his latest movie, which I guess is another swashbuckler. Did you notice that I call him Kevin, even though I've never met him? That's because I'm in Hollywood, and out here we're all on a first-name basis with everybody!"

"And what does Emily say about him? Is he ordinary people, or the other kind?"

"Well, Emily is plain folks, but as a matter of fact she doesn't have a lot to say about Kevin. So I guess I'll just have to wait and see. Now tell me about you and Joshua. I can hardly wait to get home!"

So I told her about Josh and me going fishing on East Beach and getting a Spanish mackerel at the Jetties, and about the two of us taking the dinghy and fishing in vain for bonito off the Oak Bluffs dock, and about the trouble I was having with, of all things, our zucchinis, which seemed to be defying the laws of nature by dying instead of overrunning the earth as they usually did, and about everything except the Ingalls business, which she forgot to ask about before she rang off.

Three more days, and she'd be home!

The next morning, Joshua and I were at the A & P when the doors opened. A few minutes

302

later, as we were piloting our carriage past the deli section, we ran into Manny and Helen Fonseca, who, like us, were shopping in the early morning.

"What's the latest gossip?" I asked.

"Well, I guess Moonbeam is still hiding out," said Manny. "Connie must really be mad at him this time."

"It's happened before," I said.

"Yeah, but usually somebody sees him somewhere. I hear they found his pickup in the St. Augustine's parking lot up in Vineyard Haven. Some people park there when they take the ferry to Woods Hole, so maybe he went over to America till she calms down."

"What'd he do this time?"

Manny shrugged. "Don't ask me. They're both strange birds. How's Zee?"

"Zee is in California," I said, and told them what she was doing out there and when she'd be back.

"She's certainly pretty enough to be a movie star," said Helen. "Wouldn't it be something if she got to be one! You could live in a Hollywood mansion instead of up there in the woods."

"How about me?" I said. "Do you think I'm star material?"

She laughed. "Sure, J.W., sure you are!"

"When she gets back," Manny said, "you

have her give me a call so we can do some more practice. October ain't far away."

"I'll do that," I said.

Josh and I were putting our groceries in the Land Cruiser when I saw Barbara Singleton get out of her car and walk toward the store. She didn't seem to see me, and I felt a little tingle.

I drove home and got my lock picks, then, with Joshua still in his car seat, headed up-island, wondering how long Barbara would be gone and whether Connie Berube still felt that she was in charge of security at Lawrence Ingalls's house.

It seemed to me that if Barbara had just wanted to do some grocery shopping, she'd have done it at the Up-Island Market, which was a lot nearer home. But she hadn't done that. Instead, she'd gone all the way to Edgartown. Which probably meant she had some other business at that end of the island, and wouldn't be home until she'd taken care of it. And since it was still early, and a lot of places wouldn't be open until eight or nine o'clock, she might not come home until mid-to late morning.

Which meant no one was in Ingalls's house and that no one would be for an hour or maybe two.

That left Connie the watchdog. How

would she respond to seeing me heading up to the house? Especially since she'd no doubt seen Barbara leaving it earlier in the day, and knew nobody was home.

I turned off North Road and followed the winding driveway. Passing Moonbeam's place, I noted that the old backhoe had been moved a bit and that the sewer trench had more new dirt in it. Maybe the job would finally get done someday. Maybe not.

The eldest boy, Jason junior, watched me pass, his lovely, pale, empty face turning on his slender neck as I went by. Two smaller children, as white and delicate as their older brother, stopped playing in the patch of mud that they squatted in, and watched as well. I didn't see Connie.

I parked in front of Ingalls's house, got Joshua into the sling I used to carry him on my chest, and went up to the front door. I knocked and listened and knocked and listened some more, then went around to the back of the house and raised my voice.

"Anybody home?"

No answer.

I walked over to the path that led down to the beach, and called again.

Still no answer. And no one in sight, either. I went back to the rear door, opened its lock, and went inside the house. I was getting

305

pretty good with locks. Maybe I had a potential vocation in crime.

I went to the desk in the study and picked the simple locks on the drawers. I didn't know what I expected to find, but I didn't find it. Apparently, Lawrence Ingalls was just a guy who liked things locked. There are people like that; they lock their houses, lock their cars, lock their desks, lock everything. I've never understood them, being the kind of person who almost never locks anything but my gun cabinet. And even then, the key is on top of the cabinet, where anybody can find it. Besides, I am of the school that maintains that locks only keep out honest people, a theory supported by the fact that I was now pawing through the papers in the drawers of Lawrence Ingalls's desk.

And the papers were just papers: files having to do with the work of the DEP, a file with a record of the money paid to Connie Berube for housekeeping duties, another one with a record of money (a pretty generous amount, I thought) paid to Jason Berube, Sr., for keeping up the grounds, files of past and future income tax materials, files containing those guarantees and forms that come with equipment you buy: your radio, your washing machine, your computer, all of which come with folders and papers that list model numbers, and tell you what to do if you have problems, where to call, and who to write.

I never keep those papers, but Lawrence Ingalls kept them all in neat files in the locked drawers of his desk. There was nothing there to suggest a motive for his murder.

I locked the drawers again and went to the file cabinets. Again the locks opened easily, as such uncomplicated locks are inclined to do, and again I found myself looking at neat files of papers. Records of visits to doctors, all routine, as far as I could tell; records of credit card transactions; records of the costs of building the house; records of travel expenses; records of auto and truck purchases and repairs; records of Lawrence Ingalls's whole life, it seemed. Hadn't he ever thrown a piece of paper away?

There was a lot of empty space in the file cabinets, but that wasn't too surprising, since all of the bills and other dated material, except for some older papers about ongoing environmental affairs, were less than three years old, clearly having been accumulated since Ingalls had built this house.

Early on, therefore, I was fairly certain that my search wasn't going to reveal anything having to do with his more distant past, but I looked at everything anyway, just in case. Finally I did find a travel folder advertising the charms of a Costa Rica resort area called Playa de Plata, a place I had never heard of. It was for deluxe vacations, quite beyond the reach of sunseekers in my economic class, and was, I guessed, a reflection of Ingalls's holiday interests before he had built his Vineyard house and given up foreign travel. The brochure was printed on costly paper, and was filled with beautiful photographs of beautiful people doing things in beautiful places. It promised the kinds of services and activities available to those sorts of people who were content with only the very best, and for whom expense was not an issue.

I put the folder right back where I'd found it, and locked the file doors. Then I remembered something and opened one of them again and took out the folder containing records of car and truck purchases and repairs, which I'd only glanced at before.

The key word was *purchases*. As far as I knew, Ingalls's own Vineyard vehicle had been a three-year-old Ford Bronco. I'd seen it in Joe Begay's yard, and the last time I'd looked, after Ingalls's death, it was garaged out in the barn behind this house. Ingalls had used a DEP pickup when he was on company business, as had been the case the day I'd found him on the beach.

But the folder contained not only a record

of the purchase of the Bronco, bought new the year Ingalls built his house and began vacationing on the island, but, at about the same time, the record of the purchase of an almost new 4 x 4 Chevy pickup, color gray, low mileage, and the record of the transfer of ownership to Jason Berube, Sr. Ditto for Connie's four-wheel-drive Subaru sedan.

Lawrence Ingalls had bought both vehicles.

I wondered why. Were they part of the deal that had made Moonbeam into Ingalls's groundskeeper and Connie into his house-keeper? If so, Moonbeam and Connie had struck a good bargain, because he also paid Moonbeam a particularly liberal salary to mow the lawns and trim the shrubs, especially for a man not known for high-quality work.

I rechecked the money paid to Connie for her housekeeping. It was a very correct salary, but in no way as generous as that paid to Moonbeam.

As my sister Margarite, who lived out by Santa Fe, might ask: *Qué pasa aquí?* Why would Ingalls pay a hardworking, dependable wife less than her lazy and untalented hus-band? Surely straight-arrow, ironed-shirt-and-shorts, always proper and in control Lawrence Ingalls hadn't thought that Moon-beam was worth that much more than Connie. What was with the big salary? And with the pickup and the Subaru?

Maybe Ingalls had just been a terrible male chauvinist who believed that man's work was always worth more than woman's work.

Or maybe I was doing Moonbeam an injustice. Maybe he was worth every cent, and more.

Maybe I was the Grand Duke of Russia.

I locked the cabinet doors and went out of the house.

— 26 —

"They like me," said Zee. "Or, at least, that's what they say. They say I'm photogenic."

"You're at least photogenic," I said.

"Tonight's the party, and tomorrow Drew and his family and a bunch of us are flying to the island," said Zee. "I can hardly wait! I haven't seen you and Josh for a long time!"

"Almost five days. Is this the party where you finally get to meet the stars?"

"Yes. Kevin Turner, at least. And maybe Kate Ballinger, too, and maybe Jack Slade, according to Emily. Jack is going to be the director. I guess it's a sort of get-together for the people who are going to the Vineyard. I miss you."

"I miss you, too. What have you been up to?"

She had been up to getting a snap course about the movie biz from Emily Mondry, who had been taking her around town, and with whom Zee had struck up a friendship. She was being told about such subjects as agents and actors; contracts and salary negotiations; the jobs of directors, cinematographers, producers, distributors, and writers; the meaning of all those credits that show up on the screen, and the importance attached to the size and placing of them: the logos of the studio and the distribution company, the names of actors, the executive producer (who, Emily had explained, could have his or her name up there for any one of lots of reasons, many of which had little or nothing to do with the actual production of the film), the production company, the producer, the associate producer, the director, the writer or writers (some of whom may have done a lot and others of whom may have done little or almost nothing), the composer, arranger, and conductor of the music, the film editor, the director of photography, the camera operator, and a bunch of other people like assistant cameramen, gaffers, makeup people and hairdressers, and others of whom there were too many for Zee to keep track of.

"You'd be amazed," said Zee, "at how complicated it all is. No wonder movies cost so much money and are usually so bad. It's a miracle any of them ever get made at all!"

"I'd probably be more amazed than most people," I agreed. "But there's a lot of money to be made, if it all works out."

"For some people, but not for others. The bean counters out here are very good about showing that even movies that make hundreds of millions of dollars actually lose money; that way, the real money people don't have to pay taxes or the suckers who agreed to work for a share of the profits!"

"Skullduggery in Tinseltown, eh? Is that un-American or just American?"

"Just business as usual, as Sir Winston said in his youth. The smart people take a percentage of the box office receipts, but you have to be pretty important to get that kind of contract. The best thing for most people is to get as much money as you can up front."

"In that case, since you're smart, you should demand a piece of the box office receipts. If they won't give them to you, quit!"

She laughed. "I think you'd better reconsider your decision to become a Hollywood agent, sweets. Now I've got to go prepare myself for the big party. See you tomorrow afternoon at the airport! Be there! I love you! Good-bye!"

Good-bye, good-bye. Tomorrow was already bright and shiny even though the calendar and clocks said it was really still getting dark the evening before.

Joshua, tired from another August island day, was sleeping the sleep of the just. Since he was finally beginning to snooze through the night instead of insisting on a 2:00 A.M. meal, as he had done up till now, I was pretty sure I had my time to myself until sunup or so, when Josh would need my attention once again.

I used it to first brood upon what I did and didn't know about Lawrence Ingalls's life and death; then, giving up on that, did some reading from my living room book, which, at the moment, was the Bible, Revised Standard Edition. I was actually rereading it — sort of, because I was skipping the "begats" and some of the other genealogical records that were probably important but didn't interest me, and was concentrating on the interesting stuff: war, romance, and mindless sex and violence, of which there is a lot and which explains why even us heathens call it a Good Book.

In our house, there were books in every room, so we never had to go looking for something to read. We had bedroom books on the bedside tables on each side of the bed; bathroom books (usually poetry or books of aphorisms, since we were never in there long enough to read novels or even short stories); living room books; kitchen books, read only while cooking or eating; and porch books, kept back away from the screens so they wouldn't get wet during windy rainstorms. I had been thinking about making a waterproof book box for the balcony, but so far I hadn't gotten around to doing it, so when we were up there we tended not to read, which was probably just as well.

And we had car books, so we could read on the beach or while in a ferry line, or while waiting for a spouse to come out of a store. By having books everywhere, it was possible to get quite a lot of reading done even though we were busy doing other things. The secret was to be able to alternately read pieces of a lot of books and not lose track of what was happening in any of them. People who could read only one book at a time would not benefit from our system, but both Zee and I always had several books going at once, with Dr. Spock always at hand in case of unexpected baby problems.

With all this reading going on, why wasn't I getting wiser or, barring wisdom, at least getting smarter? Was it a case of the more you study, the more you learn; and the more you learn, the more you can forget; and the more you can forget, the more you do forget; and the more you forget, the less you know?

Whatever it was, I was aware of my failure to grasp the truth of Lawrence Ingalls's murder, even as I read of the Lord telling our

Joshua's namesake to appoint cities of refuge so that the manslayer who kills any person without intent or unwillingly might flee there, and they would be a refuge for him from the avenger of blood.

I didn't think that whoever had killed Ingalls had done it without intent or unwillingly.

The next morning, right after breakfast, Quinn called. "Listen," he said. "Charles Ingalls — that's Lawrence Ingalls's old man — belongs to a club here in town. He has friends there. Aristocratic types just like himself, all of them getting old together. They drink, they eat, they get away from their wives, they sit in big leather chairs and read the stock market reports. They been doing it since they were young guys. Larry Ingalls was a member, too, but he wasn't the club type, I guess, because he never went there much. But the old man has always spent time there. After work, sometimes overnight, and like that.

"Now here's the part that might interest you. Everybody drinks and everybody talks and listens, and over the years stories circulate. Some of them get outside the walls, and one of them got to somebody I know. It seems that the old man was straight arrow at home, but when he went abroad, it wasn't just business, but it was business and bordellos. He liked Oriental meat, and when he took his boy over there to introduce him to the banking business, he introduced him to his other interests, too. Like father, like son. Well?"

"Well, what?"

"Well, now you know something you wanted to know, for Christ's sake. You know your boy Ingalls wasn't a saint like everybody thought he was. If he liked sex over there, he probably liked it over here. And if he liked it over here, he might have made somebody mad enough to shoot him!"

"We don't have any saints on Martha's Vineyard, Quinn. Even I know that. As for sex, everybody likes it here, just like they do up there where you live. Except down here, especially in the summertime, there's so much of it being handed out free that most people don't have to pay for it like you do. And that being the case, nobody down here, as far as I know, has ever gotten mad enough to shoot somebody over a woman. The worst it gets is maybe a bloody nose and then a wife switch. Keep looking."

"You're really going to owe me before this is over, buddy."

He rang off, and I thought of what he'd told me. It didn't seem like much, one way or another. The Ingalls men were not the first to taste forbidden fruits abroad, while sticking to proper cuisine at home, and I could see no particular significance in their foreign dalliances.

I loaded Joshua and his gear into the Land Cruiser and drove down to Edgartown Travel, which was being womaned by Petunia Slocum, who was some sort of distant relative of the famous single-handed circumnavigator and the only Petunia I had ever met outside of a flower bed. Petunia and I don't often meet on business, because I rarely travel anywhere, so now she looked at me with surprise from behind her desk.

"What can I do for you, J.W.?"

"Tell me about a place called Playa de Plata, in Costa Rica," I said.

She raised her eyebrows. "You must have won the lottery, J.W. Isn't that a pretty swanky place?"

I sat down across from her. "I'm a pretty swanky guy. I just don't let it show. I'm not interested in the hotel and swimming pool, I'm interested in the entertainments that are available. Both the official ones and the unofficial ones."

She put on her blank face. "The unofficial ones?"

"Yeah."

"I'm afraid I don't know what you mean," she said in a careful voice.

318

"Sure you do," I said. "I mean what sort of activities are available to those who want only the best and are able to pay for it? Who, maybe, want something that's not listed in the brochure."

She sat back and looked inquiring but neutral. "Like what?"

"Like sex."

She stared at me, and I thought I saw distaste in her eyes. "I'm afraid you've come to the wrong agency, Mr. Jackson. I wouldn't know anything about that sort of thing."

I had gone from J.W. to Mr. Jackson in not very long.

"Now, Petunia," I said, "don't get all moralistic on me. I'm not using you to help me pursue any exotic vices, because I've personally already got all the woman I can handle right at home. What I'm trying to do is get a line on a man who used to walk the wild side in the Far East, then switched to Playa de Plata. The guy is dead and gone, but I want to know what he liked to do in the way of recreation. Anything you can tell me might help in a criminal investigation."

She brightened immediately. "Why didn't you say so right off, J.W.? What criminal investigation? Are you working for the cops on this murder case? I thought you were just a civilian like the rest of us."

I sat back in my chair. "I'm not a cop and I'm not working for the cops, but I am working on the case. I know some people they don't know, so I may have some leads they don't have and know some things they may not know. One of the things I don't know is what this dead guy liked in the way of sex when he went on vacation. I thought maybe you could find out for me."

She leaned forward. "Something kinky, you mean?"

"I don't know what I mean. That's what I want you to tell me."

"Well," she said thoughtfully, "it's probably not regular prostitutes, because there are regular prostitutes everywhere and I can't see why somebody would go to one of these places just to meet prostitutes. Unless he was such a snob that he only wanted to meet really expensive ones. And if that was the only criteria, he could have found some of them right at home, probably. Where did this guy live?"

"Boston."

"Well, then, he wouldn't have had to leave town to find a really upper-class hooker. Maybe he didn't want to mess around in his hometown, where people might find out. Could that be it?"

"It could be that," I said. "How does a

wide-eyed little island girl like yourself know so much about hookers, anyway?"

She gave me a coy look. "Maybe I have a secret life."

"Gosh, Petunia, I never knew."

She faked a sigh of regret. "Me neither. But I read the *Globe* and the *Herald*, and I watch the exposé shows on the tube, so I'm an expert. You think he did his whoring overseas because he was shy about cavorting with the girls at home?"

"I don't know. I know he was married for a while, and that after the divorce he dated some women from where he worked, and that he was engaged again just before he died. But I haven't picked up anything about him soliciting prostitutes."

She stared at me, then at her desk, then at me again, smiled, and said, "I never tried to research anything like this before. It's a juicy question, though, and sure as hell a lot more interesting than booking little old ladies to Scottsdale, so I'll ask around. Maybe some people I know might know. Give me a couple of days and I'll see what I can find out about Playa de Plata."

I went on to the A & P and battled the gathering late-morning crowd to get a few things I needed, then went home to do some cooking. Zee would be arriving in just a few hours, and, if I knew anything about her appetite, she'd be ready to eat a raw kangaroo. I planned to serve something better.

Sherry and garlic flounder, in point of fact. It was actually a shrimp recipe, but I had flounder in the freezer, so I used that instead. Like a lot of terrific recipes, it was so simple you wondered why you hadn't thought of it yourself before you read about it somewhere.

I greased a shallow baking dish, and put a couple of fair-sized fillets in it, then mixed up a half cup or so of olive oil, about half as much dry sherry, three crunched garlic cloves, about a half teaspoon of thyme, maybe a quarter teaspoon of crushed red peppers, and a bit of salt. I poured the mixture over the filets and put the dish in the fridge. Nothing to it.

When cooking time came, I'd put the fish in a 400-degree oven for eight or ten minutes, just until the fish was tender, then serve it over rice, with some homemade white bread, a bottle of sauvignon blanc, and a garden salad. *Très* haute cuisine from the kitchen of J. W. Jackson.

Joshua said he might have a little taste, and I told him he could if he wanted to.

Then I vacuumed the house, put clean sheets on the bed, and did a washing. When the washing was done, I hung everything out on the line in the solar dryer. It was a beautiful day, and I was feeling good when the phone rang.

It was Joe Begay.

"I have something for you," said Begay. "I know some people who used to work for an outfit with interests over in Indonesia and thereabouts, where Carlson Bank and Trust has been doing business for lo these many years. My contacts know some old hands who were over there after the Big War, and those old hands know other people, and so on. You get the picture."

What outfit? What interests?

"I get the picture," I said, and Begay went on.

"One of the things people wanted to know in those days was whether Carlson B and T was tied with any of the governments we didn't like or with any of the criminal cartels that were getting started again after the war. Drugs, arms smuggling, piracy, money laundering. Stuff like that. Apparently it wasn't. People still keep an eye on the banks over there, of course, in case any of them have ties to, say, the export business out of the golden triangle. Carlson is clean as far as anybody can tell."

"Which means," I said, "that there's no evidence that Larry Ingalls ever had anything to do with the drug trade or any other sort of criminal activity that might have gotten him killed."

"Right with Eversharp. So, when I learned that, I asked some people over there about his private life. And guess what, he did have a private life. You ever hear of a place called Silver Sands?"

"No. What about it?"

"It's a private island off the coast of Sumatra. All one big luxury resort, no expense spared. One of several in different parts of the world run by the same outfit. Everything that money can buy and complete privacy guaranteed. The clientele is international: Asian, European, African, American, you name it. If you have the money and the right contacts, you can have your little bit of heaven on earth right there at Silver Sands, and go home a new man, ready to face the competition with a smile."

I caught the new-man bit. "What about new women?" I asked.

"Ah," said Begay. "There are women there, of course, and real beauties from what I'm told. But not many of them are customers.

Almost all of the paying guests are men. Big business types, mostly, who want to get away from it all. Some politicos, too, and a few sheiks and kings and the like. There are a few well-heeled women with particular sexual tastes who show up, too, but they're the exception. Charles Lodge Ingalls introduced his boy Lawrence to the place when it was just getting off the ground in the seventies, and Lawrence liked it so much that after he got out of the banking business, he went back there alone once a year or so for vacations."

It is a commonplace that some people prefer to have their sex with partners from races other than their own. The real or imagined exotic quality of such couplings gives them pleasure they can't otherwise achieve.

"So," I said, "Lawrence Ingalls and his father both liked Oriental women, and could pay for the best. They stayed straight at home, and did their cavorting abroad. Quinn told me as much, although he didn't know about this Silver Sands place in particular. The only unusual thing about Silver Sands seems to be the amount of money you need."

"Not quite," said Begay. "There are female prostitutes at Silver Sands, of course, but there are males there, too, so you can have one of them, if you like. But the house specialty is children. Boys and girls of any age you prefer. They're the real draw. Clients fly in from all around the world to visit them."

"Ah." If my brain had been a computer, it would have begun to hum and click.

Begay went on. "Silver Sands gets their kids from the parents, mostly. Poor people who need money so badly that they'll sell their children to whoever will pay the best price. Or sometimes the kids will sell themselves, because it's the only way they have to stay alive. It's a pretty common practice in any part of the world where there's a lot of poverty. All you have to do is read your *Globe* or *Herald* and you'll see the stories now and then. It's a kind of slave trade, and it goes on all the time, because there are terribly poor people all over the world and there's always a market for sex. The oldest profession, and all that.

"Now, in most of the brothels around the world, there's no such thing as safe sex; AIDS, for instance, is spreading in Asia and Africa like spilled milk. But Silver Sands is different. There, everybody you might want is clean, healthy, and well trained. You take your vacation at Silver Sands, you don't have to worry about taking HIV home with you. It's paradise, and worth every cent."

I had read those stories Begay had mentioned. The UN and other agencies were always trying to stop the international trade in women and children, but to no avail. There were too many poor people in the world, and too many people willing to buy or sell them. Besides, you didn't have to go to some Third World country to find boys and girls selling themselves on the streets. You could find it happening in any city in the United States. Both kids and adults without jobs doing what they thought was necessary to stay alive.

I thought of the sympathy Dostoyevsky so often showed for prostitutes in his stories. He portrayed them as poor girls given no choice as to how they had to earn money, as angels more than as sinners. He had less charity for their customers, or those who had driven them to the streets.

What went on between consenting adults didn't concern me, but I was prude enough to think that children shouldn't be used that way.

I said, "Are you telling me that old man Ingalls and Lawrence Ingalls both liked children? That they were pedophiles?"

"Not girls," said Begay. "Boys. Clean young boys. We don't approve of it over here in the U.S., but in other cultures it's not that unusual. I don't have to tell you that in some places men marry women so they can have children, but have boys for pleasure, and nobody thinks anything about it. If you called one of those men a pedophile, he'd say so what?"

Cultural ethics rearing its head once again. In the land of headhunters, hunting heads is not a sin.

"You're telling me that both Charles Lodge Ingalls and Lawrence Ingalls vacationed over there so they could have sex with boys?"

"I'm telling you that's what my sources tell me. And since the old man's still alive, I'd guess he still feels that way, although his sexual urges may have pretty much gone by now. He doesn't go abroad alone anymore, at least."

"And his wife doesn't know about it?"

"I don't know what his wife knows. Wives tend to know a lot about their husbands, and they keep a lot of it to themselves."

True. Like the cops and social workers and schoolteachers who know all the dark secrets of their towns and keep most of that knowledge to themselves, wives and husbands often know things about their spouses that they never tell anybody. And maybe it is just as well.

"Who runs Silver Sands?" I asked.

"An outfit called Paradise International, Limited, based in Bern. They run resorts all over the world. Not just the Silver Sands kind, either, although they own others like it. They have some resorts for families, some for swinging singles, some for athletic types, some on shipboard, all kinds. The only thing they all have in common is cost and quality. The best of everything but only for top dollar. No blue-haired widows in polyester on budget vacations. PI Limited is making regular deposits in those famous Swiss banks."

When I'm irked, my voice is sometimes faster than my brain. "Sumatra's part of Indonesia, isn't it? Even Indonesia must have laws against child prostitution. And Switzerland is supposed to be squeaky clean. How does the Paradise International outfit get away with running places like Silver Sands?"

Begay laughed a small laugh. "You were a cop. How do those things work in Boston?"

Touché. In Boston or anywhere else, enough money in the right hands can buy you a lot of freedom. Paradise International had enough money to buy blind official eyes in a cash-hungry Third World country like Indonesia, and Switzerland wasn't going to close down a hometown outfit that fed big and mostly legit bucks into its banks.

"Well, well," I said. "This is all very interesting. I just wonder if it has anything to do with Ingalls getting himself shot. You don't suppose some irate Indonesian finally tracked him down and knocked him off, do you?"

"No," said Begay, "I don't."

"Me, neither. One more thing, then. There's a resort in Costa Rica called Playa de Plata. Do you think some of your contacts with interests in that area of the world can find out something about the place?"

"I already know the name," said Begay. "Playa de Plata means 'silver sands' in Spanish, and is owned by Paradise International. PI has another place near Mozambique called Silberstrand. You want me to check that one out, too?"

"I don't know anything about Silberstrand," I said, "but Lawrence Ingalls went down to Playa de Plata between the time he stopped going over to Silver Sands and the time he built his house in Chilmark and stopped vacationing abroad."

"I can tell you that all three places cater to the same crowds," said Begay. "Megabucks clients, mostly male, but also the occasional woman who doesn't want to practice her private habits back home. You want particulars about Playa de Plata?"

It seemed to me I knew enough. It was tiring knowledge. "No, I guess not," I said. "But if you happen to find out that some mad Costa Rican had it in for your pal Larry Ingalls, let me know."

Begay sounded almost amused. "First, irate Indonesians, and now mad Costa Ricans, eh? Round up the usual suspects, Sergeant."

I hung up the phone and got myself a Sam Adams. The beer was cool and seemed to lave away some of the fatigue I'd felt after talking to Joe Begay. I checked on sleeping Joshua, then went out onto the porch and looked at the sea and sky. I began to feel as though there had been dust on my brain, but that the dust was now being washed away, like a shower cleans Edgartown after a dry spell in the summer, leaving the buildings fresh and white and the air pure.

It seemed to me that I could almost see the truth about Lawrence Ingalls's death. That, in fact, I already had the information I needed, but, still looking through a glass darkly, I knew only in part what later, face to face, I would know even as I was known.

When I next looked at my watch it was time to head for the airport, and Lawrence Ingalls fell right out of my mind.

I packed Joshua's traveling gear, and woke him up. He wasn't too happy about that, but when I told him his mom was coming home he perked up. I gave him a clean diaper, a powdered bottom, and a plug, and put him and his gear in the Land Cruiser. Ten minutes later we drove through the entrance of the County of Dukes County airport, where I had occasion to briefly muse once again on the matter of Dukes County not really being Dukes County at all, but instead being, officially, the County of Dukes County.

But this island idiosyncrasy, caused, I'd been told, by some casual error in some ancient official document, did not long occupy my mind. I had better things to think about. I drove in and parked, and Joshua and I walked past a waiting limo and on into the outdoor waiting area. Zee had been gone almost a week, going on several years.

The county airport on Martha's Vineyard has one of the seediest terminals on the East Coast, which some people think odd, considering the island's fame as a resort for the rich and famous. Compared with Nantucket's modern, airy terminal, the Vineyard's is a disaster, being old, beat-up, badly designed, and otherwise shabby and sadly out of date. Still, as might be expected on an island where all matters are passionately disputed by partisan factions, there are vociferous parties opposed to modernizing the terminal on the grounds that doing so would somehow serve to erode the already endangered character of the island. The pilots who use the airport are not included in this group, but are aligned with the pro–new terminal aficionados, whose voices are as loud as their opponents'.

Not being one who often flies, I was neutral on the subject. All I cared about was safety, and I didn't know whether a new terminal would affect that.

A dot appeared in the sky and grew larger. It became the plane from Boston, a flying cigar of the kind that airlines use to fly passengers into small airports away from the big cities. The cigar landed and taxied to the terminal. The propellers stopped turning and the door opened and passengers came out.

After a while, Zee emerged, and my heart thumped in my chest. Behind her came Drew Mondry, and behind him came a handsome woman followed by a girl who looked like the woman. Behind the girl came a beautiful man and a beautiful woman. Mondry's wife and child and the Hollywood stars, I guessed.

Zee saw us in the waiting area and came running. The three of us met in a flurry of hugs and kisses, with Zee and me trying not to squeeze Joshua too hard between us.

"Oh, it's good to be home!"

Drew Mondry, the handsome woman, the girl, and the two beautiful people came into the waiting area. Mondry came right to me. "Hi, J.W.!"

We shook hands, and he introduced me first to his wife, Emily, and their daughter,

Carly, then to Kate Ballinger, whose eyes flicked from my feet to my face, and whose handshake was a lingering one.

"Well," said Kate Ballinger in her famous sultry tones, "I see why Zee was in a hurry to get home."

"And this is Kevin Turner," said Drew.

Kate Ballinger's hand withdrew and was replaced with another. A manly hand this time, with a firm grip.

Kevin was so good-looking that he put handsome Drew quite in the shade. He was sun-bronzed and had bright blue eyes, and obviously kept himself very trim. He was sporting a dashing mustache, which, like his thick hair, was sun-bleached and reminded me of some actor I'd seen portraying George Armstrong Custer. Come to think of it, maybe the actor had been Kevin Turner.

Kevin had a melodious baritone voice with which he proclaimed his pleasure at finally meeting me even as his eyes kept straying to Zee.

Around us, people were starting to realize that they were in the presence of more than mere mortals, and were beginning to stare and whisper to one another.

"We'd better move along," said Drew. "You and Kate take the limo, Kevin. The driver knows where to go. I'll get the luggage and a cab, and Emily and Carly and I will be right along."

Kate and Kevin, obviously used to having awed eyes around them, bestowed smiles upon the whisperers and starers and slipped away.

The luggage came off the plane, and I gave Joshua to Zee and got her bag. Drew shook hands again. "I'll be in touch. I want to give you a job while we're here. Zee can tell you about it."

"Come on," said Zee, pulling on my arm.

"See you later, Zee," said Emily. "Nice to meet you, J.W."

"Nice to meet you," echoed Carly Mondry.

We walked out to the parking lot. There Zee almost hugged the Land Cruiser, then climbed in and took Joshua in her lap. When I got into the driver's seat, she pulled me to her and kissed me.

"Home, James," she said when we parted, breathless.

"Yes, ma'am."

I drove out of the airport. "You seem anxious to get away from your friends," I said. "The last time we talked on the phone you were having a great time."

"That was before I met Kevin Turner," she said. "Kevin Turner is an asshole!"

Zee rarely used such language, so I was impressed.

"Really?" I asked.

"Really," she said.

Joshua looked up at her. Really? he asked.

She held him in both hands and looked him in the eye. "Really," she repeated. "Really, really, really!"

That was a lot of reallies. Really.

I drove us home.

— 28 —

"He's just what I said he was," said Zee. "Kate's got an eye for men, goodness knows, but Kevin Turner really thinks he's God's gift to women. He even has that Errol Flynn mustache to perfect the image."

The sun was going down and we were on the balcony eating smoked bluefish pâté and cheese on crackers and drinking ice-cold Luksusowa martinis. Joshua was sitting in Zee's lap and listening to the conversation.

"Maybe Kate and Kevin should get together," I said. "They could feed on each other." I was feeling good.

"They may already be together," said Zee. "Part of the time, at least. But not all the time. I saw her ogling you."

"Women always ogle me," I said. "Surely you must have noticed it over the years. They can't help themselves. But I only ogle you."

"Sure you do, you liar. I've seen your head

almost come unscrewed when a pretty girl walked by."

"Never."

"Ha!"

"At least not since we got married."

"Ha, again!"

"Well, sometimes, maybe, but when it happens I'm just comparing them to you, sweets, and they always come up short."

"Yeah, yeah. Maybe I should buy you some blinders."

I gave her a kiss. "I'm already blinded by your beauty, dear. Besides, I haven't noticed that you've lost your eye for other men since we tied the knot."

She kissed me back. "Nonsense. My eyes are only for you. Officially, at least." She sipped her drink and put her head against my shoulder. "But you and I are just oglers. Kevin is a predator. He has a slick tongue and a thousand hands, and the worst thing is that women just fall all over him."

"It's a curse some of us suffer," I said. "The gals just won't leave us alone."

"Then you'd have understood the moves he put on me at Drew and Emily's party. I felt like Little Red Riding Hood at Grandma's house."

I felt an unmistakable evaporation of my good humor.

"Oh?"

"Yes, oh. He was on my case the whole evening. He doesn't know what no means."

"Is that a fact?" Kevin Turner's face appeared in my mind. He looked sleek and predatory.

"Yes, it's a fact," said Zee. "I'm just glad you weren't there."

I looked at her. "Why? It sounds to me like maybe I should have been."

"Because you might have gotten protective like you do sometimes, and I don't know what might have happened."

I thought I knew. "Protective?" I said. "Me?"

"Yes, you. But I can take care of myself, and I took care of Kevin."

"How?"

She grinned. "He told me I had a body made for breeding. I told him I was sorry the same couldn't be said for him. There was a small crowd listening."

I could see it happening. I smiled. "Good for you," I said. Then I had a happy thought. "But does putting the star in his place mean that he'll blackball you from this movie they're making?"

"Oh, no. In his private life, Kevin is the seven-letter word I said he was, but he's all pro when it comes to his work. They still want me in the movie, even though it's only a teeny part. Drew and Emily say that it can lead to better things."

Better things. "You mean bigger roles?"

"That's what they say."

Hmmmmm. I drank some martini. "What do you think of that idea?"

She shrugged. "I don't believe it, if you want to know the truth. But I don't know. I seem to photograph well, and they say that's important. And they say I can learn how to act. But it might mean I'd have to move out West and give up nursing, and I don't think I want to do either of those things. I don't know."

"Some people make a lot of money being actors. More than nurses make."

She pulled away from me. "I'm not a nurse because of the money."

I pulled her back. "I know."

She leaned against me. "I make as much money as I need. I won't take a job I don't like just so I can make more."

"Maybe you'll like being an actress," I said. "What are you going to be doing in this movie?"

"Not much, and I'll probably end up being the face on the cutting room floor. Wait here."

She put Joshua in my lap and trotted downstairs. When she came up again, she had a manuscript in her hand.

"Here," she said, giving it to me. "This is the script."

I had never seen a script before. This one was for *The Treasure Hunters*. I started reading it. It consisted of dialogue and rather cursory technical information about what the actors were doing and how the cameras were going to be used.

"Actually," said Zee, "it's not the final script, it's what I think they call a shooting script. They might change it a lot before they're through. I guess Jack Slade — he's going to be the director — has a reputation for doing that. Anyway, this is me."

She flipped through the script until she came to a character called Pirate Girl, who had one line: "This will buy you a night you'll never forget, Captain."

Zee smiled at me. "That's me. Pirate Girl. The scene is a dive on the waterfront back in the seventeen hundreds. I'm the girl the pirate captain — that's Kevin Turner, of course — chooses when he gets into port after capturing a Spanish galleon loaded with treasure from Peru. He tosses me a piece of eight, and after I bite it to make sure it's real gold, I promise him the night of his life."

"I've had a few of those with you, myself," I said. "And every one of them was worth at least one piece of eight."

"Which, now that you mention it, I never got," said Zee. She turned more pages. "And here I am again. Only this time I'm a modern girl sitting in a modern bar. The modern treasure hunter, Kevin again, who just might be the descendant of the old-time pirate captain, sees me and flashes back to the Pirate Girl scene. And I have two other teeny scenes: modern girl passing and eyeing modern Kevin on the modern street, and pirate girl passing and eyeing pirate Kevin on the pirate street. That's it. That's my whole bit. Four scenes."

"It's enough," I said. "Academy Award for best supporting actress."

"We can put it up there on the mantel, right beside your dad's best decoy. Anyway, that's how the movie's being done. The modern treasure hunters are after the gold the old-time pirate buried somewhere, and the guy leading the expedition has these flashbacks. All the actors play double roles: modern ones and eighteenth-century ones. The idea is to parallel modern swashbuckling and skullduggery with old-time swashbuckling and skullduggery."

"A fable for our times."

"Well, actually it's more a vehicle for Kevin and Kate. And Jack Slade's movies may make a lot of money, but they aren't famous for intellectual content, I'm told." She grinned at me. "The same can be said for Kevin, of course, but that doesn't keep him from being a star."

"I've always suspected that it was my lofty mind that kept me from being a leading man, and now I know. You'll be the exception to the rule: a beauty who is also a brain."

"Not all stars are dumb," said Zee. "It just happens that Kevin isn't too bright. As for you, it wasn't your mind that attracted me; my eyes never got above your belt. Didn't I ever tell you that?"

"Remember what you're learning about women, Josh," I said. "This information could prove invaluable to you in about fifteen years."

I gave him to his mother and went downstairs to fix supper.

Later, when Joshua was finally asleep after the excitement of seeing Mom come home, I added another IOU to my pieces of eight debt, and Zee and I afterward lay wound in each other's arms feeling musky and satisfied.

"What does Drew have in mind for me?" I asked. "He mentioned a job."

"I think he wants you for local knowledge. As a driver who knows where places are. Or as somebody who knows where to find things they might need when they begin shooting. Materials for a scene, maybe. You might like it. It would be something different for you."

"That it would." And I could use the money.

"Kevin and Kate will be vacationing for the next few days, but other people will be coming in all week and Drew will be working with them. Props people and electricians and lawyers —"

"Lawyers?"

"They haven't killed them all yet, in spite of Dick the Butcher's advice. There are contracts to sign, like one with John and Mattie Skye for the use of their farm, and with other people for other places they might use, and where there are contracts, there are lawyers."

"I get the picture. And since movies also mean fame and money, there are people who'll want to sue the company for one thing or another if they think they can get away with it. So that means the movie outfit always needs lawyers to joust with the other people's lawyers."

"Just like in real life," said Zee. "Anyway, Jack Slade will be coming in next week, and the camera people will be coming in, and the other working stiffs will be coming in, and all of them will be getting things ready so when it comes time to start shooting, there won't be any delays, because delays cost money and location shooting costs money, anyway. Which reminds me . . ."

"What?"

"They'll shoot the modern scenes here on the island, including the ones of me in the modern bar and on the modern street. But a lot of the scenes about the old-time pirate will be shot in Hollywood on a sound stage. That means I'll have to go out there again."

I looked at the ceiling. "Ah."

"It shouldn't take long. But if you don't want me to do it, I'll tell them to forget the whole thing." She snuggled closer. "If I have to choose between them and you and Joshua, I choose you and Joshua. No contest."

I held her close, filled with contradictory feelings. "No problem," I said. "You don't have to choose."

Early the next morning the three of us went into Edgartown to the Dock Street Coffee Shop to celebrate Zee's return. We had high-cholesterol breakfasts: juice, coffee, fried eggs with buttered toast and sausage. Delish!

The regulars were glad to see Zee, and told her extravagant stories about my behavior during her absence. She said she believed them all, but that she'd soon have me straightened out, now that she was home. From his pack on my back, Joshua listened to every word. No one said a thing about the late Lawrence Ingalls.

Out on docks where the charter boats load and unload, we eyed the *Shirley J.* and decided, it being a fine August day, and maybe the last free one we'd have for a while if Drew Mondry really did plan to hire me, we should go for a sail.

So we did that, beating first down-harbor through the anchored boats and on through the narrows into Katama Bay, then coming back and going outside past the lighthouse and over to Cape Pogue Pond, where we anchored for lunch down by the south shore.

There, while Joshua and Zee enjoyed the beach, I waded out and raked for the giant quahogs that live in the pond just offshore from the little boathouse there. They are the biggest quahogs I've ever seen, but they're deep in the seaweed and there aren't many of them, so they're hard to find. I once got seven and they were so big that the seventh sank the little floating basket I was using; today, though, it was all hunting and no finding.

No matter, while I had waded and raked, I'd used the time to think about several things.

We packed up and sailed back through a falling wind just in time to catch the last of the rising tide, which carried us and the other returning boats past the On Time ferry and into Edgartown Harbor.

We ghosted up to our stake on the last whisper of wind, dropped sail and made everything fast, and went ashore. There, who should we meet but the chief, who had spotted us coming in and had driven his cruiser down the Reading Room dock, where we kept our dinghy.

"Purely a chance meeting," he said, puffing on the pipe he had just lit up. "Thought you might be interested in knowing that even Officer Olive Otero no longer believes you bumped off Ingalls. She can't figure any way for you to have gotten your hands on the murder weapon, so you're off her list."

"Well, good for Officer Otero," I said. "Now who does she think did it?"

"I believe that Moonbeam is currently the favorite candidate," said the chief. "And since you're now officially as pure as driven snow, I'm letting that word leak out to the locals. With luck, most of the ones who've been avoiding you will stop doing that, and the others will quit congratulating you for knocking him off."

"Thanks," I said. "I probably shouldn't give a damn about what any of them think, but I do."

"Like most people would," said the chief. "It's that decent respect for the opinions of mankind that the Declaration talks about. The people who don't have it are the ones who keep guys like me in business. You were a cop. You know what I mean. Hello, there, Joshua. Nice to see you home again, Mrs. Jackson. I hear you're going to be a movie star."

Zee was surprised. "Who told you that?"

He waved his pipe. "No secrets can be kept from us minions of the law."

"All right, then," I said, "who kacked Lawrence Ingalls?"

"Well, maybe there are a few things we aren't absolutely sure about yet," he replied. "That's one of them. But we'll figure that one out, too." He looked at Zee. "As for your career on the silver screen, this movie outfit has been in touch with us hick cops about security. A guy named Mondry mentioned you as local talent."

"Oh," said Zee. "Well, don't worry. I'll still speak to you little people after I'm famous, because I'll never forget my roots. What was your name again?"

The chief drove away, and we went home.

Not much later, Drew Mondry called and asked me to go to work for him the next day.

He mentioned a salary rare on Martha's Vine-yard.

I said I would. The money was reason enough, but I had others.

— 29 —

Cassiopeia Films got down to work the week after Labor Day, when the island was largely emptied of its summer people, most of whom had gone home so the kids could go back to school or who had otherwise used up their vacation time and had taken their August tans back over the sound to America. A slightly higher than average proportion of tourists lingered on this year because of the movie makers. They wanted to watch celebrities and maybe even be lucky enough to be extras. Zee arranged her schedule at the emergency room so she could be home while I was working, and I made sure that I'd have time off to take care of Joshua when the film crew shot her scenes.

There were a lot of people involved in making the movie, and many of them had titles that I never did get straight. Grips did all sorts of handyman work, especially when cameras were being set up. The best ones I saw had strong backs and quick minds. There were also carpenters and painters and set decorators and various wardrobe people, all of whom more or less did what you'd think people with those titles would do. And there were propmen, and there was a special propman called a greensman who only did plants, and since the Skye twins' horses were going to be in the background of some of the shots on John and Mattie's farm, there was a wrangler in charge of them. And there were drivers, of which I was one when I wasn't doing other things, who drove people around, and there were people who turned out to be a stuntman and a stuntwoman for a fight scene I never saw.

No matter what the job, everybody seemed to belong to one union or another, which was in itself something different for largely un-unionized Martha's Vineyard.

There were doubles for Kevin and Kate and other actors, and there was a fencing master who coached Kevin and the other sword fighters and created a sort of ballet for them to dance while they were supposedly fighting, so no one would get hurt. John Skye, long-ago undergraduate three-weapon man, was fascinated and appalled by the movie combat. On the one hand, he claimed that anybody who actually tried to fight with swords that way would be dead in about thirty seconds, but on the other he had to admit that it looked like a lot more fun than the competitive fencing he'd done in college.

All in all the whole operation seemed like chaos to me. I never did get everybody and everything figured out, and finally stopped trying.

Since there were both interior and exterior scenes to be shot at John and Mattie's farm, the Skyes were obliged to abandon their house and find quarters elsewhere. In partial thanks for this, Drew Mondry, true to his word, made sure, to the total delight of the twins, that they and their mother got work as extras. The twins' real problem had been to talk Mattie and John into letting them sacrifice the beginning of school for the sake of their future careers as stars, but somehow the girls, great cajolers, had managed to do that. John himself, on the other hand, could not avoid going to work at Weststock College, but made it back for long weekends.

The lines of eager local would-be extras were so long that the island high school gym was taken over on a Sunday so that the decision makers could, in their to-me-mysterious wisdom, make their choices about which of the local wannabes would actually be hired. The fortunate elect were as joyful as their less successful competitors were blue.

Zee, who had learned that she would be obliged to join the union because of her one line of dialogue, was not required to go through this process, of course, but she thought that I should.

"You really should," she said to me while making kissy faces at Joshua, who was on her knee smiling up at her. "I think you'd have fun."

"I don't see a lot of people in the business who seem to be having lots of fun," I said. "Fun is a bluefish blitz."

"You look like somebody who lives on Martha's Vineyard," said Zee. "They need people like you for ambiance."

"Ambiance, schmambiance. One star in the family is enough. I'm a behind-the-scenes kind of guy, and I don't expect that to last much longer."

"Maybe I should take Joshua down and have him screen-tested. He's definitely the best baby on the island and maybe in the whole world! Yes, you are, Joshua!" She and her son beamed at each other.

"You can take him down if you want to," I said, "but if he gets a job, all the other moms will be jealous and think it's just nepotism."

"They're already jealous, aren't they, Joshua! Because you're the cutest baby anybody's ever seen!"

Joshua grinned toothless agreement, and she gave him a big kiss.

Good grief, what a pair.

My principal value was as a local guy who knew how to take people places they wanted to go, and where to find stuff people suddenly discovered they needed. I knew where the hardware stores and the lumberyards were, where catering outfits could be found, who to contact in case some Cassiopeia bigwig wanted to use a piece of property or equipment that hadn't previously been leased, or in case some emergency came up, as they regularly seemed to do.

I mostly worked for Drew Mondry, but sometimes got loaned out to somebody else who needed wheels or local knowledge. I drove people around to look at the sites Mondry and I had surveyed earlier, picked people up here and delivered them there, and in general made a good salary doing nothing very hard.

I met a lot of people imported from California and grew to like many of them in that casual way you meet and enjoy people you know you won't be with very long. Most of them were working stiffs who never got in front of a camera or wanted to, and I ended up introducing the beer-drinking component of that group to the Fireside, in Oak Bluffs, where they could have an end-of-the-day brew in casual, to say the least, surroundings. The higher-toned drinkers found their way to the classier watering holes.

One person who was not a working stiff also came to the Fireside. Kate Ballinger didn't seem like the type who would favor the place, which was rich with the odor of stale beer and the muted fragrance of marijuana, and was the traditional site of the occasional barroom brawls that spiced up Vineyard nightlife. She seemed more the snazzy inn type or the Navigator Room type, but on the second night that some other workers and I were in the Fireside, Kate Ballinger appeared in the door, looked around, and came right over.

The noise of the saloon fell off as eyes followed her across the room. Even Bonzo, who decades before had reputedly blown out a promising mind on bad acid and was rarely excited about anything but fishing and listening to birds, paused, bar rag in hand, and looked at her, wide in both eyes and mouth. Kate Ballinger was the prettiest thing to enter the Fireside since Zee had brought Joshua in to show him off to the regulars.

She smiled and said, "Hi, guys. Mind if I join you?" and sat down beside me at the bar. She looked at the bartender and flicked a finger toward my Sam Adams. "I'll have what he's having," she said.

The bartender pulled himself together and put a bottle and glass in front of her. She poured and sipped.

"Good beer," she said.

The crew members were the only unimpressed people in the room. They had seen too many movie stars to be awed by another one. They lifted their glasses and bottles and said, "How you doin'?" and "Cheers," and continued with their talk. Some of them looked with blank faces at her and then at me and only then continued with their talk.

"Good beer," she said again, taking another sip so small that you knew beer, even a fine one like Sam Adams, was not her usual drink. Then she touched her glass to mine. "Cheers," she said. "How are things going, J.W.?"

"I'm the last person you should ask," I said. "I don't have any idea what's going on."

She laughed. "I could say the same for some of the directors I've worked with. How's that pretty wife of yours?"

"I'll know in about fifteen minutes," I said.

"Oh." She tipped her head to one side, and gave me a smile I recognized from some movie I'd seen her in. "You're not staying around for another drink or two?"

It had been a seductive smile in the movie

and it had worked. Now, in real life, I could understand why it had.

I looked at my glass. It was almost empty. I still felt thirsty.

"I think this will do it for me," I said. "Zee'll have a martini and supper waiting for me. I'm about ready for both."

She arched a brow. "Ah. And when you're at home and your wife is working, do you have a martini and supper waiting for her?"

"It's sort of a rule at our place," I said. "Whoever is home looks after Joshua, does the cooking, and has the martinis waiting in the freezer."

"I see. And when you're the one at home, you do all that."

"Yeah."

She drew circles with her finger in a bit of spilled beer on the bar between us, and her hand brushed mine. "When I first met your wife out in California, she told me you were quite a guy. I can see why she thinks so." Her smile was dazzling.

"I plan to keep on fooling her as long as I can," I said. I finished my beer and slid off the stool.

"You're really leaving, then? Oh, dear. I can't charm you into having another drink so we can talk?"

The Scots have a word for it: glamour. It's a

magic spell or charm, an elusive allure. When you *cast the glamour,* you cast an enchantment. Kate Ballinger could do it, and knew it.

Zee could do it, but didn't know it. I put her face in front of Kate Ballinger's. "I have places to go, things to do, and people to see," I said as lightly as I could, and I walked away.

"See you tomorrow on the set, then," said Kate Ballinger's voice.

I raised a hand in reply and went out the door. On Circuit Avenue the air felt clean. I got into the Land Cruiser and went home. Zee met me at the door. She had never looked better. I put my arms around her and gave her a kiss. Finally she pushed herself away and looked up at me, grinning.

"Wow! Maybe I'll stay home every day!"

"I'll stay with you."

She studied me with her great, dark eyes. "The vodka is in the freezer, and the pâté and cheese and crackers are in the fridge. You grab them and I'll grab the man-child and we'll meet on the balcony and you can tell me all about your day on the set."

We went up and sat drinking and looking out over the garden and the far waters, where the last of the evening sailboats were coming in on the falling wind.

I told her about my day, including the part about Kate Ballinger.

"She has her eye on you," said Zee. "She likes conquests, and she's had a lot of them."

"I can believe that last part," I said.

"You can believe the first part, too," said Zee in the silky voice she sometimes used when talking about other women.

"I've already been conquested," I said. "By you. That's enough for me."

"You probably don't have much say in this," said Zee. "Women who seduce men don't ask their permission first."

"Is that why you never asked me? No wonder I was so easy."

She leaned over Joshua. "Is it all right with you if I give your father a kick? No? Well, okay. I won't do it this time, but next time he might not be so lucky."

Joshua blew a bubble. I owed him and he knew it. I decided it would be smart to change the subject, so I asked Zee about her day at home.

"I picked two acorn squash, did a clothes wash, had a chat with Toni Begay, and went shooting with Manny for an hour just before you got home. I put Joshua on his beach chair and put plugs in his ears and mufflers over the plugs and I let him watch, and he didn't cry at all."

"Like mother, like son. Gunslinging is in his blood, just like in yours."

"I don't know about that, but he was really good. Manny and I are going to be doing a lot of practice in the next few weeks, so it's good that the noise doesn't bother him."

"After this movie business is over, I'll be home to take care of him, and you won't need to take him down to the range."

"Another thing. You got some phone calls. One from Petunia Slocum down at Edgartown Travel, and one from Quinn. You're supposed to call them back. And Toni Begay told me that Joe wants you to call him. You're a really popular guy. What's going on?"

I told her what I knew and what I guessed about Lawrence Ingalls, and about my talk with the chief, and about what I'd asked of Petunia, Quinn, and Joe Begay.

"Well, well," said nurse Zee, for whom few human foibles were surprises, since she'd dealt with their consequences in more than one hospital.

"Well, well, indeed," I agreed. "I'll be interested to hear what they've learned, if anything."

"I'll get at supper, then," said Zee, finishing her drink and getting up. "You can make phone calls while I finish the cooking. Come on, Joshua, we're headed downstairs."

Petunia seemed most shocked by what

she'd learned. Being in the travel business, she had, of course, heard rumors of very private resorts such as Playa de Plata, but until now she hadn't actually known they existed, or that they catered so particularly to the tastes of their clients.

"Heavens to Betsy," she said. "Who'd have thunk it? What an innocent little country girl I have been."

"Maybe you should do some advertising in the *Times* and the *Gazette*," I said. "You might end up doing some very profitable business. There are probably a lot of rich, kinky people who come to this island, and they might like to do their travel business with a local, close-mouthed gal like yourself."

"I'll give it some thought," said Petunia, "as soon as I get my eyeballs pushed back in my head."

Quinn and Joe Begay were not so astonished. Their inquiries had carried them to the same information, but it was not surprising to them. Their work, like Zee's, had put them in contact with such a variety of human activities that very little shocked them anymore.

"And now what?" asked Joe Begay, as Zee called that supper was ready. "We know that Larry Ingalls liked boys and that he took his vacations in places where he could find them. What else do you need to know?"

"If you can come up with the name of the guy who killed him, that would help."

He laughed. "There are a lot of retired spooks living on this island. I know some of them. Shall I put out an SOS for bored agents willing to work for nothing?"

"Do that."

"I'll give it some thought. But don't hold your breath, buddy. These guys all worked for Uncle Sam, remember. Fast solutions to problems weren't their specialty."

"Nothing is simple anymore. Where's Holmes when we really need him?"

"I think he's still keeping bees on the Sussex Downs. But Sherlock is getting a little long in the tooth and may not want to pop over to the Vineyard. We'll probably have to handle this case ourselves."

He hung up and I went into supper, where I told Zee what my phone calls had brought me. As I was washing up the dishes, thinking things over, the phone rang again, and Zee answered it in the living room. After a minute, she came back into the kitchen.

"It's Kevin Turner. He wants to know if we'll join him for a drink at the Harborview."

"I think I'll pass," I said.

"Kate Ballinger is there, too, he says. She must be barhopping." Zee raised an eyebrow.

"I think I'll stay passed."

"Actually, I think he just wants me to join him," said Zee.

Was my pause as long as it seemed? "It might be fun for you," I said. "You've been home all day. If you'd like to go, go."

She went back into the living room and I heard her say thanks, but not tonight. Later, maybe.

She came back into the kitchen. She was whistling. She took my arm and hugged it.

The next morning when I went to work, Drew Mondry had some news for me.

"Kate Ballinger's decided she needs a private driver. She's selected you for the job."

"I thought I was working for you."

"And I'm working for Cassiopeia Films and Kate's their star. Who do you think swings the most weight? Sorry, J.W."

— 30 —

Drew wasn't happy. I wasn't sure whether I was happy or not, but unlike Drew, I had some choices.

I thought about all of the money that was being spent on *The Treasure Hunters*, and how much more was going to be spent.

"How long do you guys expect to be shooting down here?" I asked.

Drew cocked his head to one side. "Two weeks. Maybe three. Why?"

That was longer than I'd been in Vietnam. "What if I don't want to be Kate's private chauffeur?"

Drew was uneasy. "I hope you won't decide that, J.W."

"What would happen?"

He took a deep breath. "You'd get fired."

"By you?"

He shrugged and nodded. "I hired you, I'd fire you. I'm sorry. But if I didn't fire you, they'd fire me, and I can't afford that."

"Star power, eh?"

"Yeah. Look, I don't blame you for being mad —"

"I'm not mad," I said. "Not at you, not at anybody. You don't owe me anything. You didn't have to give me this job, and I didn't have to take it. It was just a deal we both agreed to: you'd give me money and I'd work for you. Now the deal's over, that's all."

"I'm glad you feel that way. I —"

I interrupted him. "I'll tell you what I'll do. I'll drive Kate Ballinger around while she's here, but it'll cost you a lot more money than I'm getting now." I named an extravagant figure, and his eyes widened. "And a couple of other things: I won't drive her anywhere before seven in the morning or after five in the afternoon unless the shooting schedule makes it necessary, and I wear my own clothes and not those chauffeur clothes I see some of the other drivers wearing. That's the deal. If you take it, fine. If you don't, no hard feelings and I'm bound to East Beach to do some bonito fishing."

A grin wriggled its way onto Drew's face. "You've got a lot of gall! So you'd quit, eh?"

"Here on the Vineyard, if somebody isn't on a job anymore, we say he got through. Nobody gets blamed; the guy didn't quit, and he didn't get fired, he just got through. I'll get through working for Cassiopeia Films if your bosses don't like the deal I just offered."

His grin got bigger. "You'll just get through, eh? I like it. Stay right here. I'll talk to some people."

He went away and I watched things happening for a pretty long time. We were at John and Mattie's place, and the crew was setting up a scene by the front door.

After a while Drew came back.

"You're not through yet," he said, smiling. "Come on, I'll show you Kate's personal car."

We strolled toward a clump of parked cars parked in a meadow beside the driveway.

"You have to do any serious arguing?" I asked.

"I did until Kate said it was a deal. After that, it was no problem." He pointed to twin, fair-sized house trailers parked by the barn. "That's Kevin's dressing room and that's Kate's. They had to get identical ones so neither nose would be out of joint. Kate's in hers right now, waiting for you."

"I'm just her driver. I'll wait with the car."

"You're a hard case." He laughed.

The car was a new Ford Explorer. I was surprised, because I'd expected a Porsche or BMW or something sporty like Kevin drove. The keys were in the ignition. Maybe they didn't have thieves in Hollywood.

Drew shook my hand, said he was glad I was still around, and went away. I got into the Explorer and spent some time figuring how everything worked. It was the newest vehicle I'd been in for several years, including the Range Rover I'd driven for Drew. Four-by-fours are a lot plusher these days than they were when my old Land Cruiser had come off the line.

"Hi," said a feminine voice. The face that went with it was Kate Ballinger's. I got out of the car, and she put her hand in mine and left it there a moment. "I'm really pleased that you've agreed to be my driver, Jeff," said Kate, looking at me with her magic eyes. "I want to go everywhere on the island and see everything. Do you mind if I call you Jeff?"

"Most people call me J.W., but Jeff's okay."

Her eyes moved down over me, then came back up. "I thought maybe your wife was the only person who called you that. I wouldn't want to intrude."

"You won't be intruding," I said.

"I have to be here all morning. After that I should be free. Would you care to have lunch with me? I thought you might know a good place for us to eat, and that afterward you could take me on a tour."

"I can take you wherever you want to go," I said.

"I'll bet that you can, at that." Her smile was feline. "I'll meet you at my trailer when I'm through here."

"How will I know when you're through?"

"The guys will all stop work and start eating lunch out of boxes. Ciao."

"Isn't that some kind of pug-faced dog?"

She laughed and walked away. She had great hips, and knew it.

Since I was getting paid for doing nothing, I watched the scene in front of the house being shot and then shot a couple more times. Kate, the heroine, and Kevin, the hero, approached the house when suddenly the door was thrown open in front of them and Martin Paisley, the actor playing Neville Black, the brains behind the caper, displayed excitement on his face and waved his arms, encouraging them to hurry. Kate and Kevin exchanged looks and hustled into the house. Obviously Martin had some important news.

Then Jack Slade, the director, had the greensman and his assistant move a bush, and the light guys change some lights, even though the sun was bright, and shot the whole thing again.

Then a camera was moved and there were more adjustments, and the scene was shot a third time, which apparently was the charm, since Slade was satisfied.

The actors' mouths had moved, so I knew there was dialogue, but I was too far away to hear it. When I considered the time and the cost of the talent it took to shoot that one insignificant shot, I began to realize why it took so much money to make a movie, and why my new salary was really no big deal, except on principle.

Just before one o'clock, work stopped and people went over to where the caterers had lunch boxes and soft drinks waiting. Kevin and Kate headed for their house trailers, and I followed Kate. She looked back and waved, then went into the trailer.

I leaned on the wall beside the door, and she came back out in less time than I expected. She had new makeup on her face, and had changed into a denim shirt, ivory-colored shorts that matched her hair, and sandals. She took my arm and smiled her mystic smile. *La belle dame sans merci.*

"Come on, Jeff," she said, pulling me toward the Explorer. "I'm starving! Get me out of here before they put me back to work!"

Eyes followed us to the parking lot. I got behind the steering wheel and she sat beside me.

"What do you like to eat?" I asked. "High-brow, low-brow, or middle-brow?"

"You decide. Then you can show me the island."

I wanted beer with my lunch, so I took her into Edgartown and found a parking place on North Water Street, up toward the Harborview. We walked back to the Navigator Room, which not only offers good food, but serves it up with Edgartown's best view of the harbor. People looked at Kate, but couldn't be sure it was really her because of me. I didn't look like a bodyguard or anyone else who should have been with Kate Ballinger, so probably it wasn't Kate Ballinger at all. But it sure looked like her.

The Navigator Room was mobbed, but Arthur was leaning against a support post when we came in, so I took Kate over to him and said, "Arthur, do you have a table for two? For a quiet lunch?"

Arthur recognized Kate immediately, but he had met celebrities for decades, and was unimpressed by their fame. He was, however, sympathetic to their occasional need for a tad of special consideration to compensate for the lack of privacy that is a product of that fame.

He looked around the room. On the far side, near a window, a busboy was clearing a table. Arthur raised a forefinger, and a waitress appeared. He murmured to her and pointed a finger at me. She nodded, then turned and smiled at me.

"Follow me, please."

"Thanks," I said to Arthur.

"You owe me a fresh bluefish," said Arthur. "Enjoy your lunch."

We sat by the window and the waitress took our order: beer and a burger for me, salad and white wine for Kate. We looked out at the yacht club and the boats. I pointed out the *Shirley J.* swinging at her stake.

"What a cute little boat," said Kate.

"Catboats are pretty, not cute," I said.

While she decided to let that pass, she glanced around the room, wearing her famous smile for everyone who happened to be looking toward her. A lot of people were. At other tables, I saw customers catch that smile, look again, then lean toward each other and speak, then look at her again. "I think this is where we'll be shooting the bar scenes," she said. "Do you come here often?"

"Sometimes. Zee and I do most of our socializing at home alone."

"How nice."

Our drinks came and she touched her glass to mine.

"Thank you for being my driver."

"Thank you for the salary. I can use it."

She pretended to pout. "Oh, dear. I was hoping that you were doing it for me, not just for money. I hoped that we could be friends."

"Maybe we can."

She touched my hand. "Oh, good. I don't meet many men like you. Your wife is a lucky woman."

I used the hand to lift my glass to my mouth.

"I'm the lucky one."

When my hand returned to the table, hers was waiting for it. "Zee is a really beautiful woman. And your little boy is so sweet! You're right. You are a lucky man." She paused. "She doesn't mind you working for me, I hope."

"She doesn't know about it yet."

Something changed in her. A thinly hidden feral quality appeared in her eyes and body, as though a lioness had emerged from her den and spotted her prey.

"Ah. I hope she won't be unhappy."

"Why should she be?"

Her hooded eyes beamed at me, and I felt the power of her charm. "Oh, it's so good to find two people as loving and trusting as you and Zee. It's so rare these days. I never meet people like you anymore. I know we're going to be friends!"

Our food arrived just in time, and I scarfed mine down while she picked at hers. I waved for the bill and for once got immediate attention, just like the heroes in movies. It was clear that our waitress had been watching us. When she brought the tab, I pointed to Kate.

"Her treat."

Kate looked surprised, but recovered quickly, dug out her card, and handed it to the waitress, who hurried away.

"My treat?" she asked, leaning forward. "I thought the gentleman always paid."

"I'm just the chauffeur," I said.

She didn't take long to think that one through. "Well, you're a gentleman as far as I'm concerned, and in the future I'd really like to have you pay. It looks so much better, don't you think? Then I'll pay you back, of course."

"Where would you like to drive?" I asked.

"You will pay the bills from now on, won't you? I'll give you the money ahead of time, if you like."

"I give two island tours," I said, and described the two-wheel-drive tour and the four-wheel-drive tour. "We can do either one."

The waitress came back and Kate not only signed the chit but, when the awed girl requested her autograph, gave her that as well.

"Are you telling me that you won't even pretend to pay our bills?" Her eyes had a deep light in them. It looked like anger to me.

I finished my beer and touched her hand with mine. "Whenever I invite you to lunch, Miss Ballinger, I'll pick up the tab."

I climbed out of my chair. She looked up at me from under lowered brows, then surprised me by suddenly laughing.

"I knew I'd like you, Jeff! Please call me Kate. I know we're going to be friends!"

She stood, and I followed her out to the street. Arthur waved and arched a brow as we went by.

"So she's sure you're going to be friends," said Zee. "How nice."

"She's sweet. I think she wanted to hold my hand."

"I think Kevin wants to hold more of me than that. He called again while you and Kate were off in Gay Head or wherever it was you went."

"It was Gay Head. We did the two-wheel-drive tour. Tomorrow she wants me to take her out to Cape Pogue. Apparently Drew has given the Chappy beaches rave reviews."

"She just wants you out there alone where nobody can see her jump your bones."

I bounced Joshua on my knee and bitty-bum-bitty-bummed a bit of the "William Tell Overture" for mood music. Joshua thought galloping was great, and grinned and drooled.

Zee sipped her martini and smiled at her men. "While you're out on the beach, Kevin wants to take me to lunch. The next day we're shooting the Main Street scene, and he says he wants to talk with me about it."

"The Main Street scene is the one where the modern hero sees the modern girl and has a flashback to the old days when the pirate saw the pirate girl. Is that right?"

"That's it. In the script I walk past him, turn my head and give him a casual smile, and walk on. I don't think there's much for Kevin to explain."

"I'd lie about my motives, too, if it got me close to you."

"You're already close to me. Kevin just doesn't give up very easily. He has a concrete confidence in his charm. I thought I'd cooled his jets in California, but here he is, back at the hunt."

"You want me to punch his lights out?"

"Good grief, no! Besides, he might punch your lights out. No, I think I can handle Mr. Turner without any help. The thing I'm not so sure of is if you can handle Kate Ballinger all by yourself."

"O ye of little faith. I'm impervious to all charms but yours."

"Pardon my rolling eyes. Here, have some pâté."

I took the cracker and ate it. Delish.

"I think I'll take the day off and watch when you do your scene," I said. "In case you end up on the cutting room floor, I want to be able to testify in my memoirs that you actually did have a film career."

"What if Kate wants you to be her friend some more? Maybe she'll fire you."

"Break my heart. Besides, if she fires me, I'll quit. Then who'd drive her around?"

"I'm sure she can find some man to do the job."

I thought Zee was right about that. "Besides," I said, "if you're going to be working, I'll be taking care of Joshua. So I can't be chauffeuring beautiful, sexy movie goddesses around, even if I want to."

"Which, of course, you don't. Did I tell you I met the chief downtown? I was coming out of the A & P, and he was there talking with that new traffic cop they've got trying to keep the traffic jam from jamming. Guess what? Connie Berube has officially reported that Moonbeam is missing. I think it's an historic first. She's thrown him out of the house before, but she never asked anybody to look for him until now."

Joshua yawned and simultaneously wet his pants. Had that ever happened to the Lone Ranger? We went downstairs, where Zee got to work in the kitchen and I got to work on Joshua, changing him and putting him into his playpen, where he soon began to snooze in spite of his efforts not to. Later, as I stacked the last of the dishes in the drainer, Zee sidled up and put her arms around me, pressing her front against my back.

"I don't like other women making a play for my man."

"They just can't help themselves," I said. "You have to forgive them."

She gave me a sharp squeeze. "I'm serious."

I thought about how I felt when men ogled her. "I'll tell her to quit tomorrow," I said.

She turned me around. "No. I'm your wife, but I'm not your keeper. But she's a witch, and her spells are the man-catching kind, so be careful." She put her arms up around my neck and pulled my lips down to hers. Her tongue was like a fire. Kate Ballinger wasn't the only witch on the island.

"Stay here," I said.

I went into the living room, picked up comatose Joshua, and put him into his bed. Then I came back into the kitchen, picked up Zee, and carried her to ours.

The next morning I took Kate Ballinger on the four-wheel-drive tour.

She was staying in a house owned by a famous pop singer who lived up off Lambert's Cove Road, and as I parked the Land Cruiser and walked to the Explorer, I had occasion once again to wonder how all these famous people happened to know one another. Not many of the island's more renowned visitors had ever asked to stay at our place, that was for sure.

Kate was again decked out in shirt, shorts, and sandals, and this time was carrying a basket and a canvas bag.

"Good morning, Jeff! The caterers packed us a lunch, and I brought along beach towels. What a lovely day!"

I opened her door for her and she took the opportunity to give me a fast kiss. Then she put her gear into the Explorer and climbed in after it. I got behind the wheel and we headed for Katama.

"The only thing wrong with this car is these damned bucket seats," said Kate, giving me her enthralling smile. "If we were lovers, it would be really frustrating to have to sit this far apart."

"It's an imperfect world."

"Maybe we could both sit in the backseat and you could drive with your feet."

I laughed at her unexpected humor, and felt some ice thaw inside of me. Uh oh.

Kate crossed her long legs and they caught my eye. She grinned at me. She wore pale lipstick, and her eyelashes were long and her eyelids slightly lowered.

"I can hardly wait to see these beaches Drew Mondry was so wild about," she purred. "He says there are almost no people out there at all."

"Fishermen, mostly," I said. "More blue-fish are coming back south, and there are bass and bonito and Spanish mackerel."

"You're a fisherman."

"I am."

"Are you a hunter, too?"

"Not as much as I used to be."

"Are you a good shot?"

"Not as good as my wife."

"Really?"

"Really. I'm probably as good with a rifle or shotgun, but she can shoot rings around me with a pistol."

"How fascinating. My husband doesn't do any of those things. He's an executive. He plays golf and tennis. They bore me, I'm afraid."

"I didn't know you had a husband."

"He doesn't travel with me. He stays home and makes money."

"When he isn't playing golf or tennis."

"That's right. Could I learn to shoot? That sounds like it might be fun. Skeet. Isn't that what they shoot?"

"That's one of the things."

We came to the end of the Katama Road,

and I stopped beside the deputy sheriff's pickup. He came over as I rolled down the window.

"New truck, J.W.? You win the lottery or something?"

"It belongs to the lady," I said. I looked at Kate. "I hope you brought your money, because this trip is going to cost you two beach stickers, one here and one over on Chappy."

"You're the most costly driver I've ever had!" She dazzled the deputy with her smile. "How much do you need, Officer?"

He told her, and she gave him the money. We filled out the papers, got our sticker, and headed east. Twenty minutes later, on Wasque Point, we ran into a Trustees of Reservations patrol, and went through the process again.

"This is getting to be an expensive trip," said Kate.

"No problem for a woman of your caliber," I said. I gestured toward the line of trucks on the point. "Fishermen after blues. If I'd brought a couple of rods, we could join them."

"Fish are slimy."

"I'm afraid our engagement is off. I could never marry a woman who thinks fish are slimy."

I put the Explorer in gear and we drove north along East Beach. I pointed out the Cape Pogue lighthouse far ahead.

"Your Zee is no doubt as good at fishing as she is at shooting," said Kate.

"She is, indeed. In fact, we met right there on Wasque Point one year when the blues were just coming in for the season."

"Wonder Woman! How can I win you from Wonder Woman? I eat fish after they've been cooked. Does that count?"

"It counts, but not enough. Love me, love my live bluefish."

"You're making this very difficult for me."

"I'm just your ordinary manly man," I said, "with manly standards about fish and women. Zee thinks I'm a hopeless case, so you probably shouldn't try to change me. Maybe you could learn to love golf."

She laughed, but shook her head. "No, I don't think so. Can we stop along here somewhere? I have my bathing suit on under my clothes, and I'd like to swim and then get some sun."

I pulled out of the track and parked. There was no one else in sight. Overhead the September sun was bright, and in front of us Nantucket Sound was blue and cool. I could see Muskeget off to the southeast. Kate put two towels side by side on the warm sand, then peeled off her shirt and shorts, revealing a bathing suit that apparently had been designed for a fairy's child.

"Your husband is an idiot to let you out of his sight," I said, looking her up and down.

Her hair was long, her foot was light, and her eyes were wild.

"Come on," she said. "Let's swim."

I took a breath. "You swim. I didn't bring my bathing suit."

She looked both ways along the beach. "You don't need one. Come to think of it, neither do I."

A moment later, she was naked. My pulse jumped.

"Come on." She put out her hand.

"I'm your driver," I said. "Not your knight-at-arms."

"I don't know what you mean. Come on. It'll be fun."

"Take your swim. I'll wait here."

She walked to me and put her hands on my shoulders and looked at me with her siren's eyes. My will began to fade. "You don't find me attractive?" She took my right hand and placed it on her left breast. Her nipple was hard. As I touched her, she took a short, sharp breath.

I put Zee between us, and moved my hands to her waist. "You are a great beauty," I said, holding her away from me. "In fact, you're the second most beautiful woman I know. Now, go take your swim before some fisherman comes driving by and asks you for your autograph."

She stepped away and looked at me wide-eyed. "The second most beautiful? No man ever told me that before! My God, Wonder Woman's not even here, but you'd think I was a potted plant! There must be something wrong with you, or else I've totally lost my touch!"

I held up my left hand and touched the ring on my finger. "You haven't lost your touch," I said, "but this means I'm married. You're tempting but I'm taken."

She shook her head and studied me for a long minute, then smiled an ironic smile. "I don't know whether to laugh or cry. I didn't know there were any really married men left. Just my luck to run into one. You sure you don't want to take a swim?"

"I'll pass this time."

Her smile turned into a crooked grin. "Well, since I'm naked anyway, I guess I'll just go in like this. That way I won't have to wear a wet bathing suit for the rest of the day."

She turned and walked into the small surf. I tried not to watch her, and to think about

Lawrence Ingalls instead. I didn't do too good a job of it, but I did remember one thing that I'd been forgetting.

When Kate came out of the sea, it was the birth of Venus, and I almost forgot what I'd remembered. As she dried herself with her towel, she looked at me.

"That was good," she said. "It cooled me off. I have two more weeks here. I'm not through with you yet."

"You might be," I said. "I'm taking tomorrow off." I told her why.

She shook her head. "Drew said you were a hard case, and he was right. But if you're trying to get fired, it won't work. I want you around where I can get my hands on you."

"Figuratively, of course."

"No, not figuratively."

I gestured toward Wasque Point. "There's a Jeep coming along toward us. Maybe you'll want to climb into some clothes."

"Damn," she said. She glanced down the beach, and reached for her teeny-weeny bathing suit.

When the Jeep came by, she was sunning herself on the dry towel. The fishermen in the Jeep waved and looked at me enviously. I didn't blame them.

— 32 —

Early the next day, Edgartown's finest closed off Main Street from the Old Whaling Church to the Dock Street parking lot and redirected traffic through the village's other narrow streets. The lucky locals who'd gotten jobs as extras were given directions about how to stroll along Main and look like summer tourists. The Skye twins and Mattie were among them. Cameras were set up, power cables were strung, Kevin Turner's trailer and a couple of lesser trailers were parked in the lot by the town hall, and when the sun was where Jack Slade wanted it to be, action began.

Joshua and I watched from inside the Bickerton & Ripley bookstore, where we had as good a view as most people.

A whistle blew and the extras moved along the sidewalks. Some cars came down the street. The chief played a traffic cop at the four corners, and a couple of the selectmen sat on the bench in front of the town hall, pretending to be old-timers watching the passing crowd. After a while, another whistle blew and everybody went back to where they'd started and, at the sound of the starting whistle, strolled along the street once again. They strolled four or five times before Slade was satisfied.

"You two should be out there," I said to the owners of Bick & Rip, who were also looking out of their window since there was no business to be done while the street was closed. "You could provide local color."

"We just want to get our shop and our sign in the scene," said Dana. "Be good publicity."

"Especially if the movie's any good," said Marilyn. "But even if it's a loser, well, they say that any publicity at all is better than no publicity."

"I can see it now," I said. "You'll have so many customers that your store will be famous and you'll be able to sell it and live off the interests of your investments. It'll be great."

"Hey, there's your better half," said Dana. And sure enough, there was Zee, looking spectacular in a light summer dress I'd never seen before. Something from Wardrobe, no doubt.

"And there's the star himself," said Marilyn, as Kevin Turner appeared, smiling and waving to those extras who could not restrain themselves from oohing and aahing and pointing.

While various assistants got the crowd to act more professionally, Kevin and Zee and the director and some others talked and gestured. Then the whistle blew once again and the extras and the cars once more moved along the streets. This time, though, Kevin was part of the crowd, looking thoughtful and walking down the sidewalk just as Zee, peering casually into storefront windows as she went by them, came walking the other way. As she and Kevin passed each other, she glanced at him and gave him a smile. Their eyes met for a fleeting moment. He froze but she walked on. He stared after her, then raised a hand as if to call her back. But after one faltering step after her, he stopped, frowned, and put his other hand to his forehead. The whistle blew.

They did it again.

Then they set up cameras in the street right at the spot where Zee and Kevin met and shot the scene again, only this time without the cars or most of the extras.

Then they put cameras on the sidewalk so that they faced Zee as she came toward Kevin and shot the scene again. And again. Then they replaced those cameras with others at different angles, and shot it again. And again.

I was glad I'd chosen another line of work, but Zee and Kevin and the extras patiently repeated and modified their actions until at last the director was satisfied.

A half hour later, Main Street was again open to the public, and Cassiopeia Films had moved on, to South Beach this time, where Kate and Kevin would be shot walking the sands side by side before realizing that their blood was running too hot for them to resist it any longer, and they fell to earth in a passionate embrace. Maybe Kate had just been practicing yesterday. As for me, I preferred to make love where I didn't get sand in my crotch.

"Well, what do you think?" I asked Dana as the street got back to normal. "Is there a place for me on the silver screen?"

"Joshua might make it big," she said.

Another diplomat. I walked out and found myself face-to-face with the chief, who had abandoned his traffic duties once the cameras were turned off.

"How's show biz?" I asked.

"I hear the academy already has me up for best supporting actor. They know talent when they see it."

He hoisted up his belt. It, like the belts of all

cops these days, was loaded down with pistol, ammo, radio, cuffs, and all that other stuff that forces their owners to walk that instantly recognizable cop walk with their arms arched away from their bodies.

"You should wear suspenders with that belt," I said. "Some day it'll fall down and take your pants with it. With your luck it'll happen just as somebody robs the bank, and there you'll be, right in the middle of the street with your pants and your gunbelt down around your ankles."

He dug his pipe out of a pocket and blew through the stem. "Zee tell you we got a missing person out on Moonbeam? They found his pickup up there in Vineyard Haven, but nobody's seen Moonbeam."

"Maybe he went over to America."

"Nobody saw him on the boat, and Moonbeam's hard to miss. Connie thinks he's gone for good this time, but she wants us to find him if we can."

"She seem upset?"

"What did he ever do for her besides give her all those kids? She did say she wished he'd finished covering up that sewer line out back of their place before he took off, but that she'd figured out how to use the backhoe and is doing it herself. If she doesn't need him to run the backhoe, she probably doesn't need him at all, but she may be like a lot of married folks: they get used to having somebody around, and they want 'em there even if they're not much good. You see a lot of that. You remember the Bickersons on the radio? Nah, you're too young."

"I remember the Bickersons," I said. "My dad had some tapes of them. Old-time radio show."

"Yeah, that's them. There are a lot of couples like that: bicker and pick on each other all the time, but can't live away from each other. The really mean ones fight, but when one of them calls the cops and the cop comes and tries to straighten things out, they both jump on him. Maybe Connie and Moonbeam are like that."

"I didn't know Connie could run the backhoe," I said.

"Neither did I," said the chief. "But Moonbeam is no genius. If he can run one, probably anybody can. Hell, maybe even you could do it."

As a matter of fact, I could. I'd run one the summer before I'd lied about my age and joined the army, digging trenches for foundations and water lines for a nonunion construction outfit in Somerville. I figured I still could run one if I had to.

"Aside from Moonbeam being among the

missing, how's the murder investigation coming along?" I asked. "Anything new?"

He filled the bowl of his pipe from a plastic tobacco bag. I inhaled the scent of the tobacco.

"The state is running the investigation," he said, "and they don't always tell us dumb, small-town cops what they're doing. What I'm still doing is trying to find out if anybody saw Moonbeam or anything or anybody on the beach that day. So far, no luck."

But a little light had been flickering in the back of my brain, and with his words another one suddenly joined it. Then other little lights joined them and made one bigger light. And in that light I saw a shadowy form, and wondered, not for the first time, just how dull I could be.

"Are you busy right now?" I asked.

The chief heard something in my tone, and tilted his head a little to one side. "Nothing that can't wait. Why?"

"I want you to take a ride with me."

"Where?"

"South Beach. There's a guy there named Drew Mondry. He has a videotape I want you to see."

"A video of what?"

"Martha's Vineyard. It was taken the day Lawrence Ingalls was killed. It's just possible

393

that the guy who shot the tape got a picture of the murderer."

The chief's cruiser was parked in front of the courthouse. We got into it and drove to Katama. It was Joshua's first ride in a police car. As the chief drove, I told him about the helicopter and the videotape.

The film crew was setting up at the Herring Creek end of the beach, but had taken a break for lunch. Drew Mondry was eating out of a box at an aluminum table under an umbrella. He said he had the tape at the hotel where he and Emily were staying. He tossed the remains of his lunch into a garbage barrel, and the four of us drove to the hotel, where he found the tape and put it into his VCR.

"Do you want to see anything in particular?" he asked.

"The beginning," I said. "The part I didn't see before. The shots the cameraman in the helicopter took when he was flying over Chappy and along Norton's Point Beach."

Drew rewound the tape to the beginning and turned on the TV.

There was a sweeping shot of the Vineyard as the helicopter came over the sound from the mainland. Then the camera was looking down at Cape Pogue and the lighthouse, and then was panning south along East Beach. There were fishermen at the jetties, and two of them waved as the helicopter passed over them.

The plane flew south along the beach, recording the new Dyke Bridge, the towels and umbrellas of the swimmers and sun-bathers who had crossed it to reach the beach, and the occasional 4 x 4 parked or moving along the edge of the sound toward new fishing grounds.

Wasque Point came into view, and there below the helicopter were the Skyes and me. The helicopter made a circle over us and we all waved, then the plane went west over Norton's Point Beach. It flew over Lawrence Ingalls's pickup and looked down upon his body, but didn't hesitate because, probably, another body lying on the beach was just another body lying on the beach, and the cameraman had no way of knowing that this one was dead. Then the plane flew over a car going west toward Katama, and I said: "Stop. Rewind."

Drew rewound the tape and we looked down once more at Ingalls's body and then at the car going west before the plane passed over it and went on toward Katama.

"You can stop it again," I said to Drew. Then I looked at the chief. "Well?"

"Let's see it again," he said.

We saw it again, then one more time just to be sure.

"I think we can get this enhanced, if we need to," said the chief. "But I don't think there's much doubt about it. That's Connie Berube's car." He looked at me. "You don't seem surprised."

"I've stopped being surprised at how dumb I can be," I said. "I forgot all about this part of the film until you mentioned looking for witnesses this morning. I saw the rest of the tape with Drew, when the two of us were scouting locations, but I never saw this part because Drew had already been driven around Chappy and had seen everything there he needed to see. Dumbness."

The chief stuck his pipe in his mouth and chewed on the stem.

"I guess I'd better get in touch with Dom Agganis and Olive Otero. But I want to make a copy of this first, so we'll have one for ourselves." He eyed me. "You weren't not surprised because you felt dumb. You were not surprised that it was Connie's car. You expected it to be Connie's car."

I nodded. "Yeah. Because I think Connie killed Ingalls. And Moonbeam, too."

The chief frowned slightly and waited for more.

I told him about Silver Sands and Playa de Plata and what went on there. "Lawrence Ingalls's old man introduced him to Silver

Sands," I said, "so maybe the taste for boys is a genetic thing. Later, Ingalls stopped going to the Orient and started to go down to Central America instead. He could get what he wanted and didn't have to travel so far to get it. An occasional vacation was all he needed, because like a lot of people, I guess, he didn't need sex all of the time. The rest of the year he was pretty abstinent.

"Back home he even went out with girls. He even married one early on. For show, maybe, or maybe because he wanted to be straight and hoped he could be. His family is a very proper one, and his father not only married but had a family, even though he took his vacations at Silver Sands. But Lawrence Ingalls's marriage didn't last. Probably because his wife found out about his taste for boys and maybe about his father's taste, too."

"Marriages break up for lots of reasons," said the chief. "Besides, Ingalls was engaged to Beth Harper, so maybe he wasn't the child lover you say he was."

"Maybe. But a lot of pedophiles marry for appearances or because they're bisexual. Besides, Ingalls was a pretty straight-arrow guy, except for his sex drive, and I imagine he wanted to be married if he could manage it.

"The thing is that after his divorce, Barbara, his ex-wife, stayed very close to the family. I've wondered why. It is not unknown for people to like their daughters-in-law and sons-in-law better than their own children, but it's not the usual thing. In this case, I think it's probably been for two reasons: because they really do like her and because they don't want her to spill any family secrets she learned while she was married to Lawrence. So they've taken good care of her all of these years. She's up at Ingalls's house right now, looking after things just like she was a member of the family. I'll bet she's never had to actually work for a living since she divorced Ingalls."

"You're stretching things," said the chief. "Even if you're right, you'll never be able to prove any of this."

"I don't want to prove any of it," I said. "I'm just telling you why I think Connie killed Ingalls and Moonbeam."

"I think I'm getting the picture," said the chief, "but you go on and spell it out."

"I'll make it short. Ingalls had been coming to the Vineyard for several years, but two or three years back he stopped going to Playa de Plata and built a house right here on the island, just beyond Moonbeam and Connie's place. He hired Connie to clean the house a couple of times a week and he hired Moonbeam to take care of the grounds. That's okay, because they can use money, but about that time, Moonbeam all of a sudden has that new pickup of his and Connie has that Subaru sedan of hers. He's never had that kind of money in his life. Where did the cars come from?

"He got them from Ingalls, and he got them for selling his boy Jason to him. Moonbeam and the boy would go up to Ingalls's place to work the grounds, but Moonbeam was the only one who stayed outside the house. Jason would go inside with Ingalls.

"They say that Moonbeam's ancestors all married their cousins or even closer kin, so incest wasn't anything new to him. And they say he got Connie from a whorehouse down in Kentucky, so he was used to dealing in human flesh. And even if that's all nothing but gossip, it's a sure thing that Moonbeam would sell anything for the right money."

"Even his own kid?"

"Yeah. Connie's gotten restraining orders on him in the past to keep him from abusing his kids, so it wasn't too big a jump for him to sell Jason to Ingalls. Of course, he wouldn't dare tell Connie about the deal, because she'd have killed him."

"Which is exactly what you think she did."

"Yeah. Now, Connie isn't the highest form of human life I've ever met, but she's got fire in her, and I think that when she found out about Moonbeam's deal with Ingalls, she went up to Ingalls's house and got that pistol of his and killed them both. She knew Ingalls was going out to the beach that morning, and she followed him out there and shot him. I figure she didn't care if she got caught or not, but she almost lucked out and got away without anybody seeing her there.

"I don't know if she shot Moonbeam first or second, but when she was done with her killing, she wiped the gun clean and put it back. Maybe nobody would ever have tied it to the killing if Beth Harper hadn't tried to shoot me with it."

The chief nodded. "And then she let it out that Moonbeam had gone missing again just like he's done in the past, and all of us believed her, especially after they found Moonbeam's pickup up there in Vineyard Haven where she parked it. And she iced the cake by asking us to put out a missing persons on him."

"But she knows where Moonbeam is, and I think I know, too."

The chief nodded again. "Up alongside that sewer line Connie filled over with the backhoe. Come on. I have to talk to some people and get some warrants. I hope you're wrong about this, J.W."

I hoped so, too, but I didn't think I was.

— 33 —

The children had been taken inside the house by a rep from the DYS, but Connie, hard-faced, arms crossed, stood among the reporters and law enforcement people who watched as I slowly uncovered the sewer line with Moonbeam's old backhoe. I didn't have to dig up the whole line, because the dirt that Connie had recently added still looked new, and if Moonbeam was there, he'd be under that part. I worked slowly because I didn't know how far down he'd be, and we finally found him just before noon.

Guys with shovels did the last of the digging, and the photographers recorded everything. The DA, who not long before had been hinting that I was a prime suspect, and then that Moonbeam might be, now made a statement to the reporters about the tragic nature of the case, about solid police work, and about the perseverance of his office that had led to this latest grim discovery.

A reporter stuck a mike in front of Connie's

face as Olive Otero cuffed her and took her to the state cruiser. Connie had nothing to say.

The reporter pointed the mike at me. "Any statement you'd like to make, Mr. Jackson? There'd been a lot of heat on you for the last few weeks. How do you feel now?"

The question irked me. Why do reporters always ask survivors how they feel? "In the course of justice, none of us should see salvation," I said. "We do pray for mercy."

"Mercy? Justice? Do you think justice is being done, finally?"

"Ask me after the trial, if they have a trial," I said, climbing into the Land Cruiser. "Meanwhile, you can quote me as saying I think the police have done a hell of a job."

I drove away.

At home, Zee and Joshua were eager to hear what happened. I told them.

"You look wiped out," said Zee. "Here, hold your kid, and I'll bring out some lunch."

We sat in the yard under one of our big table umbrellas and had sandwiches and beer. I began to feel better.

"What do you think will happen to Connie?" asked Zee.

"I don't know. I think she'll go to trial, but you never know how a trial will turn out. The kids are the real problem. The Department of Youth Services will take them, but I trust the

DYS here in Massachusetts about as far as I can throw Boston City Hall."

"I'll tell you something," said Zee. "I don't think she should have killed those men, but in a way I don't really blame her, either. Imagine how she must have felt when she found out what they were doing to her children!" She looked at me with fierce eyes. "If anybody ever tried to hurt Joshua, I might shoot somebody, myself!"

Powerful words from peace-loving nurse Zee. I decided to change to a cooler subject.

"What's next in your movie career?"

But she had already started thinking about something else, and a little smile was playing on her lips.

"What?"

"I said what's next in your movie career?"

"Oh. What's next is the modern barroom scene where the modern hero catches another glimpse of the modern girl he saw on the street and has another flashback to the pirate girl. They're going to shoot it down in the Navigator Room tomorrow."

"Is this the scene where you get to say your line?"

"No. That'll be in the old-time pirate bar scene that they'll shoot in the studio. I'll have to go out to the Coast to do that, and to shoot the old-time pirate street scene that the hero

403

flashes on after he sees the girl in the street scene we shot yesterday. You're sure you don't mind if I go out there one more time?"

Her voice was right there at the table, but her mind was somewhere else.

"I don't mind," I said. "What are you thinking about?"

She gave me a sphinxish smile. "I was thinking about your boss, Kate Ballinger, and about my wooer, Kevin Turner."

"Is Kevin really your wooer?"

"He's trying to be, although I don't think he wants to make an honest woman out of me. He is hard to discourage."

I noticed that my right hand had become a fist, and made it back into a hand. "I'll discourage him, if you want me to."

"Never mind discouraging Kevin. I can handle Kevin. How about Kate? Are you having any luck discouraging her?"

"You're a woman. You know how hard it is to resist me. Don't be so hard on poor Kate. She probably can't help herself."

"Actually, you're getting easier to resist every minute."

"You're not," I said, leering. "I don't blame Kevin Turner for lusting after your bod. Of course, being the manly guy I am, I may have to challenge him to a duel for doing it."

"You can be manly in some other way,"

said Zee. "I think a friendly but telling gesture might be better. Didn't Kate say she might want to learn how to shoot? I'll tell you what I want you to do. I want you to invite her down to the Rod and Gun Club tomorrow after work. Manny is going to be giving me a lesson then, and maybe he'll give her one, too. I'll invite Kevin to come, too, and we can all be friends together."

Joshua was so taken by this idea that he transmitted his lunch into his diaper. Or maybe he was just agreeing that Kevin Turner was a shit.

It was going to take all the next morning to shoot the barroom scene, and since Kate had to be there and there wasn't any place for Joshua and me to watch what was going on, he and I went fishing instead after I dropped Kate off. In a week or so the Bass and Bluefish Derby was going to start, so it was an excellent time for a little surf casting and scouting action.

"Remember, you're still working for me," said Kate, adjusting the collar of my polo shirt with the logo of Cassiopeia Films on the pocket. "I'll need you at noon."

"I'll be here," I said, looking over her head and seeing Zee watching us from across the room. Zee waved her fingers at me, and gave me a big fake smile.

Joshua and I drove first to Wasque, where Joshua watched me and some other guys catch nothing, then cruised up East Beach, stopping at the Yellow Shovel and at all the little points between there and the new Dyke Bridge, where pilgrims still came to have their pictures taken and real fanatics still brought empty vials and bottles to fill with water from beneath the structure where, decades ago, the nation's most famous automobile accident had taken place.

We caught nothing, and all the time I was brooding about Connie Berube. She was a killer, but I couldn't forget what Zee had said about shooting anyone who molested a child of hers. When I looked deep inside myself, I couldn't really find much disagreement with that sentiment. But I was the one who had nailed Connie, so now what? I thought about that as I fished.

We took the inside road up to Cape Pogue Pond and tried at the mouth of the Narrows, then farther along at the Cedars, then off Quahog Point. Nothing. Across the pond, over on North Neck, the giant new house looked bigger than usual, for some reason. Chappy was getting more crowded all the time.

Joshua thought it would be better if I took him for a walk instead of trying to catch fish that obviously weren't interested in my lure, so I put my rod on the roof rack and carried him along the beach, where we looked at rocks and shells and watched the gulls working the shallows. Later, as I was strapping him back in his car seat, a truck came by and stopped. Zack Delwood got out. I finished with Josh and shut the door.

Zack looked up and down the beach. No one was in sight. "Got your pistols with you this time, tough guy?" He came toward me.

"Not this time," I said.

"I hear they got Moonbeam's old woman for killing that fucking Ingalls. Now I'm going to get you for trying to stick me with the rap."

"I never tried to finger you," I said.

"You're a liar. You and the chief are thick as thieves. The two of you would have hung it on me if you could."

He was about my size and age and could do some real damage if I let him. I faded back, fell down, and got up again as he closed in on me. I swung a clumsy-looking left and as he tipped his head to let it go by, I came around with a right and threw a handful of sand into his wild, angry eyes.

He bellowed and dug at his eyes, and as he did I stepped to the side, pivoted, and drove a foot into his knee. Injuries to knees, one of God's worst designs, end a large percentage of professional athletic careers. Zack screamed and fell, grabbing at his leg.

Blind and crippled, he was a pitiful sight. He gasped and groaned.

"I think it's a dislocated kneecap," I said. I got a hold of his injured leg. "This is going to hurt." Zack cried out as I straightened the leg and popped the kneecap back into place, then sighed and panted as the pain lessened.

I got water from the pond and helped him rinse out his eyes.

"I didn't finger you for the Ingalls killing," I said. "Do you understand me?"

He nodded. I walked over to his truck. Automatic transmission. Good; he could drive with one good leg. I went back to him. By then he had recovered until he was about half of what he had been before he had started the fight. "I've decided to raise some money for Connie Berube's defense fund," I said. "I need help. I think you should be a volunteer. You collect from your friends, if you have any, and I'll collect from mine. Maybe we can do her some good. What do you say?"

"Help me up."

I did, and we hobbled to his truck.

"You could have killed me," he said.

"There's been enough killing."

"I got kids," he said. "I don't blame Connie Berube for what she did."

We got him into the truck. "See your doctor about that knee," I said.

"You didn't fight fair," said Zack.

"There's no such thing as a fair fight," I said. "Somebody's always got the edge."

He thought that over, then nodded. "Yeah, I guess that's right. Okay, I'll help with the money. I'll be in touch." He drove back toward the Dyke Bridge.

I still had some fishing time left, so I wasted some of it at Bernie's Point, then drove on to the Jetties, where there were already some people fishing for bonito and Spanish mackerel. There, after failing to catch anything on my favorite Roberts Ranger, I replaced the Ranger with a two-and-a-half-ounce Hopkins and, somewhat to my surprise, nailed a four-pound blue at the very end of my cast. Everybody else immediately abandoned the bonito and Spanish mackerel, grabbed their big rods, put metal on their leaders, and tried for blues.

"Imitation is the tribute mediocrity pays to genius," I said to Walter and Iowa, who were casting beside me.

"If bullshit was money, you'd be the richest guy on Martha's Vineyard," said Walter.

There was a little school of blues way out there, and we got a few of them before they moved off.

"Not bad," said Iowa, tossing a fish into his box. He looked at Joshua. "Why didn't you bring your mom out here instead of this guy? It would be good for her to hang around some real men for a change."

Joshua gave him his best toothless smile.

"When are you going to get this kid a rod?" asked Walter. "It's time he learned how to cast."

"I thought you were going to custom-make one for him," I said. "For free, of course."

"What a cheap bastard you are. Say, how's Zee doing in the movie biz? She having fun?"

"I think she is," I said. "I know that she's inviting Kevin Turner and Kate Ballinger to come down to the Rod and Gun Club and watch Manny Fonseca give her her shooting lesson later this afternoon."

"That's great. They must all be getting along pretty good, then. Hey, that's really something about Connie Berube, isn't it? Who'd have thought it?"

Who, indeed? I told them about the defense fund for Connie and got some money from most of the guys there. I asked them to spread the word, and they said they would.

I looked at my watch. I had just enough time to get my fish into the freezer before I had to pick up Kate Ballinger. "See you later," I said. I loaded Joshua and our gear into the truck and headed for home.

Back at the Navigator Room, now open for business once again, I handed Joshua to his mother.

"How'd it go?"

"Five takes," said Zee. "I thought it was right the first time, but what do I know?" She put her finger under Joshua's chin. "You catch any fish, cute stuff?"

"Cute stuff and I got three fish," I said, and told her where and how. Then, without mentioning my encounter with Zack, I told her about the defense fund.

"Good," said Zee. "But next time, you can be in the movie and Josh and I will go fishing. Oh, hi, Kate."

"Hi," said Kate, coming up to us.

"Well, I'll be running along," said Zee. "See you later, Kate. Five o'clock at the shooting range?" She kissed me and walked away. I watched her. Dynamite bod. Madonna and bambino; Caravaggio would have loved to pose her.

"Come on, Jeff," said Kate, "you're supposed to be paying attention to me."

"Yes, ma'am." I looked down at her. "Where shall I drive you?"

"To distraction," she said, with some snip in her voice.

But instead she took me to lunch at a new place where I had never been before. The food wasn't bad at all, and they had beer.

"This is the fashionable place to eat, I'm told," said Kate as she nibbled on her salad.

"So I've heard."

"Don't you come here?"

"This is an historic first."

"Well, do you like it?"

"It's fine."

"We could come back in the evening, after we leave the shooting range."

"You and Kevin and Zee and Joshua and me?"

"I was thinking of just you and me." She touched my hand with her cool fingers. It felt good.

"Where would you like to have me drive you?"

"How about to my place?"

I understood why Odysseus had himself tied to the mast. "I go with the Explorer," I said. "If we can get the car into your bedroom, it's a deal." My voice sounded thin.

Fortunately, she laughed. "You are the most frustrating man! What should I see that I haven't seen?" There was a pause, and her laughter became a crooked smile. "Besides your body, that is."

I took her on two walks. First through the

Menemsha Hills down to the beach near the old brick factory, and then along Fulling Mill Brook, between Middle Road and South Road.

It was half past four when we got back to the Explorer, and Kate was tired but exhilarated.

"Beautiful! I never would have known those places were there if it wasn't for you!"

"Local knowledge. That's why you're paying me the big bucks."

"I knew there must be some reason." She looked at her watch. "What kind of clothes do I need to take a pistol-shooting lesson?"

"The ones you're wearing will do just fine."

"You don't want to go by my place and watch me change, I suppose. Oh, never mind. If the car can't get inside, neither can you. I know, I know. To the shooting range, James."

We were the last ones to arrive. Manny Fonseca's truck was there, the BMW that Kevin Turner was driving was there, and Zee's little Jeep was there. Joshua, his ears plugged and covered with mufflers, was in his stand, where he could watch what was going on, and the adults were at the twenty-five-yard mark on the range.

Manny, who loved to talk about shooting

almost as much as he loved to shoot, was in his element. A couple of pistols were lying on the table beside the yard marker, including Zee's Beretta 84F and her .45. Manny was talking with Kevin about what he and Zee were going to be doing. Kevin, who, I suspected, had probably had some pistol training to prepare him for his heroic roles, listened with patience that I deemed at least partially feigned.

We joined the others and Manny and Kate shook hands. Manny was pleased to meet her, as what man wouldn't be.

"What we're doing here," he said, "is teaching Zee how to shoot this here forty-five, because that's what she'll be using in this competition that's coming up. Now, Zee shoots real good with that Beretta of hers, but she's still not used to the forty-five, so that's what we'll be working with today." He eyed Kate. "Zee says you might want to learn how to shoot, yourself. That right?"

Kate eyed the table full of pistols. "I think I'll just watch for a while. Then I'll decide."

He nodded. "Makes sense. Okay, then, you folks just put these plugs in your ears and stand right over there."

He and Zee, with mufflers over their ears and shooting glasses protecting their eyes, got to work. They took turns shooting. The air was filled with the bellow of the pistols, and the targets down the range gradually disintegrated into paper fragments. Manny's hits were closer bunched than Zee's, but as she continued to shoot, hers improved.

"Jesus," said Kate as the clips were reloaded.

"That was right-handed," said happy Manny. "Now we'll try it left-handed."

He walked down and replaced the destroyed targets with new ones, then once more the air was filled with sound. Kate winced and Kevin wore an expression of studied interest. The new targets disintegrated and were replaced.

Manny talked, and Zee listened. Then they shot some more. Left-handed, right-handed, and two-handed. From twenty-five yards and from ten yards and from other yards. Finally they stopped.

"That's probably enough for today," said Manny. "You did good, but you're still pulling a little to the right." He looked at Kate. "You want to try?"

"Before she does, I'd like to take a few shots with the Beretta," said Zee.

Manny looked at her. "With the Beretta?"

Zee nodded. "I'm just getting started with the forty-five, but I'm pretty good with the

Beretta. I'd like Kevin and Kate to see me at my best."

Manny could understand that. "Well, sure. I'll set up new targets."

"I've got a couple right here," said Zee. She handed him an envelope, and Manny peeked at the targets. "Set 'em up, please, Manny, and I'll tell Kate and Kev about this weapon."

Manny made an odd sound, and went down the range while Zee snagged her Beretta from the table.

"Now what we have here," she said, "is a Beretta 84F. Wooden grips, .380 caliber, thirteen rounds, double action. It fits my hand well. And this is an extra clip, so I can get off more than two dozen shots pretty fast." She smiled at Kevin and Kate. "I'm going to shoot the first clip right-handed and the second one left-handed. Manny's teaching me to shoot with my left hand in case I ever get shot in the right hand and have to return fire. Police officers are trained to do that."

Manny came back, gave Zee an odd look, and took a stand behind her.

"This will only take a minute," said Zee, turning toward the range. It took less than that.

The rest of us turned and saw that two full-face publicity photos, one of Kate and one of Kevin, were the targets. The faces smiled at us from twenty-five yards. We only had a second to take this in before Zee began to shoot. First Kevin's photo disintegrated as Zee put thirteen bullets through it. Then, as Kevin gasped, Zee popped the empty clip from her weapon, slammed home the second, and blew Kate's picture into shreds.

A silence seemed to echo over the range.

Zee put down her empty pistol and began to refill a clip. She smiled at Kevin and then said to Kate, "You want to take a few shots now? You might like it."

"My God, no!" said Kate, wide-eyed. "I think I get the message!"

Kevin was staring at Zee. "You must be crazy! You've got to be crazy!"

Zee filled the clip and snapped it back into the Beretta. She looked at him, then knelt and picked up the other clip from the ground. She began to fill it.

Kate tugged Kevin's sleeve. "I don't think she's crazy, Kev. Come on, you can drive me to a bar. I think we could both use a drink. Nice to meet you, Mr. Fonseca."

"You're crazy," said Kevin again, still gaping at Zee, but allowing Kate to pull him toward the BMW.

"Crazy!" he yelled one last time as he spun the car around and it roared away.

I looked at Zee and felt a grin on my face.

"Crazy," I said. Then I went over and got Joshua out of his seat. I took the muffler off his ears and took out the earplugs. "You have a crazy mother, Josh. What do you think of that?"

Joshua smiled. He thought it was just fine.

— 34 —

"The worst thing was missing the opening of the derby," said Zee. "While I was out there slaving away under the lights in Hollywood, you were here catching fish! And winning a daily, while you were at it. I saw that new pin on your hat."

We were on the balcony with Joshua.

"I thought the worst thing would be being away from Joshua and me," I said.

"I mean besides that."

"How did it go out there in La La Land? The last I heard, Kevin was so mad that he wanted you out of the movie altogether."

"I may be, by the time all the editing has been done. But I guess not even Kevin is all-powerful, because I did my two pirate-girl scenes out there. The one in the pirate street and the one in the pirate bar. And I got to say my line."

"I can hardly wait to see the movie."

She grinned and put her head on my shoulder. "Me, too."

"It's going to be great being the husband of a famous star. I'll be a power figure and the bimbos will all hover around me. The only problem is that they won't dare get really close because they'll be afraid you'll shoot them."

She shivered. "You know, maybe Kevin was right. Maybe I am crazy. I actually shot those pictures all to pieces!"

"Pictures aren't people," I said. "You celluloid princesses should know that better than most. Besides, I thought it was pretty funny. And even if it wasn't funny, it sure was effective. Kevin and Kate lost all interest in us."

She snugged closer. "You don't think it was sort of wacko?"

"No. You're a nurse. You cure people, you don't kill them. You certainly cured Kevin and Kate, at least."

"Not really. Out in Hollywood, they were up to their old tricks again."

"But not with us."

"No, not with us. I'm poison now to Kevin, but, you know, I sort of like Kate, ever since she started leaving you alone. Did I tell you that there are some people in the business who want me to go out there again?"

I felt a familiar little chill inside me. "No, but I'm not surprised. What are you going to do?"

"California is so far from the bluefish! But I'm going to think about it, and we'll talk about it. Meanwhile, I'm going to join the derby and go fishing in the morning, and you're invited to come along. And after that, I have some other plans we should discuss. What's happening with poor Connie Berube?"

"Poor Connie is being charged with two murders. The sheriff got warrants to search Lawrence Ingalls's place and came up with the bills of sale showing that Ingalls originally bought Moonbeam's pickup and Connie's Subaru. And I guess they found some videotapes, too, and ice cream and kids movies and such stuff that Ingalls used to keep the Berube boy happy. On the bright side, the Connie Berube Defense Fund is doing pretty good. A lot of islanders are coming through and we've even got some mainlanders involved."

Zee sighed. "What a mess that whole situation was. There's just no telling what human beings will do, is there?"

We sat there looking out over our garden, over the pond beyond, over the barrier beach, and on out to the sound beyond, where the darkness was settling in the east. Above, the night sky showed an early star. Zee's mother, Maria, believed in a God who lived up there somewhere. Maybe he knew what was going on.

"What are those other plans?" I asked. "The ones we need to discuss."

She leaned over and peeked at Joshua, who was almost asleep in his carrier.

"There are three more," said Zee, coming back to me. "First, I plan to shoot in that competition next month. That's the little plan. The big plans are for a sister for the cub, there, and an addition on the house so she can have her own room. Every little girl should have a room of her own." She looked up at me. "What do you think?"

I put my arm around her. "It's okay with me if you want to go shooting," I said. "And I can build the room without any help. But I'll need assistance getting Josh a sister because I've never done a daughter before. In fact, I'm trying to recall how we got Joshua. Maybe you can remind me."

"I'll show you," said Zee. "And don't worry; you'll remember right away. It's like riding a bicycle. Once you know how, you never forget."

THREE RECIPES PREPARED
BY J. W. JACKSON IN THIS BOOK

SMOKED BLUEFISH PÂTÉ

8 oz. whipped cream cheese
½ tsp. prepared horseradish
1 large finely diced red onion
5–6 oz. shredded smoked bluefish
Dash of Worcestershire sauce
1 tsp. lemon juice

Optional ingredients: *a pinch of cayenne*
pepper
salt to taste
a little Grey Poupon
mustard

Mix ingredients and serve with crackers.

J.W. eats this in every book. He loves smoked bluefish pâté!

SHERRY AND GARLIC SHRIMP
(OR FLOUNDER)

*1–1½ lbs. large shrimp, shelled, deveined,
   and patted dry*
½ c. olive oil
3 Tbsp. dry sherry
3 large garlic cloves, crushed
½ tsp. thyme, crumbled
Salt to taste
⅛ tsp. red pepper, crushed (or to taste)

Arrange shrimp in single layer in a greased baking dish. Mix remaining ingredients and pour mixture over shrimp. Bake in preheated 400-degree oven for 8 minutes, turning the shrimp once. Serve with pan juices spooned over shrimp.
Rice and steamed spinach are excellent accompaniments.

J.W. cooks this dish in chapter 26 of this book, but he doesn't have any shrimp, so he substitutes flounder. Delish, just the same!

Black Bean and Rice Salad

2–3 1-lb. cans of black beans, rinsed and drained
1 lb. frozen corn kernels, cooked (or 1 15-oz. can)
2 c. long-grain rice, cooked
1 large bell pepper, red or green, diced
½ c. red onion, chopped
1 tsp. salt
Dash of oregano
Good Seasons Mexican Salad Dressing to taste

Optional ingredients: *shredded cheddar cheese or feta cheese*
sliced black olives
marinated artichoke hearts
chopped cilantro
oregano
chili powder
cumin

Mix and serve. It's very good with rice pilaf, wild rice, or basmati rice.

J.W. serves this dish in chapter 3 of this book. It is, of course, excellent!

Philip R. Craig grew up on a small cattle ranch southeast of Durango, Colorado. He earned his M.F.A. at the University of Iowa Writers' Workshop and is a professor of literature at Wheelock College in Boston. He and his wife live in Hamilton, Massachusetts, and spend their summers on Martha's Vineyard.